BLIZZARD HEROES

Sydney Carr

Author's Note.

This book is the third in the 'Heroes?' series by Sydney Carr. Although it is not essential that 'Heroes?' and 'Instinctive Heroes' are read beforehand, readers may find that by doing so they would add to their enjoyment of this book.

I have described the locations I have used in this book as I remember them in 1963's Ashington and Northumberland. Treshinish House is fictitious.

All the characters in the book are fictional.

I have written the dialogue, where appropriate, in Geordie/Pitmatic dialect with the words spelt phonetically; these are not spelling mistakes or typing errors. For those readers not familiar with this dialect, I have listed the Geordie/Pitmatic words I have used along with their meanings at end of the book. The pronunciation of Geordie/Pitmatic words, I leave entirely to the reader.

PROLOGUE

The Big Freeze of 1962/63

The winter of 1962/63 was the coldest for 200 years in Britain. It began just before Christmas in 1962 when high pressure moved to the northeast of the British Isles, dragging bitterly cold winds across the country.

A belt of rain in Scotland turned to snow as it moved south, reaching southern England on Boxing Day when it parked over the country, bringing snowfall of up to 30cm.

The blizzard that followed created snowdrifts up 6m deep. Roads and railways were blocked; telephone lines brought down and, some small villages cut off for several days. The snow was so deep that some farmers were unable to get to their livestock and many animals starved to death.

The country quickly froze solid due to the very low temperatures, with snow and ice remaining everywhere despite there being plenty of sunshine. The weak winter sun did not warm things up, however, as the lack of cloud cover allowed temperatures to plunge. The conditions caused the cancellation of most horseracing meetings and football matches.

The temperature remained below freezing until the 25 January when a brief thaw began that unfroze the rivers and helped with the clearing of roads to remote communities. However, over in the frozen wilderness of Siberia, a wind began to circle the Steppes, gathering pace, and collecting freezing air and ice particles as it rose higher into the atmosphere. There, the wind changed direction and headed west over Russia and on across Europe, gathering speed as it stormed towards the British Isles, covering most of Northern Europe in blizzard conditions.

In Britain, Friday, February the 8th was initially, another day of striving to keep roads ice-free, relieving snow-bound communities, recovering abandoned vehicles and, rescuing cattle. The majority of the population was unaware that a blizzard, driven by gale force winds of up to 80 mph, was racing across the North Sea toward them.

The A68

The A68 runs from Darlington, north-west up through County Durham and on into Northumberland where, it eventually crosses the Border high up at Carter Bar, atop the Cheviots. From there it descends into the Scottish Lowlands and meanders up to the A720 and on into Edinburgh.

In Northumberland, it follows the route of Roman 'Dere Street' for much of this stretch until it reaches the huge and remote military ranges at Otterburn. From there it follows the river Rede up into the hills, passing the mile and a half long Catcleugh reservoir that can look peaceful, benign, and beautiful in summer but can also look cold, and foreboding in winter. Two inches of ice, topped off with several inches of snow had covered the reservoir for many weeks but the three-day thaw thinned the ice considerably, reducing it to less than an inch thick in places

The hamlet of Rochester straddles the road between Otterburn and Catcleugh, with Redesale Army Training Camp to the east of the road just beyond the hamlet. The camp sits in a wide, shallow-sided valley but the landscape becomes wilder as the road carries on up through upper Redesdale, into the edge of the massive Kielder Forest. Four miles from Rochester, the road passes the collection of white council-like houses built in the early 1950s to house Forestry Commission workers and their families; the remote hamlet of Byrness. In 1963, it was ill-served by public services and often cut off during heavy snowstorms. Beyond Byrness, the valley narrows at Catcleugh Reservoir with two isolated farms, on the opposite side of the road. The forest ends beyond the reservoir with only a couple of lonely farms before the road climbs steeply to the Border at Carter Bar.

Jack Gray – 9 am. Friday 8th of February 1963

Stamping the snow out of the cleats of his calf-high, scuffed, brown-boots, Jack Gray pulled up the thick collar of his waxed, heavy-cotton, stockman's overcoat that bore the scrapes, and stains of many years of use and abuse. Glad to have finished his latest recovery task, he pulled his worn, yellow gauntlet from his right hand and stroked the scar that spread like pink rivulets from the corner of his left eye, down his cheek to his chin. The longest and most vivid scar pulled down the corner of his mouth, the disfigurement providing the left side of his face with a permanent and disconcerting scowl.

The scars on his otherwise handsome, square-jawed, Nordic face were courtesy of a German high-explosive tank shell that destroyed much of the house in Arnhem that he had been fighting from, as part of Lieutenant Colonel Johnny Frost's 2nd Parachute Battalion during WW2. The blast left him concussed, bleeding from severe lacerations to his face and arms and, with a broken right arm. Partially buried under rubble, he was unable to free himself when German soldiers stormed the house.

Taken prisoner, poor initial and subsequent treatment by his Germans captors resulted in the scarring that marred his good looks. After his release at the end of the war, his disfigurement robbed him of his ability to approach women casually, believing they would find him hideous or repulsive. He became morose and remained unmarried, fighting to overcome his loneliness, nightmares, and depression through hard work that kept him almost permanently active. As well as looking after the family house, land and a small collection of mixed livestock, he ran a recovery service and, worked part-time as a Range Warden on Otterburn Ranges.

At 39-years-old, just under six feet tall and muscular; he was in his physical prime but it was his mental scars, and his loneliness that he knew would overpower him if he did not constantly work to push them from his thoughts.

Thirty minutes earlier, the wind played havoc with his thick, tousled, blonde-hair when he looked up at the sky and watched mushrooming grey clouds bulldoze their way across, blocking out the winter-sun as they raced eastwards like a massive sky-borne avalanche; a clear and intimidating warning of the impending storm.

Now, with wind-driven snow battering him outside a garage in the village of Bellingham, 8 miles South West from Otterburn, he finished lowering a broken-down, coal merchant's Bedford, delivery-wagon from the suspended tow on the rear of his WW2, Scammell Pioneer, 6x4-recovery truck. Having spent almost an hour winching the truck from a deep ditch that it had skidded into the day before, he was keen to head home before the road became unpassable, even for his mighty Scammell. He did not want to leave Maggie, his widowed mother on her own in their remote farmhouse in upper Redesdale.

Treshinish House, Jack's home was located at the edge of the pine-tree forest surrounding the upper reaches of Catcleugh reservoir. A working farm up until WW2 when 18-year-old Jack had left to fight for his country, subsequent events changed the farm forever.

Diagnosed with terminal cancer in 1943, his father died shortly after Jack became a prisoner in 1944. Prior to his death and worried about Maggie being on her own and, the welfare of his livestock while Jack was a prisoner in Germany, he sold most of his land and animals to the neighbouring Fenwick's Farm,' half a mile up the valley, toward the Scottish Border.

The house itself is a traditional Northumbrian, stone-built farmhouse with a central, oak door set in a large stone porch that led through an internal door to a wooden-floored hall. Two tall Georgian windows flanked the porch on both sides, with a row of five across the top. A spacious and comfortably furnished front parlour sat on the left of the hall, while on the opposite side stood a room of equal size, originally a dining room, but now set up as a tearoom come café that Maggie ran in the summer months. Two, large, Norwegian, cast-iron, Jotul wood-burning stoves sitting inside imposing, stone fireplaces provided heating.

A central staircase led to the five bedrooms and bathroom off the landing upstairs. At the rear of the house, an Aga provided heat and cooking facilities in the huge welcoming country kitchen, lined with well-worn pine cabinets and, a wooden drainer with a huge Belfast sink. All set around an eight-foot-long, battered, pine table and, ten chairs that all bore the marks of long and useful lives. A rear parlour or snug was on the other side of a back door that led to a short hall with doors off to a boot room, toilet, and scullery, and an end door leading out to the rear of the house where a small courtyard lay, surrounded by single story outhouses.

A huge, open barn with its back to the north-west sat on one side of a large cobbled square at the front of the house, with two smaller enclosed barns, and a workshop on the other side. The cobbled yard Jack kept clear of snow, led directly onto the A68.

Wearing a navy-blue Guernsey Jumper over a striped, blue shirt, slim, fit and strong-willed, fifty-nine-year-old Maggie, hitched up her green, serge trousers, before opening the front door. Feeling the full ice-laden blast of the gathering northeast gale, she quickly forced it shut against the wind, glad that she fed her half dozen beasts in the barn earlier and silently prayed that Jack was safe, and would be home before the snow arrived, as it surely would.

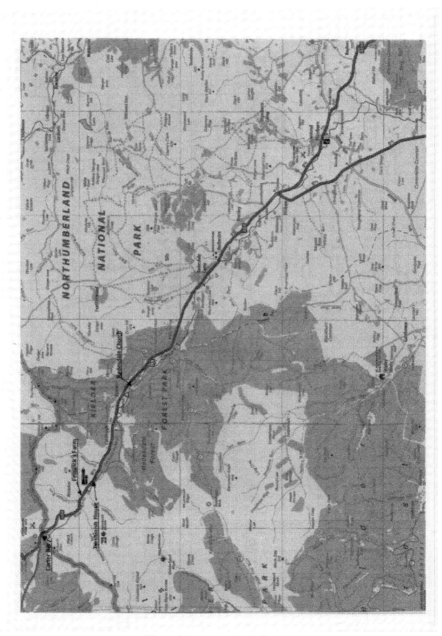

Map of Upper Redesdale

Table of Contents

CHAPTER 1

Friday 8th February – 4:45 am
Deep Underground

Coal dust clung to thirty-eight-year-old Bill Carter's sweat-soaked, ragged tee shirt, as he laboured on his knees, bent almost double in the backbreaking, two-foot-ten-inches height of the coalface in the 'Duke' pit, six-hundred feet below Ashington. His muscle and sinew sculptured arm rammed his oval filler's shovel under the pile of coal that sparkled through the dust where light from his miners' head-lamp reflected off the sharp edges and smooth surfaces of the heaped black gold.

Over halfway through his shift, Bill worked rhythmically, in smooth, muscle memorised movement, scooping a full shovel full of coal, throwing it with accurate, practised ease onto the belt, scooping up the next load in the blink of an eye. The lights from the headlamps of the other men working along the low coalface provided his only companionship as he concentrated on clearing his allocated ten yards required to earn his wage for the shift.

Sandwiched between two layers of stone, the men working the previous day and night shifts had undercut, drilled, and blasted the seam of coal. Now the ten fillers, including Bill were hard at work shovelling the bounty onto the conveyor belt that dumped the coal onto the larger 'Mothergate' conveyor at the end of the 100-yard long coalface. This conveyor carried the load that the fillers worked so hard to win, off along the 10 foot high and wide 'Mothergate' to the main trunk conveyor that raced the coal from all of the faces in the 'Duke Pit' to the metal tubs waiting to be filled near the pit-shaft bottom.

Through the pitch-black Mothergate tunnel, Bill's coal rode silently along the belt, rising and falling as it crossed the heavy-duty rollers toward the trunk belt. Nearing the end of the Mothergate, it slid past a scene that could have been a tableau straight from Madame Tussaud's Chamber of Horrors. The still-bleeding corpse of Harry Weedon, the Coalface Deputy, lay next to the belt, twisted and silent, glazed eyes staring up at the girders above, as blood seeped from the gaping wound in his skull.

The massive figure of 19-year-old Geordie Robertson stood motionless next to him; his heavy, brutish face, contorted with a mixture of rage and fear made even more grotesque by the spectral light that shone up from the dead deputy's lamp at his feet. He stared at the dead eyes that appeared to have sunk into Weedon's thin, dirt and blood-streaked face, the light from his lamp reflecting off the dead man's false teeth, exposed by his grimace of death

Shuddering, he dragged his horrified gaze from the ghoulish face to his own, blood-soaked fist that still clutched the short metal fishplate he used to bludgeon Harry Weedon to death. A cold shiver ran down his back and he cast the plate onto the ground as if it was burning his hand.

Despised by his fellow deputies, Weedon was an arrogant, greedy, and selfish man, loathed by the men who worked under him and hated by many of the poorer folk of Ashington who had fallen into his evil grip.

Having borrowed money from him with extortionate pay back charges, the poor wretches found themselves trapped with no foreseeable way of paying off their debts to rid themselves of the detestable Weedon. He tried, but more often than not, failed, to portray himself as jovial and generous, but his weasel-like features and sarcasm betrayed him for the crook he was. Along with the hulking Bill Robertson, Geordie's father, he had operated a lone-shark swindle for several years from his home, a colliery, yellow-bricked, terraced house in Sycamore Street, one of many lined up back to back in the 'Hirst' area of Ashington.

Far too big, to work comfortably underground, Big Bill Robertson worked in the colliery shunting-yards driving one of the small Saddleback, steam trains -nicknamed 'Tankies.' The brute of a man was Weedon's enforcer and debt collector, but as the numbers of people who found themselves in the Loan Shark's grasp grew, he took on young Geordie to help collect the weekly payments that few of his poor victims could afford.

He also needed the protection the father and son provided as on more than one occasion, an angry client refused to cough-up the financially crippling repayments or, threatened violence or, threatened to inform the police. Bill and Geordie used their huge physical presence to intimidate non-payers and, when they thought it necessary, dole out the occasional thump or full-blown beating, something they both took pleasure in providing.

Weedon had also been involved in illegal betting but that ended with the introduction of the 1960 Betting and Gaming Act that resulted with betting shops opening in almost every town and village after the 1st of March 1961. In early December of 1962, along with Big Bill, he rented a small shop in one of the Avenues between the austere lines of colliery terraced-houses in the Hirst and having obtained a gambling license, he opened a betting shop.

However, obviously unaware of the impending big freeze, after initial success, business came almost to halt at the end of December when the freeze forced the cancellation of racing fixtures and football matches. The conditions also stopped whippet racing in the Welfare grounds, which was a blow to the many owners, and punters in Ashington.

His loan swindle and other petty crime he was involved in, made him sufficient cash to enable him to leave the colliery and coal mining, a job he hated but which provided him with a legitimate income and cover for his illegal operations.

Ten minutes earlier, he had been sitting at his 'Deputy's Kist', his workstation made out of wooden chocks and short planks fashioned into a seat and table above the kist or chest in which he kept his tally book and the other paraphernalia required for his job. A large piece of brattice cloth hung from the girders behind his back to provide shelter from the steady flow of directed air that flowed along the roadway.

Seeing a head-lamp approaching from the main roadway, he put down the black, hard-backed book he had been writing in, pulled the scruffy jacket he was wearing tight around his scrawny frame and to the hulking shadow behind the approaching light, said, 'How Geordie, is that ye lad?'

'Aye Harry, Geordie answered as he stopped and leaned over the Kist in an unintentionally intimidating manner, something that was hard not to do when you are 6 feet 3 inches tall and weigh 18 stone – most of it muscle.

A bully in school, Geordie Robertson had only come unstuck twice in fights, the first time with Rafe Trevelyan and the second with Ian Trevelyan. However, since then he had gained 5 inches in height and several stones in weight and having spent many hours in the gym training and sparring, neither of the lads posed a threat to him now.

After leaving school at fifteen, his reputation for violence rocketed as he bullied and battered his way through the Working Men's' Clubs and dance halls in the area, establishing himself as the 'hard-man' of Ashington. Such was his reputation as a fighter; no one, young or old, was brave enough to challenge him as he swaggered his way around town.

'Aa've finished teking the last load of props and gorders inte the barrier and want a word we ye,' Geordie said brusquely.

Working with a pit pony, Geordie was the 'Timber-Leader' responsible for delivering pit props, girders, tub rail-lines and anything else the miner's on the coalface required.

Weedon lent back and spat, 'Torn your frigging lamp away from me face forst ye stupid big git ye!'

Pushing his helmet up so that his headlamp shone up into the girders, Geordie growled, 'There ye gan we yer frigging insults again, I've warned ye before, ye canna speak te me like that man!'

'Aah'll talk te ye anyway Aah bliddy want, ye sackless dummy and, ye'll de as Aah tell ye, ye work for me, divin't ye forget that.'

Gritting his teeth, Geordie glared with narrowed eyes at the skinny, weasel-like Weedon, and hissed, 'Aye, and that's what Aah want te talk te ye aboot, noo that am deeing more collecting noo that me fatha is working in the betting shop with ye when he's in night-shift.' 'Aah want more money, it's me that has te gan doon Chinky Toon and kick on peoples doors for yer money and am working in the betting shop as weell when Aah can, so Aah want more money for deeing that.'

Pushing himself up from his seat, Weedon thrust his face up toward Geordie, who still towered over him and snarled,

6

'Work in the betting shop, that's a frigging joke, ye cannit coont te ten let alone run a betting shop, yer a frigging disaster, a pissing joke. My lad can run the betting shop on his own but ye, all yer good for is howking people, yer even ower bliddy big te work on the coal-face. Howking folk and sweeping the shop, that's all yer fit for so shut yer fucking gob and de as yer telt or ye 'll get nowt and ye can piss-off.'

Snorting in disbelief, Geordie's anger and frustration got the better of him.

Grabbing the planks on top of the kist, he threw them across the conveyor belt, snarling, 'Aah'll fucking kill ye, ye skinny, little bastard if ye speak like that te me again!'

Weedon grabbed Geordies tee shirt and began to speak but Geordie raised his right arm and knocked him backwards, shocking the smaller man. Leaning back against a girder, Weedon grabbed the metal fishplate he used as a paperweight and swung it at Geordie who blocked it with his left arm as the Deputy continued to lash out with the nine-inch long lump of steel.

Pinning Weedon against the tunnel wall, Geordie wrestled the fishplate from him, but Weedon began kicking him with his steel-toe-capped pit boots, catching him on the shin. Wincing in pain from the kick, Geordie reacted instinctively and swung the fishplate at his attackers head, striking him with a sickening thud just above the left ear. Blind with rage, he struck him twice more in almost the same spot, smashing Weedon's cheekbone and the left side of his skull, spilling bits of brain and blood as the Deputy collapsed like a stone onto the dust-covered tub-way.

Dead within seconds, Weedon looked like a scruffy, half-stuffed rag doll, discarded by a petulant child.

Transfixed by the sight before him and the realisation of what he had done; mounting panic and shock engulfed Geordie as he stood rooted to the spot. Unable to think coherently, he let out a slow, agonized groan that grew to a full-blooded howl, ending with him screaming, 'Fuck, fuck FUCK!' at the top of his voice.

Lowering his head, he tried to calm himself and think rationally, but, unable to control his emotions, panic took control of him. His first thought was to run but he managed, just, to stop his impulsive reaction. Looking down at the lifeless Weedon, revulsion engulfed him and he felt the need to hide the gruesome evidence of his murderous attack. Bending down, he lifted the lifeless Weedon to his chest as if he was a small child and effortlessly threw him across the conveyor belt where the corpse hit the stone and girders of the Mothergate wall and fell behind the conveyor.

Struggling to stop himself from again screaming in panic-driven desperation, he turned and began shuffling quickly out of the Mothergate tunnel, frantic to escape from the scene of his brutal attack.

Desperately, he tried to rationalise the thoughts racing through his head as he tried to think what to do as he scurried along:

'I left me pony Tom in the barrier, the bugga can stay there, am not ganning te the stables, the'll kna sumats up.'

'Nee bugga'll miss that bastard or see him lying behind the belt so Aah've time te get oot the frigging pit and away.'

What the fuck am a ganna dee?'

'Get oot the pit and piss-off before any bugga finds oot what Aah've done, am not hanging for that skinny, little, bastard.'

'What excuse dee Aah give te get oot the bliddy pit between shifts?'

The light from his head torch bounced wildly on the tunnel walls in front of him as he continued his manic shuffle toward the pit shaft bottom and the cage that would carry him to the surface as he tried to process what he should do:

'The bugga at the shaft bottom is gannin te want te kna why I want te gan up top!'

'Aah'll gan through the baths then hyem, nee bugga'll be up yit.'

'Aah kna, Aah'll tek the money my Dad keeps in the tin under the stairs and bugga off in his car, doon sooth te wor Alf's at Nottingham.'

'Nur not there, the fucking polis will find oot aboot family doon there and will gan looking for me.'

He shuffled on along roadways, passing an old man, sitting watching coal spill from one conveyor onto another before he eventually stumbled past the noise and controlled chaos of the loading point where coal poured into waiting tubs. The men working there were far too busy to stop working and speak to Geordie but a couple of them looked at him and then at each other, raising their eyebrows to silently, questioning what he was doing.

Geordie hurried on his thoughts still changing rapidly from problem to problem:

A place of sanctuary, a memory of a happier time came to him, 'Jedburgh - Jedburgh, that's where Aah'll gan, the owld converted railway carriage that we stayed in on holiday a few years ago. Aye that's it nee bugger'll be there this time of year, Aah'll break in and hide up there until Aah figure oot what te dee, the police winnit think Aah'll gan north.'

'Just got te get oot of Ashington and away...'

'Noo, who am Aah ganning te get oot the bliddy pit – pretend am hort, that's it, Aah'll mek on am hort and tell the owld fella at the shaft bottom that Aah hev te gan te the Medical Centre – that's it.'

Sweating from his thirty-minute race out, he fastened the bottom two buttons of his tight fighting denim jacket and slowed as he passed through the metal, air doors near the shaft bottom. Stuffing his right hand into the opening of his jacket, he blinked in the bright overhead lights as he approached the benches at the waiting area for the cage to the surface.

The old man on duty put down the book he was reading as Geordie approached, stopping for a second to take his identity tally from the board where it hung with the tallies of all the other men who were working in the pit.

'What's up we ye lad?' he asked as wild eye and sweating, Geordie approached saying, 'Aah've wrenched me bliddy showlder and the deputy telt me te gan up te the Medical Centre.'

Thinking that the look on Geordie's face was due to his injury, the man slid the concertina safety gates open and raised the cage door to let Geordie enter, closing them behind him before tapping the electric clapper that informed the winchman high above in the Winder House to wind the man-riding cage to the surface.

A blast of freezing air slapped Geordie in the face as he stepped out the cage and hurried passed the Banksman toward the lamp cabin. The familiar sounds and sights of the tubs full of coal rumbling past, rail wagons below the walkway banging and clattering as they were been shunted to and fro, and glaring arc lights did not register with him as he raced to the lamp cabin hatch. Dumping his lamp with its heavy battery and, his tally on the shelf below the hatch, he raced past racks of timecards before thumping down the open stairs and across frozen slush in front of the silent and deserted colliery offices, and on, into the Pit-Head-Baths. The cold air helped to clear his head a little and he forced himself to slow before entering the warmth of the damp-smelling, empty shower block.

Stripping off his pit clothes, he stuffed them into his dirty locker, one of the hundreds of narrow galvanized lockers built in two tiers in the 'Dirty' side of the baths. Grabbing his towel and soap, he hurried into one of the open-top, tiled shower cubicles and turned on the water, stepping under the flow before the hot water reached the showerhead. Shivering, he remained there, allowing the water to heat up slowly as it began to sluice away the coal dust and grime from his massive frame.

He showered in record time and quickly half-dried himself before striding to his locker in the clean side. Unlocking the door, he pulled out a packet of Capstan cigarettes, fumbling with shaking hands as he pulled one out; lighting it with a match from a flip pack. Placing his meaty left hand high up the on the lockers to steady himself, he took a long slow drag. It did little to calm his mood and he stubbed it out on the metal door. Casting the cigarette onto the floor, he pulled on his clean clothes, thick socks, denim jeans, tee shirt, a thick woollen, crew-neck jumper, rubber-soled leather boots and, a huge ex-RAF, blue, greatcoat.

Dressed, he set off quickly for the short walk to his home in the long terraced Ninth Row, one of eleven long, dreary rows of houses lined up in two blocks next to the colliery.

The clear, night sky was awash with stars and black ice glistened under street lamps as he hurried along the deserted and silent row, crunching over ridges of ice where snow that had turned to slush in the thaw of the past three days had frozen overnight. His thoughts in turmoil, he barely noticed the increasingly strong icy wind that pushed him toward his home as he pulled up the collar of his greatcoat to protect his frozen ears.

Nearing home, he tried, unsuccessfully to mask the sound of his approach by walking on tiptoes as he passed the streamlined shape of his father's two-tone, 1959 Vauxhall Cresta before pulling the front door key from the pocket of his greatcoat.

It was 6:30 am; well over an hour since he had murdered Weedon when he silently crossed the small backyard and carefully opened the front door to his home. Stepping inside, he quietly closed the door behind him and stood motionless for a minute in the small hall at the foot of the stairs, listening for any sound while the familiar smells of his home engulfed him.

He felt no remorse for the murder, blaming Weedon for his own actions as anger welled up inside him as he thought of the trouble Weedon had caused him, realising his life would never be the same again.

Gathering his thoughts, he turned back to the door, took down a knitted-woollen skullcap, and pulled it over his cold head and ears before silently walking into the unlit kitchen where the remains of yesterday's fire still glowed in the centre of the black-leaded, kitchen range.

Turning immediately right, he bent down next to the cupboard under the stairs and gently pulled open the triangular shaped door that gave a cat-like squeal, the sound making him wince. Reaching inside, groping behind a large cardboard box in the dark, he searched for his father's money tin.

Stretching as far as he could, his hands touched the smooth metal of the twelve-inch-long tin that he grasped before pulling it out, surprised at how heavy it was. Sinking back on his haunches, he prized open the lid and putting his right hand into the box, felt the cold metal of his father's point three-eight calibre, Webley revolver; a stolen souvenir from WW2 lying on top of a wad of notes and some loose ammunition.

Lifting the revolver out, footsteps on the stairs startled him and grabbing the large bundle of notes from the bottom of the tin with his left hand, he stood up. His father, 'Big Bill' Robertson, wearing striped pyjamas that barely covered his enormous bulk, stepped into the kitchen and switched on the 100-watt light bulb dangling from the centre of the ceiling, filling the room with a, white light. Both men lowered their heads and squinted under the bright light, Bill trying to grasp what was going on.

Seeing the empty tin on the floor and, his wild-eyed son with the revolver in one hand and a fistful of money in the other, he snarled, 'Waat the bliddy hell are ye deeing lad?'

Panic gripped Geordie again as he stammered,' 'Aah've got te getaway, Aah need yer money and the car, so aah can get away.'

'Haad yer friggin horses lad, yer not teking my money or car, what the hell de ye need te get away for,' spat Bill with venom.

'Aah've killed Harry Weedon;' Geordie spluttered, 'the fucka attacked me with a fish plate and Aah took it off him and smashed his frigging heed in so Aa've got te get away man.'

Shocked by his son's outburst, Bill stood in stunned silence for a few seconds as he tried to digest what his son had just said before almost shouting, 'Ye've done waat ye stupid bastard?'

Geordie's face turned red with rage; as a young boy, he had suffered many a beating from his father until he had grown too big and intimidating for him to handle. He was not going to let him stop him from escaping.

'Listen!' he snapped, 'am buggaring off and am teking this money and yer car, am not ganning te fucking prison; now get oot me fucking way or Aah'll shoot ye,' and quickly brought the revolver up, pointing it at the huge figure in front of him.

Stepping forward, Bill raged, 'Ye useless bastard, yer not getting me involved in this, give me the gun and me money, and ye can fuck off te bliddy hell as far as am concerned.'

He lunged with both hands at Geordie who raised his left hand to ward off his father as his mother Pat, still pulling on a faded striped dressing gown over her lean frame, stepped into the hall at the bottom of the stairs and looked in.

Bill grabbed his son's shoulders and squeezed, a look of hatred in his eyes that changed to shocked astonishment as Geordie struggled to break free and squeezed the trigger of the revolver. The deafening bang caused Pat Robertson to scream as Big Bill staggered backwards clutching his stomach, blood spurting between his fingers as he fell to the ground, knocking over two kitchen chairs as he fell.

Geordie exploded; his fear, anger, frustration and, attack by his father had pushed him over the edge; stepping forward he stood over his father and pointing the revolver at the centre of his father's head, squealed, 'Yer frigging, big bastard, Aah fucking hate ye,' and squeezed the trigger.'

The point thirty-eight calibre bullet travelled the few inches from the revolver, before smashing through the centre of Bill's forehead, instantly blowing bone, brains, and blood from the back of his head, across the floral wallpaper and curtains behind him, changing the previously cosy kitchen into a scene of carnage.

His mothers' piercing scream startled Geordie as she launched herself at him. Caught off guard and reacting instinctively, he swung the revolver in a wide arc, smashing it into her unprotected face, knocking her half-conscious, in a heap on top of her dead husband where she rolled over, clutching her smashed cheekbone and nose; unintelligible moans bubbling from her bloodied mouth as she sank back in pain and despair.

Looking at the terrible scene before him, Geordie had to fight the rising bile in his stomach as fear-induced panic once more took control of him. Stuffing the money into his pocket, he bent down and took the four spare rounds of point thirty-eight ammunition from the tin, dropped them into his pocket and snatching the keys for the Vauxhall hanging from a hook above a tall wooden Rediffusion radiogram, hurried out to the car.

Lights were coming on in neighbouring houses as he fumbled for a second or two to open the car door, before pulling the old blanket off the windscreen that his father had placed there the afternoon before. Stuffing the revolver into his greatcoat pocket, he climbed into the car and with trembling hands, put the keys into the ignition, and pulled out the choke. Depressing the clutch, he turned the key, praying the car would start; the engine whined a couple of times and then burst into life. After switching on the headlamps, he slipped the gear into first, let out the clutch, and drove off down the row, wheels spinning, and the car fishtailing as he fought to hold it straight on the icy road.

Pulling his overcoat on over his pyjamas, tall and thin, Tommy Bones from the house next door was the first out into the street, watching as the tail lights of the car disappeared around the corner at the bottom of the row. Joined by his wife who, in slippers and wearing a large brown dressing gown, asked 'What's happened?'

Her husband looked at her and answered, 'Buggared if Aah kna Pet but am certain those bangs wor shots,' and he headed toward the Robertson's back door, where another man from the house on the other side joined him.

Tommy shouted through the open door, 'Bill, are ye alreet?' Not hearing a response, he stepped into the kitchen where he stopped suddenly when he saw Bill and Pat lying in a bloody pool against the blood-spattered kitchen wall.

He took a moment to gather his thoughts before turning to the other neighbour who had followed him, 'Ray ye best run roond to the police station and tell them tha's been a morder here and ask them to phone for an ambulance as well and Aah'll see what Aah can dee for Pat.'

Ray nodded and hurried out the house to jog the few hundred yards to the police station as Tommy and his wife gently helped Pat to her feet and through into the sitting room. There they lowered her down onto the settee in front of the fireplace that still provided warmth from the coals that had been burning the night before. The calm atmosphere of the room provided a surreal contrast to the savage events that had just taken place a few feet away.

CHAPTER 2

Friday 8th February – 6:15 am
The Grundy's

Acouple of hundred yards away in the cramped and cold bedroom of the house in the Third Row that he shared with his two younger brothers when he was on leave, newly promoted, eighteen-year-old, Lance Bombardier Jake Grundy quietly touched the shoulder of eleven-year-old Billy. Sitting up with a startled expression, Billy carelessly dragged the bedding off nine-year-old Roger, curled up foetus like below an untidy heap of blankets.

Roger sniffed, and squinting up at Jake, asked in a whisper, 'Are we ganning noo?'

Jake held his forefinger to his lips and whispered, 'Aye, come on, noo be quiet, we divvint want te wake anybody up,' and handed Roger his National Health spectacles and, his clothes.

Jake had already pulled on his army long johns, woollen socks, string vest, and thick khaki shirt but shivered from the cold as he silently wound up the blind that hid the frost-covered window in the sloping roof, allowing moonlight to illuminate their bedroom. While the two younger boys dressed, Jake pulled on his wool pullover and green combat suit before bending down to slip his feet into his old slippers. Not wanting to wear his studded army ammunition boots that would have woken the rest of the house, he rolled up his green webbing ankle gaiters and shoved them inside his boots ready to carry them downstairs.

Shivering from cold and the excitement of their escape, the two younger brothers finished dressing in their school clothes and looked at Jake expectantly. He re-arranged their bedding, trying to give it the appearance that the boys were still in bed, and then giving them a nod, he again held his finger to his mouth before silently opening the door and leading the boys quietly down the steep stairs to the front door.

Glancing back to make sure they were both ready, he handed them their thick duffle coats that were hanging on the wall by the door. Once they had pulled their coats on over their jumpers and shorts, he slid the bolt from the back door and led them out to the bronze-green, 1 ton Austin, four by four, cargo truck that he had driven home the night before.

The truck was relatively short at only seventeen-feet long, with a small two-seater enclosed cab and a canvas covered superstructure over the rear cargo bay. It did have excellent ground clearance due to its raised suspension and heavy-duty military wheels that, allied with four-wheel drive, provided the vehicle with excellent cross-country performance.

Opening the passenger door he was about to help them inside when Billy said, 'Haad on Jake, I need te gan for a piddle.'

'OK, but be as quick as ye can,' Jake said, 'we've got te get away before any bugga wakes up.'

Billy grimaced and answered, 'Divin't worry, am not hanging aboot in the netty, it's freezing in there,' and ran across the road to their outside toilet, lined up with other toilets, coal houses and sheds opposite the terraced houses.

Jake smiled and turning to Roger who was wiping the almost permanent dewdrop from his nose with the sleeve of his duffle coat, asked, 'Aah suppose ye want gan as weell?'

'Not in there!' Roger sniffed, 'Aah'll gan te the toilet at Mrs Trivlin's, it's warm in there and she has propa soft netty paper.' Despite not being able to pronounce Trevelyan correctly, he always called Jane by the name he knew her by before she married Edward Thompson.

Trying not to laugh, Jake said, 'OK, but it's Mrs Thompson now man, can ye not get that right?'

Roger grinned, 'Aye , alreet, Aah'll caall Mrs Trivlin, Mrs Tomsin noo.'

Jake helped Roger to climb up onto the leatherette seat in the cold cab just as Billy came running out of the outside toilet, saying, 'It's bliddy freezing in there man.'

Waiting until Billy had climbed up next to his brother, Jake whispered, 'Sit here until I gan back and close up the hoose, they kna am leaving early but winnit think that Aah've got ye two with me.'

Pulling his duffel coat tightly around him, Roger looked down at Jake and said forlornly, 'Am hungry, can we have a sammich or something Jake?'

'Missus Thompson will give ye breakfast Roger lad, noo just keep yer heeds doon for a bit and here, put me boots on the floor in there,' answered Jake as he handed up his boots before pushing the door quietly closed.

Walking to the back door, he opened it quietly and was startled to see his father, forty-two-year-old Albert, in a long striped nightshirt, shivering at the foot of the stairs; freshly lit cigarette dangling from his bottom lip as he rubbed his scarred hands in an effort to warm them. He had burnt his hands three years earlier when he had tried and failed to dig his wife, Flo, from the burning wreckage of their terraced, colliery house in the Sixth Row when an RAF jet fighter had crashed into it.

Because the injury to his hands had prevented him from returning to work underground, the NUM had secured him a job as an attendant in the Pit Head Baths, as well as a small compensation payment from the Ministry of Defence.

'Are ye ready for the off then Jake lad,' Albert asked, unaware that his two youngest sons were sitting in the cab of the army truck.

Controlling mounting anger and frustration, Jake replied, 'Aye Dad, I didn't want te wake ye's, look Dad, am sorry aboot last night but ye have te believe me, she's bliddy evil, she's bleeding ye dry and hitting the lads and bugga knows waat else. Ye've got te get rid of her.'

Albert screwed his face as though he was in pain and seemed to shrink a little making him look rather like a sad, circus-clown in his long nightshirt with thin hairy legs appearing to dangle from below the frayed hem. A spark suddenly appeared in his eyes, and lifting his head, he said forcefully, 'ye've got it wrang, Edna is a lovely woman, she wouldn't hurt a fly, them marks on the bairns are from them messing aboot - ye kna tha always fighting each other.'

Jake tried to interrupt but Albert stopped him, 'Nur, Aah winnit listen te ye anymore, she looks after me and the hoose and keeps the bairns clean and tidy and tha far better behaved noo.'

That was too much for Jake, 'Aye tha better behaved because tha terrified of her, she's threatened to have them put in a borstal or sent te a home and, she's ower bliddy young for ye Fatha but it's pointless arguing with ye, ye winn't bliddy listen. Aah phoned Ronnie last night and he's coming up from Catterick tomorrow to sort things out, so am off, Aa'll just clean the windscreen and gan, Aah might be able te get back tonight if the QM will let me.'

Albert did not say anything; he seemed to shrink again as his son left, closing the door behind him.

A few minutes later, Jake was just finishing scraping ice from the windscreen of his truck, when he heard two muffled bangs – 'Bliddy hell, Aah wonder what that was?' he thought as he climbed into the cab and smiling at his brothers started the engine.

Putting the truck into gear, he slipped the clutch and felt the large military tyres bite into the scattering of frozen slush as he drove carefully down the row, turning right onto the avenue that led from the colliery to the main road where he turned right into High Market.

He smiled reassuringly at Billy and Roger who had sat up to look out of the frosty side window of the truck as his thoughts took him back to June of last year when he had passed out of the Junior Leaders Regiment as the Junior Leader – Regimental Sergeant Major.

It had been the best day of his life, the end of two years of intense, demanding, and often exciting training that had changed him from a feckless and mischievous schoolboy into a determined and motivated young man. He had also grown to five-feet-ten inches and gained well over a stone, all of it muscle thanks to being a member of the gymnastic display team. The highlight of the day had been the parade when his father, brothers and friends had watched him march the Regiment on to the Parade Square of the ex–RAF camp.

After the parade, the young soldiers and their families and friends were enjoying refreshments in and around the Junior Soldiers' NAAFI, as the officers and SNCOs from the Regiment, mingled with them discussing with the parents, what their sons had achieved during their time there. Jake had just been congratulated, again, by the Commanding Officer and was taking some mild ribbing from his four pals who had travelled from Ashington to watch the parade, when, his older brother, Ronnie interrupted and said, 'Jake, I need to talk to you,' and led him to one side.

A corporal in The Kings Own Northumbrian Border Regiment, he had travelled down from Catterick with his beautiful Chinese wife Mary, and their two-year-old, daughter, Florence. Immaculate in his Service Dress, he wrinkled his brow and staring intently at Jake, asked, 'Do you know that Fatha's talking about getting married again and that she's already moved in?'

'Waat - not that frosty-fyeced, black-haired, miserable bugga who's been hanging roond me fatha for the past twelve months; hur with that fat, brat of a son?'

Ronnie smiled, 'Aye that's the one Jake, Mrs Bliddy, Edna North, I only found oot when I went up to see him and the lads at Christmas, she was sat in the sitting room, bold as brass with hur fat kid on her knee and Dad and wor two on the settee watching tele. He was right sheepish about it but not hur, she just turned and said, "Hello; Albert'll mek ye's both a cup of tea in a minute," whey man I was just ganning te say something but Dad jumped up and half-pushed us both in to the kitchen, closing the door behind him. He was really embarrassed and said that he had been lonely since Flo had been killed - but he didn't look very happy seeing as how they are planning te marry in spring!'

Jake looked shocked, 'She's a lot younger than him why on Earth would she want te marry him, he's not exactly handsome is he and how on Earth did she get hor hooks inte him?'

'Aye Dad's forty-two and she's ownly twenty-seven not much older than I am. She has a canny figure and isn't bad looking in a hard, nasty sort of way. Dad had started to go to the Bingo at the Tute where she was a regular, and she wheedled her way into his company. She then got him to take her to the Bingo at the Piv once a week and from what I have been told, he paid for her.'

Jake shook his head in disbelief, 'Do you think she is after his compensation money?'

'It looks that way but as far as I know, tha wasn't that much money. Apparently, she was married and lived in a colliery hoose in Pegswood but her old fella killed himself, suffocated in the back of his car. Folk say she had been buggaring aboot with other fellas and she had debt's all ower the place.'

Frowning, Jake butted in, 'But hoo come she was at the hoosy at Ashington Tute?

'She had to leave the colliery hoose after her husband killed himself, and was living in a bedsit above a shop in Station Road; she's probably got debt all over Ashington now!'

Jake looked over at his Dad standing next to Billy and Roger who both looked very morose and asked, 'How have Billy and Roger teken to hor moving in with her spoilt brat and knowing that they are ganna get married?'

'That's what am worried about, they didn't seem happy at all but when I asked if everything was OK they said everything was great and that's all they would say – not like them is it?'

Jake nodded, 'Nur it's not, ye cannit shut them up most of the time.'

Ronnie continued, 'Mind she has the hoose looking spick and span but I think she's stopped Dad from working in his shed at nights and weekends and ye kna how much time he used to spend in there tinkering with broken mopeds. Anyway, when ye get up there try and find oot what's ganning on, I was only there a couple of days and she tried to be nice as ninepence but most of the time, she had a face like a slapped arse!'

To his shame, Jake had intentionally not spent that much time at home on his leave. Not wanting to be near the odious Edna, he had been out with his pals most nights and they had all spent a week at Butlin's at Skegness where Jake had lost his virginity to a buxom lass from Northampton. On their return, he had tried to get the two boys to talk about their father and Edna but all he got from them was an unenthusiastic, 'She's OK.'

When he asked his Dad why he stopped mending mopeds in his shed, his Dad had told him that it was not fair on Edna him spending so much time across the road in the shed and, she didn't like him walking into the house in his greasy overalls.

He had left it that but on return to camp had felt guilty that he had not spent more time with his younger brothers and found out why they were so unhappy.

Jake's thoughts leapt back to the present when he pulled up outside Hotspur House, the large, Edwardian House where the Thompsons/Trevelyan's lived. Grabbing his boots and gaiters from the floor of the cab, he jumped out and walked round to the passenger side, hunching his shoulders against the cold east wind that was howling down the road.

Helping his two brothers out of the cab, he ushered them up the drive, past Jane's, Morris Minor Traveller, to the kitchen door at the side of the house where they found the stunning, raven-haired Jane Thompson holding the door open for them.

Stepping back inside, she ushered them quickly into the warmth of the kitchen that smelled of toast and porridge. She had endured a loveless and abusive marriage to Nick Shepherd until he had gone off the rails and murdered a police officer, a crime for which he paid the ultimate penalty. After his death, she had reverted to her maiden name Trevelyan until she married Edward Thompson, a decorated WW2 hero who now owned his own electrical business. Her three boys, however, had all kept the Trevelyan name.

Once they were all in the warm kitchen, she smiled as she helped Billy and Roger take off their matching duffle coats, saying, 'Hello boys, take your coats off and take a seat at the table while I get you some hot porridge and honey to warm you up,'

Roger who had crossed his skinny legs, asked hurriedly in his best, posh-voice, 'Canna, please use yor netty, sorry, canna please use yor toilet Missus Triv, sorry Aah mean Missus Tosmin, I mean Missus Tomsin, please?'

Just managing to surprise a giggle, Jane, said, 'Of course Roger, you know where it is and you don't have to ask when you need to go.'

Roger hurried to the door to the hall saying over his shoulder, 'Thanks very much Missus Trivlin.'

Gunner Ian Trevelyan, Jane's son and Jake's lifelong friend had watched from the far side of the table where he was devouring his second bowl of porridge, 'Come and sit doon Jake,' he said, 'and have some porridge, did you manage to get away without anyone knowing?'

Putting his boots down Jake pulled up a chair in between Ian and Billy and replied, 'Just aboot, Aah got them two into the truck but my Dad had heard me and come doon the stairs. But - he didn't kna the lads wor already oot so, hopefully, they won't kna the've gone until the witch wakes up and gans inte get them up for school.'

Placing three bowls of porridge on the table, Jane asked, 'Did you leave a note like we discussed last night Jake?'

'Yes Mrs Thompson, just like we discussed, I wrote that I was bringing the lads here because they were doing a presentation at school with yor Tommy and they wanted te practice before they went in.'

Jane nodded, 'Good I'll wake Tommy in a few minutes and bring him down for his breakfast,' and turning to Billy asked, 'Have you got your money for school lunch, or, is it already paid Billy?'

'Swallowing a mouthful of porridge, Billy spluttered, 'If ye mean school dinnas Mrs Thompson, nur we divvin't have school dinnas anymore, she stopped paying for them so we gan home for sumat te eat, she niva makes owt so we have jam and bread or sumat else but she alwas meks sumat nice for fat Howard.'

Jake's brow furrowed as he asked, 'When did she stop paying yer school dinners?'

'Ages ago, just after she moved in,' Billy said, worried that he had said something he shouldn't have.

Jake was about to say something in anger but Jane stepped in, 'Not to worry, I'll come and collect you both, and Tommy at lunchtime and bring you back here for lunch, hopefully, Ronnie will be here by then and he will be able to discuss matters with your father.'

The door swung open and Roger strolled back in and stood looking covetously at the large bowl of porridge next to an empty chair.

'Go on sit yourself down and tuck in,' Jane said smiling, 'I've got more bread in the toaster for when you finish your porridge.'

Roger sat down and picked up his spoon, 'Thanks Missus Tri..., sorry Tomsin.'

Ian stood up and looking at Jake who was finishing his porridge, said, 'Come on Jake, get your boots on we need te get back to Redesdale camp before half-past-eight or the QM will have our guts for garters!

Jane looked at her son in his green combat suit and black beret and thought how handsome he looked but sighed quietly. It had been an upsetting time for her when, last June, just after Jake had finished his leave and gone off to join his new regiment in Essex, that Ian had dropped his bombshell!

Jane, her husband Edward, Mike, Ian, his younger brother Tommy and, Rafe, Jane's much younger brother had all been sitting at the kitchen table, finishing dinner when Ian cleared his throat and almost whispered; 'Mam, I am going to join the army.'

A look of shock and confusion clouded Jane's face but it was Rafe who spoke first in his refined voice,' 'What! When did you decide that; you are studying for your 'A' levels; you are joking; surely?'

'I am serious, I want to join now,' Ian replied as he mentally prepared himself for what he was sure was going to be a long drawn out discussion, if not argument – it was both. He told them that seeing how much Jake had changed and having listened to his stories of army life, he was even keener to join up but talking to Jake's officers at the Pass-Out Parade had shocked him. He had realized how different they were to him; all of them, without exception, had spoken with posh, educated accents that left him feeling out-of-place and insecure.

Jane and Edward had argued that the officers were no better than he was and that he was every bit as intelligent as they were. Rafe then tried to talk him around but his posh accent and upbringing just added weight to Ian's argument.

Jane became a tad angry when Edward said; 'You can join up as a soldier and still be picked up for a commission or even apply for one when you are ready,' as she knew then that she had lost the discussion. A few weeks later, Ian caught the train to Oswestry and became Gunner Ian Trevelyan.

Having requested to join the same regiment as Jake, on completion of his training in August, he joined 204 Regiment Royal Artillery, stationed just outside Southend-on-Sea in Essex. The Regiment was in the process of discharging the last of its National Service soldiers, a result of which, it was receiving large numbers of recruits from Oswestry in order to bring it back up to strength.

Ian had turned down the chance to join the potential officers' cadre at Oswestry and within a few weeks of joining 204, was training to be a surveyor.

Jake was selected for promotion to Lance Bombardier after having served only four months of regular mans' service due mainly to the Regiment being short of NCOs and, him having been a Junior RSM, He had qualified as a signaller while at the Junior Leaders Regiment. On joining the regiment, he was allocated to the Battery Commanders Party and, passed his grade 2 signals course and, his driving test.

Pushing back his chair, Jake bent over and pulled on his boots, fastening his ankle gaiters over the top and tucking the bottom of his trousers into the thick elastic he had strapped around the gaiters.

Standing, he pulled on his beret and looking at Jane, said, 'Thanks for your help again Mrs Thompson and am sorry for coming aroond last night and dropping this on yer but I didn't know what te dee after Billy towld me that Edna was hitting and nipping them as well as stopping tha pocket money. Mind, it was when he said that she had threatened to fetch the police and have them sent to borstal if they said out, that got me really mad.'

Billy told Jake the night before, that just after they moved in; Howard told his mother that Billy and Roger had stolen crisps from Wilkinson's shop in Highmarket at lunchtime. She confronted the boys, calling them thieves and worse and threatened to go to the police and have them sent to a borstal if they ever told their father how she treated them.

Kissing his mother on the cheek, Ian said, 'I'll hopefully be back tonight Mam,' and walked to the door pulling on his woollen khaki gloves just as Edward, who had been washing and shaving upstairs walked in.

'I've just been listening to the weather forecast lads,' he said, 'it doesn't look good, the thaw is over and they are forecasting blizzard conditions later today so you need to get back before it hits us – we won't expect you home tonight Ian.'

A worried looking Jake said, 'Thanks Mister Thompson, we should be back at Redesdale before nine-o'clock - if the roads are clear,' then pointing to his two brothers, added, ' but am worried aboot these two. If Aah divvint get back tonight and wor Ronnie doesn't get up from Catterick, who's ganna sort the problem with my Dad and that aaful woman; and these two, where are they ganna stay?'

Billy and Roger both looked very worried, Roger pushing his spectacles back up his pointed nose, sniffed and said, 'Not we that horrible woman.'

Jane looked at Edward who nodded and then turned back to look at Jake saying, 'We will look after the boys Jake. If neither you or Ronnie get back, Edward and I will go to see your father and discuss the situation with him; we have seen the bruises and nip marks on the boys, there is no way we will allow that woman to lay hands on them again. I will make beds up for them in Ian's room this morning, so, don't you worry about it; we will take of them.'

Jake, gave a long sigh of relief as the tension drained out of him, 'Thanks very much Missus thompson, I canna tell you hoo relieved I am te hear that, I kna ye'll look after these two, mind, not that the deserve it, eh lads?' he said, nudging Billy.

Grinning, Billy said, 'Aye thanks very much Missus Thompson.'

Ian put his arm around Jake and said, 'Right, now that that's sorted, let's get ganning.'

'Aye, well gan canny and don't take any risks lads,' Edward said as Jane handed Ian a flask of hot tea and a bag of sandwiches and other goodies.

Ian took them and said, 'Ta, I'll call you from camp at lunchtime once I know what the situation is,' and opening the door, he and Jake hurried out closing the door against the strengthening wind that had blasted into the kitchen.

Inside, having felt the blast of cold air, Jane looked at Edward and asked, 'Will you take the boys to school in your van this morning sweetheart?'

Edward ruffled Roger's hair, 'Aye, of course, Pet, we don't want the bairns blown away in the gale, do we.'

Once in the truck and driving out of Ashington along the Pegswood Road, with snow from previous storms piled high on either side, Ian asked, 'Are we going back the way we came, Jake?'

'Yep, Morpeth then alang to Belsay and up the A696 to Otterburn then the A68 to Redesdale, let's hope the roads have all been salted.'

'Look at that sunrise,' said Ian, pointing to the red and yellow sky, burning just below the eastern horizon.

Concentrating on the road ahead, Jake replied, 'Aye, red sky at night, shepherds' delight, red sky in the morning, we're in for a frigging storm!'

Two weeks earlier, As the Regiment prepared for a three-week live-firing camp at Otterburn, Jake and Ian had marched in to see their Battery Sergeant Major – BSM and asked permission to be in the fatigue party from the Battery that would be part of the Regimental Advance Party under command of the QM. They would be driving up to Redesdale Camp, arriving on Thursday the 7th of February. The Advance Party had to take over the camp and prepare it for the Regiment's arrival on Sunday the 10th.

The BSM was sceptical at first but when Jake told him that, he was hoping to get a couple of nights at home to sort out a family problem he had agreed. The two lads had reported to Staff Sergeant Hobbs, the Battery BQMS, who briefed them on the jobs they would be doing, mainly moving bedding from stores to bunks at Redesdale, and helping with kitchen fatigues. He had asked if either of them could drive and when Jake had said yes, he told him he would be driving an Austin truck that would be loaded with 'Q' stores.

It was half-past seven with the sun rising slowly behind them when Jake approached Morpeth on almost deserted roads, following the route that Geordie Robertson had taken fifty minutes earlier.

CHAPTER 3

Friday 8th February – 7:15 am
The Ninth Row

The blue Bakelite telephone rang nosily in the hall of DI Jamie Norman's semi-detached house in Wansbeck Road as he dipped another toast soldier into his soft-boiled breakfast egg.

Julia, his wife, who had just poured him a cup of tea, asked,' Shall I answer it, sweetheart?'

Leaving the toast sticking out of his egg, he said in his soft Scottish lilt,' 'Och, no, I'll answer it, tis probably for me,' and walked into the hall.

'Sergeant Jameson here sir; 'the Duty Sergeant at Morpeth Police Station said, 'we have a suspected murder in the Ninth Row, a couple of uniforms are there from Ashington and have the scene under control.'

Jamie asked, 'Any idea when it happened?'

'Yes, according to neighbours, two gunshots were heard at about six twenty this morning, and they saw the son, a

George Robertson driving off in the victim's car, the victim was identified as William Robertson by a neighbour who was looking after Mrs Robertson. She had allegedly, been assaulted by her son, she's been taken to Ashington hospital.'

Having scribbled most of the information the sergeant gave him on a note pad next to the telephone, Jamie said, 'OK I'll drive around there now in my car, get DS Dodson to meet me there, did uniform get the make and number of the car?'

'Yes sir, we have circulated details, a two-tone, blue Vauxhall Velux and we've got three local cars out looking for him and HQ at Newcastle is pushing cars out, I will phone DS Dodson now.'

'Better tell him to bring DC Cotton.'

'Will do Sir, this is our first murder since the McArdle case.'

'Aye Sergeant it is,' replied Jamie and placed the handset back on to its rest.

A few minutes later, he carefully brought his 1961, charcoal, Hillman Minx to a halt behind the white, police Sunbeam Rapier parked outside the Robertson's house in the Ninth Row. Taking his keys out of the ignition, he shoved them into the side pocket of his tired and well-worn Harris Tweed jacket and looked at himself in the rear-view mirror.

Noting that his hair was its normal unruly dusty-blonde mop, he licked the palm of his left hand, rubbing it across his head in a futile attempt to tame it. Ignoring his failure, he grasped the knot of his tartan tie and tried unsuccessfully to straighten it. Pleased that he had spruced himself up, he rummaged unsuccessfully through his jacket pockets for his notebook, then picking up his overcoat from the passenger seat, after a quick rummage through its pockets, he found the notebook in the inside pocket. Satisfied that he was ready, he opened the door and stepped out into the bitter wind that was now howling down the street and pulled on his overcoat.

Much had changed for the tall, bespectacled Scotsman in the last four years but 1962 had been a year to remember. Promoted to Detective Inspector in January, in August he finally closed the Joe McArdle murder file when the body of the chief-suspect, Joe's brother Pat, turned up in their car in Sheepwash quarry after the council drained and cleared it prior to landscaping. The badly decomposed corpse revealed that Pat's neck had been broken and the empty whisky bottle inside the car indicated that he was probably drunk when the car crashed.

The pathologist's verdict was that the cause of death was, a broken neck probably caused when the car crashed twenty feet into the quarry. The coroner's inquest result was suicide, committed after having murdered his brother in a drunken argument. Jamie wasn't convinced but knew that due to the lack of evidence, clues, or witnesses, he was unlikely to provide an alternative answer.

However, the main event of 1962 and perhaps his life, was his marriage in May to Julia, a petite and pretty, thirty-year-old, primary school teacher who he had met the year before. She was his opposite in all most everything – especially neatness but they gelled almost instantly. After a short, passionate courtship, they were married at the Holy

Sepulchre Church at the Store Corner, a hundred yards from Wansbeck School where she taught the local primary age kids, including Roger Grundy and Tommy Trevelyan.

Hurrying past the squad car, Jamie crossed the small yard and knocked on the door of the Robertson's house and, not waiting for an answer; opened the door where a young, uniformed police officer stopped him, saying, 'Careful Sir, the body is just inside the kitchen.'

Squeezing into the tiny hallway alongside the officer, Jamie looked through the kitchen door to Bill Robertson's bloody corpse, 'I don't suppose the doc or photographers have shown up yet?'

'Not yet sir, but an ambulance has been and taken Mrs Robertson to Hospital, I made them take her out through the garden door and back through the next door neighbour's to the ambulance so as not to disturb the scene.'

'Good lad, did you manage to speak to her?'

'Not much sir but she said that her son had shot him, that's Geordie Robertson, he's well known to uniform for fighting.'

Jamie nodded, 'Did she say anything else?'

'No Sir, but the neighbour who was with her said that Geordie drove off in his father's car, I've radioed through the description and license number.'

'Jamie looked at the dead man and muttered, looks like two wounds, belly first judging by the blood and his position and, the gore on the wall from the head shot.' 'Probably a revolver, any idea what weapon he used or where he might have got it from'

'No Sir, no idea but I reckon Mrs Robertson will know,' and staring past Jamie, he said, 'The neighbour did say that he heard two shots like.'

'What time was that?'

The PC looked at his notebook and replied, 'Approximately six-thirty, sir.'

Jamie looked puzzled, 'Right, I wonder why they were up and about so early?' Not expecting a reply, he added, 'My DS and DC are on the way, tell them I'm next door speaking to the neighbours and, let me know when the doctor or photographer turn up; I need to get down to speak to Mrs Robertson but not before I know things are in hand here.'

CHAPTER 4

Friday 8th February – 7:20 am
The Dawsons

Forty-year-old Sarah Dawson closed the lid on her cheap green suitcase, flipping the catches shut before casting an eye around the cosy kitchen come living room in the miners' terraced house at Prestwick, north-west of Newcastle. Having lived in the three up and two down house with her late husband and children for the past eighteen years, she was both sad and excited as a new phase in her life was about to begin.

She had taken pride in keeping their modest home clean, tidy, and comfortable, but she would not be unhappy when she finally moved out in a few weeks' time.

The room's neat appearance was currently marred by her ten-year-old son, Davy, who was trying to stuff a pair of shoes and, a football strip into the small suitcase he had open on the table in the centre of the room.

Fastening her thick, beige, full-length coat over the two thin jumpers she had pulled on over her slim figure, Sarah picked up a tartan headscarf and fastened it around her head, looking in the mirror over the fireplace, ensuring it was tucked neatly inside her coat collar.

Looking at Davy and seeing him struggle, she resisted the temptation to help him, not wanting to interfere with his packing, as she knew it would annoy him, he was a strong-willed and independent boy who liked to complete his own tasks.

Despite been keen to set off, she also did not want to upset him as he left his home for the last time and said quietly, 'Davy Pet, we need to go soon, please hurry up and put your bag in the back of the car, Rosalind's already in and it's very cold out there.'

As he finished closing his suitcase, she walked around the room ensuring everything was in its place and the window locked. Satisfied that everything was as it should be, she picked up Davy's quilt-lined overcoat and helped him on with it before ushering him out the door. Picking up the two suitcases and stepping outside, she leant her head into the wind and quickly carried them to the boot of her 1958, red, Ford Consul.

The car had been her husband, David's pride, and joy until his tragic death when he drowned after slipping on ice and falling into the sea while fishing off the pier at Amble in early January. Banging his head as he fell, he was unconscious when he hit the ice-cold and very choppy sea. No one amongst the half dozen folk on the pier was brave enough to jump in to rescue him and instead waited forlornly for the local lifeboat. The crew struggled for forty-five, difficult and dramatic minutes before they managed to recover his body from amongst the rocks near the mouth of the river Coquet.

Having to wait until the Coroner's Inquest was finished, Sarah, and her children were only able to bury David in the local church, four days earlier. Given four weeks leave of absence from her job as the office manager and senior typist at a well know law firm in Newcastle, she was taking her two children to stay with her parents at Dalkeith, near Edinburgh. She thought it best that Rosalind and Davy were comfortable at their grandparents while she arranged for somewhere for them to live, as they were required to vacate the colliery-owned house, their entitlement to the house, having died with David. A miner all his working life, at the time of his death, he was a Deputy at the 'Lizzie Anne Pit' of Prestwick Colliery, just off the A68.

Their married life together had not been going well, David had become set in his ways, spending far too many weekends fishing with his pals rather than sharing his days off work with his family. This had led to many arguments and the slow disintegration of their marriage that was all but over. Much to Sarah's regret, their last conversation, like many before it, had been short and tense.

Seventeen-year-old Rosalind was halfway through a secretarial course at a nearby technical college and wanted to stay to help her mother but Sarah believed that her being at home would not benefit either of them during the coming weeks.

Pushing with all her might to close the boot lid against the increasing wind, she managed to close and lock it before hurrying back to lock the door, checking twice that it was secure. She held onto the handle for a few seconds, almost reluctant to let go as she said goodbye to her old life, not looking forward to returning in a couple of days to organise removals.

Sitting alone in the back of the car, Davy was busy tucking a tartan travel rug around his legs as Sarah climbed in the front next to the very pretty, Rosalind who had the same striking auburn coloured hair as her mother.

Having started the car earlier to defrost the windscreen and warm the inside, she asked, 'Are you both tucked in and warm?'

'Yes Mam,' Davy answered quietly.

Rosalind gave her mother a worried look and said, 'I am warm now Mam but look at the weather, are we going to be OK?'

'We'll be fine Pet, the A696 is clear to Otterburn and the A68 over Carter Bar has been open for over a week; the forecast yesterday said there might be some snow later today but we'll be at your grannies in a couple of hours or so; that's why we are starting so early.'

Driving slowly down the narrow, icy back lane, she turned onto the cleared main road through the village and onto freshly gritted A696. Although the road was clear, high banks of snow thrown up by snowploughs lined the road on both sides. Concentrating on the road, she did not notice the pastel pink that tinged the surrounding snow-covered fields as the morning sun cast its red glow across the sky.

Fifteen minutes later with both her children nodding off, she drove through the sandstone hamlet of Belsay and noticed a huge bank of ominous, grey clouds, building in the east.

CHAPTER 5

Friday 8th February – 7:50 am
A696

Knowing he would have to drive past the Police Station in the imposing, pseudo-castle, just past the bridge over the Wansbeck, fear had gripped Geordie Robertson when, at six-forty, he had driven into Morpeth. He hoped and prayed that police would not yet be looking for him. The town was quiet, and he only passed one car as he drove through, breathing a sigh of relief when he was clear of the police station.

His relief was short-lived, having negotiated the as yet; quiet streets of Morpeth and heading across to Belsay, the stupidity of his panic-driven plan hit him.

'The car, the car ye stupid bastard,' he thought to himself; 'Ivry bugga is ganna be looking for it, I need te get rid of the frigging thing once am clear.' His mind in turmoil as he tried desperately to think what to do, he brought the car to a sliding halt and tilting his head forward, rubbed his face with both hands, muttering, 'Think for fuck's sake, think.'

Taking his cigarettes and matches out of his greatcoat pocket, he lit one and took a long drag, confused thoughts fighting each other as he tried to make sense of his predicament. After what seemed like ages but could have only been a couple of minutes, he stubbed the cigarette out in the ashtray of the car and pulled the money he had taken from his father's tin box, out of his pocket.

After counting it carefully, he said aloud, 'Fucking hell, £320 quid!' Then he thought, 'Bugga staying in the owld carriage, I'll have te ditch the car somewhere, in the sea or a loch and then Aah'll catch a train up inte the wilds of Scotland and stay in a B&B somewhere quiet until things quieten doon,' and stuffed the money back into his left-hand greatcoat pocket.

Still hoping that the police would not expect him to go north, he drove off, his mind struggling to make sense of his racing thoughts. Not concentrating on the road, he almost slid off the road twice and, had skidded to a halt in front of a five bar gate when he had taken a ninety-degree bend just before Belsay far too fast. Panic still clouded his mind, forcing him to hurry on but he did eventually slow down when he drove through the picturesque village of Kirkwhelpington, half hidden beneath deep snow from previous snowstorms.

Once clear of the village, he did not notice the building clouds as he as he once again, drove recklessly on; not slowing as the road climbed past snowbound pastures to wild moorland. Worrying that he would not make it across the Border, as he drove past the windswept junction at Knowesgate, he grinned when he saw a large snowplough truck coming from the opposite direction.

The sight of the vehicle lifted his mood slightly, 'Good they are keeping the road clear; I should be able to get over Carter Bar OK,' he thought.

A few minutes ahead of Robertson, with both her children asleep, Sarah continued to drive steadily northwest. The increasing wind that was beginning to blow snow from the drifts on the side of the road, forced her to switch on her windscreen wipers and, as the temperature plummeted, she turned the car's heater up to maximum.

The first seeds of doubt on the wisdom of attempting the journey began to unnerve her; however, seeing that the road was still clear and vehicles were still coming from the opposite direction, she decided to drive on as far as Otterburn, where she would pause to consider conditions before continuing.

On the road between Morpeth and Belsay, Jake was concentrating totally on the road ahead, driving carefully, well aware of his lack of driving experience. He was not going to take any risks as he headed for the A696. Sitting next to him Ian looked at his Pal, studying the concentration on his face, admiring him for what he achieved in three years, he was no longer the butt of anyone's joke. Ian realised he admired him for having made the change from a mischievous fool to a confident, smart young NCO with a very caring nature. He also realised that he was proud of his pal.

Aware that the storm was due to hit earlier than expected and, that it was likely to last at least twenty-four hours; the police at Hexham dispatched PC John Carlisle and PC Colin Wilson in a Sunbeam Rapier patrol car to assess the effects of the storm on the A68 trunk road up to Scotland. They knew that if the snow was as heavy as forecasted, that they may well have to close the road before it begins the climb up to Carter Bar.

The officers had come across several abandoned cars that had failed to make it up one or two of the short but steep hills on the switchback stretch of the road before Colt Crag Reservoir and saw that a snowplough was having difficulty clearing windblown snow as it attempted to climb the slippery hills.

Losing radio communications with Hexham, they stopped at a roadside telephone box in the remote hamlet of West Woodside that straddled the A68, just over five miles from Otterburn. Six-foot-three John Carlisle climbed out of the passenger seat and nipped into the phone box. Calling Hexham, he advised that the A68 was unlikely to remain open when the snowstorm arrived and that several cars and lorries were already stuck on the road. Hexham informed him that they heard from the police in Kelso that they had already closed the A68 south, three miles north of Carter Bar.

They instructed the two officers to continue on to Redesdale Camp and close the road north. Hexham was already liaising with the Camp Commandant at Otterburn Army Training Camp for the use of facilities at Redesdale Camp should there be any stranded travellers or drivers.

Fifteen mile away, after having dug away the snow from the front of the coal merchant's truck, Jack Gray attached the winch and began dragging it out of the ditch when the first snowflakes fell. The Scammell winch made short work of the job but it was going to take Jack, the coal merchant and his two sons, another thirty minutes of battling the weather and equipment to set the suspended tow before they could drag the disabled truck to Bellingham.

CHAPTER 6

Friday 8th February – 8:08 am
Ashington

'Isn't that the DI's car? Detective Constable Will Cotton asked the huge, overweight Detective Sergeant Bob Dodson, as he brought the Blue, Austin Cambridge to a smooth halt behind Jamie Norton's Hillman, parked outside the Robertson's house.

'Aye it is lad, the Jock git has probably solved this one already, a few statements te tek and we can all gan back te the warm office, eh,' Dodson replied, chuckling as he stubbed out the cigarette he had been smoking in the ashtray that failed to contain his many stub ends.

DS Cotton pulled up the collar of his grey, gabardine overcoat and stepping out of the car, ignored the bitter wind playing havoc with his Brylcreemed hair as he avoided the frozen ridges of slush, determined to keep his highly polished black oxford shoes clean.

Dodson joined him on the pavement, struggling to fasten the buttons of his scruffy tweed car coat round his vast belly and gasped, 'Which bugga is it, these hooses aall look the same te me?

Pointing to the green painted door of the Robertson's house, the dapper, younger man replied, 'That one Sarge, the one with the tin bath hanging on the wall.'

Before they stepped off, Jamie Norman opened the door adjacent to the Robertson's and raising his voice against the noise of the wind, ordered, 'In here,' and stepped back inside, standing to one side to allow his massive DS access to the kitchen, followed by the slim DC.

Sitting at the kitchen table, Tommy Bones turned to look up at the two detectives as they stepped in, taking up most of the free space in the small room. Standing next to a shelf by the door leading to a tiny pantry, her four-year-old son clamped to her left side, Tommy's portly wife, Isobel poured boiling water from the electric kettle into a waiting teapot, and then smoothing her hair, smiled, and asked, would you like a cup of tea?

DS Dodson nodded and pulled out a chair to sit down but Jamie stopped him, 'Not you Sergeant, you don't have time, you're coming to Ashington Hospital with me; DC Cotton will have a cup of tea with you and your husband Mrs Bones, and then he will take statements from you both.'

Turning to the DC, he said, 'Take a statement from Mr and Mrs Bones then go to the house at the other side of the Robertson's and take a statement from the couple there, Mr Bones has told me that he didn't get on with the Robertsons.'

Tommy interrupted, 'Aye that's right, Aah divvin't kna who was worse, the fatha or the big ugly son, the wor both nasty buggas. Big Bill has just bought a betting shop with Harry Weedon and his son, another nasty couple of buggas, the three of them are up te all sorts of badness; tha bliddy money lenders as weell. Bill and Geordie dee the collecting if ye kna what I mean.'

Jamie furrowed his brow and answered, 'Yes I think I do know what you mean, where can I find this Harry Weedon?'

'Doon the Hirst somewhere, am not sure which street but one of the NCB hooses, he works at the colliery, he's a deputy doon the Duke pit.'

'Thanks for that,' Jamie said and turning to his DC said, 'after you've taken statements from Mr and Mrs Bones and the couple at the other side...'

Tommy interrupted, 'The Turnbulls.'

Jamie smiled at him, 'Thanks Mr Bones,' and to DC Dodson, 'The Turnbulls – and when you have finished here go round to the colliery and see if you can find where Weedon lives and anything else about him and the Robertsons. After we have been to the hospital, we'll call at Ashington Police Station and see if they have anything on them,'

Cotton replied, 'Right oh Sir,' and unfastening his overcoat, took out a notebook from the inside of his Burton's off the peg, pinstriped suit.

Jamie nodded to DS Dodson, come on Sergeant, we need to establish what type of weapon, Robertson has, I'll show you the murder scene and then we'll go to the hospital in my car and I'll fill you in with what I have so far; Cotton can drive the team car around to Ashington Nick when he is finished here.

A few seconds later, the young constable in the Robertson's house, opened the door for the two detectives saying, 'Forensic and the photographer are here sir and the doctor has been and gone.'

Jamie nodded and said, 'Thanks, what did the doc say?'

'Not a lot sir, the victim has only been dead an hour or so and that he probably died from the gunshot wound to the head...'

'Yea, as per normal,' Dodson interrupted, 'stating the bliddy obvious and he will confirm it after the post mortem, I suppose.'

Jamie smiled, 'Steady Sergeant, your cynicism is showing.'

After discussing the known facts with Dodson, the two of them looked around the kitchen, Jamie pointing to the open door below the stairs, 'I wonder why that door is open, could that empty tin on the floor have anything to do with what happened here?'

Dodson bent over and grunted as his belt cut into his belly, 'Could be sir, I'll have Forensics check for prints and taken for evidence.'

'Aye, we need to know what was inside it and, if George Robertson's prints are on it,' Jamie said before turning to the constable, 'Get on to Ashington and let them know the body can be removed once the photographer and forensics are finished, we are going to interview Mrs Robertson.'

Hundreds of feet below them, after a hard shift clearing his ten yards of coal, a coal-dust covered, Bill Carter crawled out from the two-foot-ten-inch high coalface, into the ten-foot-high Mothergate and stretched his tired frame, then rubbed his eyelids, trying to remove some of the dirt before pulling on his tattered, ex-army, khaki jacket.

Looping the long, carrying strap, of his ex-army gasmask bag, containing his flask and bait tin over his head, he swung the bag behind him and asked the two dirty-faced, fillers who came out after him, 'Any bugga seen Weedon?'

'Aah hevn't seen the git since we had wor bait, said one as he took a long swig of luke-warm tea, straight from his thermos flask.

'Nah, the bugga's probably asleep at his kist,' said other before spitting out a gob full of chewing tobacco and jumping on the conveyor quickly followed by his mate.

Keen to get out, Bill placed both hands on the three-foot-wide conveyor belt that was free of coals and neatly jumped onto the moving belt, landing in a comfortable kneeling position, behind two other fillers as two more came off the face and joined them for their journey out of the pit.

Deep in conversation, the two men in front of Bill rode past the unseen, twisted body of Harry Weedon to the side of the belt, next to the girders of the tunnel wall. Thinking of a fag, and the sausage and eggs he hoped his wife would have prepared for him, Bill saw what he thought was a hand sticking up from the dark shape lying next to the belt as he rode toward it. Directing the beam of his headlamp at the fast approaching shape, he saw, Harry Weedon's blood-covered face lying behind the hand.

It took a couple of seconds to register before Bill acted, leaping off the belt, he grabbed two steel wires that ran in parallel above the conveyor and squeezed them together, signalling to the loader end operator on the trunk belt to stop the conveyors. During the few seconds, it took the operator to switch off the power and the belt slow to a halt; the two men behind Bill had also seen Weedon and jumped off. The first two men walked back from up ahead, one of them shouting, 'Waat the fuck's happened?'

Looking over the belt, Bill's headlamp illuminated Weedon's hand that appeared to be pointing to the roof, 'This is why we hevn't seen Weedon for half the shift.'

One of the men climbed onto the belt next to the dead deputy and said, 'Bugga me, his heed's smashed in, hoo the hell has that happened?'

'Is he deed?' another asked.

'As a frigging Dodo.' The man on the belt replied.

'Couldn't hev happened to a nicer sodding man,' one of them muttered sarcastically.

Pointing at the bloody fishplate at his feet, Bill said, 'Diven't touch the body or owt else, cos by the looks of this fishplate some buggas, smashed his heed in.'

'Whey it wasn't me, as much as Aah would hev like te have smacked the twat on the heed,' said one.

Shaking his head, Bill said, 'Aah wud as weell but Aah wouldn't say owt more, Jacky, Aah think we'll not be getting home soon the day. Aah think ye should aall gan and wait up by the trunk belt, Aah'll bide here and mek sure nowt gets touched, one of ye needs to gan and find the Owerman.'

The men agreed, and walked off along the roadway, leaving Bill to protect the scene.

Waiting until they were out of sight, he climbed onto the belt and leaning over, held the back of his filthy hand close to Weedon's mouth to see if he could feel any breath and said, 'Whey yer not se frigging clever now are ye?'

Jamie Norton and DS Dodson walked up to casualty reception at Ashington Hospital, Jamie pulling out his warrant card, showing it to the attractive receptionist, 'I'm Detective Inspector Norman and this Detective Sergeant Dodson; we need to speak to Mrs Patricia Robertson please.'

'Just a second,' she replied and made a telephone call.

A few minutes later, a young Doctor approached them and asked, 'DI Norman?

Thrusting out his hand, Jamie shook the younger man's hand and said, 'Yes, how do you do Doctor, we need to speak to Mrs Robertson as a matter of urgency.'

Squeezing the tip of his nose as though he was about to blow it, the doctor thought for a second or two before replying, 'Mrs. Patterson has a broken nose, lost some teeth and, has lacerations and severe bruising to her face. She is obviously in a state of shock. We have just finished stitching her cheek back together so I would prefer it if you would come back later.'

Dodson coughed, 'Sorry Doctor, Mrs Robertson is the only witness to her husband's murder...'

Interrupting his DS, Jamie gave him an angry look and said to the doctor, 'I understand but, it is imperative we ask her just three questions, we will be as quick as we can.'

The doctor reluctantly agreed and led them to a cubicle where a nurse was busy cleaning blood from around an almost closed eye on Pat Robertson's bruised and swollen face.

'Mrs Robertson,' Jamie said as he quietly approached the hospital trolley she was lying on, 'I am very sorry to disturb you at this dreadful time but can you please just answer a couple of very quick questions?'

Without speaking, she nodded, 'Yes.'

'Did your son, George Robertson – shoot your husband?'

She sighed deeply and paused for a second as tears welled up and spilt from her eyes, 'Yes,' she whispered.

Jamie grimaced at having to ask again, 'I am very sorry Mrs Robertson, I cannot begin to think how much of an ordeal this is for you but was that a yes?'

Turning her head slightly, she glared at Jamie and snarled, 'Yes my evil lad shot his fatha.'

'Thank you, Mrs Robertson, did he shoot him with a revolver?'

Beginning to tremble, Pat Robertson, took a deep breath and said slowly and clearly, 'Yes he shot my husband with the old army gun, Bill kept under the stairs, and then he did this to me.'

Jamie looked at DS Dodson, who was writing in his notebook, and raised his eyes before continuing, 'Thank you very much, Mrs Robertson, just one last question, did your husband keep the revolver in a green tin under the stairs?'

Nodding her head, she answered, 'That's right, alang with the money Bill made in tha betting shop, I suppose the waster has teken that as weell,' and slumping back she turned her head away.

The Doctor stepped in front of Jamie and said quietly, 'That's enough now please, you may be able to speak to her again in two or three hours, if, she is up to it.'

It was just before nine-o'clock when Jamie thanked the Doctor and the two detectives hurried back to Jamie's car, Jamie saying, 'Well that is pretty much cut and dried, we'll call in at Ashington Police Station and I'll brief the Inspector there and let Morpeth know what we've just heard'

Puffing from the brisk walk, the DS said, 'Right sir, Aah'll see what they have on Robertson and the Weedons and see if there has been any news on George Robertson, that's if we get there, here comes the snow.'

The wind blasted the snow into the faces of the two detectives as they scrambled to get into the sanctuary of Jamie's car.

In the Third Row, Albert Grundy had not gone back to bed after Jake left, instead, he had dressed for work in the pit baths, stoked the fires in the kitchen and sitting room, and made a pot of tea. After toasting and buttering some bread, he sat in front of the kitchen fire to eat it and drink a mug tea, as he mulled over his conversation with Jake.

Just after seven-thirty, knowing how much Edna hated cigarettes, he threw the butt of the one he had been smoking into the back of the fire and climbed back up the stairs with a cup of tea and knocked on the door to the bedroom she shared with her chubby, eleven-year-old son Howard.

'Hear ye are pet, he said as he placed it on the cabinet next to her bed.

She sat up and giving Albert a hideous, forced smile, said loudly, 'Howard, get yesell up and doon stairs, Albert'll mek yer breakfast.'

Lying in the put-me-up collapsible bed next to her, he farted loudly and groaned, 'In a minute man,' and pulled the blankets tighter around him, not wanting to leave the warmth of his bed for the coldness of the bedroom.

Albert left the room and stepping into his boy's room, pulled the bedclothes back and said, 'Come on ye two…' but stopped in mid-sentence when he saw the bed was empty. A worried look clouded his face as he said aloud, 'Bliddy hell where are they?'

Turning to leave, he saw the note Jake had written lying on the chair at the foot of the bed and picking it up, quickly read it:

'*Dad, Am taking Billy and Roger to Mrs Thompson's they are going to practice a presentation for school with Tommy before they go to school. See you later, Jake*'

Not sure what to make of Jakes's letter, Albert hurried downstairs and dropped more bread into the toaster.

Wearing a red, cotton housecoat, pulled tightly around her to show off her figure, Edna followed him into the kitchen and hurrying over to the fire that burned brightly in the range, turned her back to it, and hitched up the back of housecoat to warm her shapely backside.

Her hair that had been heavily lacquered the previous day, looked like a bust, black, shredded-wheat, and without makeup, her pale, face looked even more severe but Albert did not notice that, he was trying unsuccessfully and surreptitiously, to snatch a glimpse of her bare bum!

Looking through to the sitting room, she asked brusquely, 'Where are yor two buggas, are they not up yet?'

'Jake took them roond te Mrs Thompsons this morning, he said 'tha rehearsing a presentation with Tommy before they gan te school.'

Glaring at Albert, Edna hissed through tight lips, 'And ye believe that eh? That sodding son of yours is trying te split us up, isn't he?'

Looking as though he had just burnt his lips, he spluttered, 'Nur Pet, he wouldn't dee that man, Aah telt ye why he's teken them.'

'Divvin't be stupid,' she barked and walked quickly to the foot of the stairs, yelling, 'Howard, get yersell doon here – noo,' and walked back to the fireplace, staring at Albert.

Hearing her frightening tone and recognizing the danger in not obeying, Howard pulled on his shorts and hurried downstairs and into the kitchen. Wide-eyed and just a wee bit scared, he asked, 'Waat Mam?'

Arms crossed, feet tapping and engine running, 'Edna snapped, 'Billy is in your class at school isn't he?'

'Not sure where this was going, he answered timidly, 'Yes Mam.'

Sensing victory, she asked, 'And is he doing a presentation at school today with Tommy?'

Howard looked puzzled, 'Nur Mam, not that Aah kna.'

Turning to Albert who was pulling on his old gabardine overcoat, Edna curled her lip in a disconcerting sneer and said, 'A' telt ye he's up te summat, whey am not having it, he's not ganning te interfere with ye and me, Aah'll gan te school before dinner time and fetch the laddies home and find oot waat's ganning on.' Then she smiled a sickly, sweet smile at Albert and in a voice laden with false affection said, 'Eeee, Albert Pet, am sorry te have spoken te ye like that, ye just gan off te work and Aah'll sort things oot here,' and kissed him on the cheek.

Not wanting to be involved in any more nastiness, Albert snatched up his bait bag and pulling on his flat cap, said, 'Aye OK Pet, Aah've got te get off to work now and scurried out the back door. He paused to suck in a breath of ice-cold air before he hurried on, wondering what she had meant by 'Find oot waat's ganning on.'

CHAPTER 7

Friday 8th February – 8:20 am
Redesdale

Curled up on the front bench seat of the Ford, Rosalind Dawson woke up as her mother brought the car to a stop on the side of the road and looked up at the sky.

Pushing back in her seat and stretching, she stifled a yawn, and asked, 'Where are we?'

'Just past Otterburn,' Sarah answered, 'I am just checking that the road is okay to go on.'

Worried that she had not seen any vehicles coming in the opposite direction for a while, she wondered if it was wise to continue.

Leaning forward to look up at the sky through the windscreen, Rosalind said, 'Those clouds don't look too good Mam.'

Sarah replied, 'Yes Pet, that's what I was thinking,' just as a civilian Land Rover followed by two cars drove past, heading north.'

That made her mind up, 'Well if they are going on, then so am I,' and engaging gear she drove after the cars, forming a small convoy heading toward Carter Bar.

She believed she would be safe enough behind the three vehicles in front but struggled to keep close to them as the wind increased, blowing spindrift snow from the fields. On through Rochester and past the turn of for Redesdale Camp she drove, managing to keep them in her sights, then to her relief, on entering Kielder Forest, the shelter afforded by the trees enabled her to close up a little on the three vehicles but her relief was short lived.

After two miles, the three vehicles in front turned left into Byrness leaving them alone on the road just as the snow-laden, storm clouds rolled overhead

A few seconds later, when the first flurries of snow whipped across the windscreen of the car, Rosalind sat bolt upright and placing both hands on the dash, shouted in fright, 'Mam?'

Slowing down, Sarah saw a large van with flashing headlights; appear through the snow, coming toward them. Leaning out of his window on the lee-side of the van, the driver frantically waved her down in the road that, due to the banked snow, was barely wide enough for both vehicles to pass.

Stopping next to the van that sheltered her from the worst of the wind, she wound down her window and squinted up at the driver who shouted down, 'Ye need to torn aroond Missus, the road up to Carter Bar is blocked halfway up with drifting snow, I had a hell of a job turning aroond and getting back.'

Sarah nodded and shouted, 'I was just about to; where can I turn around?'

Lifting his cap with a grubby hand, he rubbed his bald head with the other and yelled, 'Not hear ye'll get stuck, gan te the end of the reservoir, there's a big farmhouse on the left we a muckle big yard that's clear of snow.' 'Ye can torn there but divvint hang aboot, this fresh snow is ganna block this road,' and winding his window up he drove on.

Sarah wound her window up, shutting out the now ferocious wind-blasted snow and said to her daughter, 'Right we'll get turned around, and head back.'

Looking in her rear view mirror as she slowly pulled to the middle of the narrowed road she saw through the now intense snow, headlights and stamped down on the brake pedal, screaming, 'Look out!'

Minutes earlier, still driving far too fast, Geordie Robertson had almost lost control again as he avoided a lorry that failed to climb up the short steep hill that dropped into Otterburn. Forced to slow down he cursed the worsening weather as he noted that there was, quite a few cars parked outside the village pub, strange for that time of day. He worried, correctly, that they may be travellers who had decided not to risk trying to drive over Carter Bar.

Once through the village, he increased speed again, determined to drive over the Border ridge before the storm broke. Joining the A68 a mile or so further on, he realised that he had only passed one car coming in the other direction and wondered why.

He had also been tempted to stop for something to eat at the roadside café in the gaunt, stone-built house in Rochester but despite his grumbling belly, fear of not clearing the Carter Bar or, of been caught by the police drove him on.

After he passed the entrance to Redesdale Training Camp, he was driving along a mile-long, wide-open, and treeless stretch of road as strong crosswinds buffeted his car when he saw snow clouds avalanching across the sky toward him. Instead of slowing, he increased speed, wanting to get up and over the Border before the snow hit.

Reaching the edge of the massive Kielder Forest, the buffeting of the car reduced slightly as he raced on past snow that was now piled up to six-feet high on the edges of the road. As he approached the turnoff to the Forestry Commission hamlet of Byrness that sat a hundred yards to the left of the road, he ignored a van with flashing headlights and sped on into what was now almost a whiteout.

The windscreen wipers slapped back and forth at top speed in a vain attempt to clear the fast piling snow, when to his horror he saw red lights a few yards in front. In the blink of an eye, he stood on the brake and clutch pedals and, pulled the steering wheel hard to the right. The tyres bit into the snow for a second and then lost traction as the big Vauxhall slid past Sarah's Ford, missing it by a millimetre before smashing into the long bank of snow, blasting snow twenty-feet into the air where it was whisked away by the storm.

The car ploughed its way fifteen-feet along the snowbank, only stopping when it hit a telegraph pole, snapping the pole and the lines it carried.

Bracing himself just before the impact; prevented him from flying through the windscreen but he had taken a blow to his nose and the side of his head and, bruised his chest and legs. He sat still for a few seconds, trying to gather his thoughts.

Realising he could not stay there and seeing that his door was up against the snow bank, he climbed over to the passenger seat and opening the door fell out into the storm. The Vauxhall was sitting on the snow bank with its battered front, several feet above the ground and through the snow that the wind drove into his face; he could see the telegraph pole had smashed in the front of the car.

Furious at having to swerve off the road and seeing that his car was going nowhere, he allowed the wind to push him back to the Ford as Sarah wound down her window. The noise and blast from the wind shocked her, Rosalind, and young Davy who had woken when his mother had screamed her warning and slid to a halt.

Geordie slid up to the Ford and placing both his hands on the roof of the car to steady himself against the storm, glared down at Sarah, blood trickling from his nose.

Looking up at the bruised and bleeding face of the hulking figure and still in shock, Sarah asked, 'Are you alright?

His huge face distorted with rage, he snarled, 'Do Aah look alright ye stupid bitch?'

Beginning to worry what the huge youth was going to do, Sarah stuttered, 'I, I'm sorry, em, I was just turning around, can, can I...'

He did not allow her to finish, he needed a replacement car, and she was sitting in it, he yelled at her, 'Get oot the frigging car now.'

Fear now gripped her and she started to wind the window up as both Rosalind and Davy shouted at Robertson. Ignoring them, he grabbed the door handle and wrenching the door open, pulled the car keys from the ignition, and grabbed Sarah by the arm in an effort to drag her out.

She clung onto the steering wheel with her daughter hanging onto her screaming, 'Leave my Mam alone.'

He did, but only to pull the revolver out of his greatcoat pocket and point it at her head, shouting, 'Get oot the fucking car noo, ora'll blow yer fucking heed off.'

Terrified what he might do and for the safety of her children, she clung tightly to the steering wheel until Geordie smashed his massive left fist into the side of her head. Rosalind screamed as he dragged her half-conscious mother from the car but when Sarah again tried to resist him, he swung the revolver into her face, as he had done to his own mother; she fell unconscious into the snow as the storm blasted around them. Opening her door, the wind almost wrenching it off its hinges, Rosalind struggled round to her fallen mother.

Squeezing into the driving seat and slamming his door shut, Geordie pushed the keys into the ignition and switched the engine back on and shouted to the shocked Davy who was still in the back, 'Get the fuck oot noo.' Davy fought to open the passenger door but the wind held it shut.

'The other fucking side ye bliddy idiot,' the huge youth screamed at the frightened boy who slid over the seat and climbed out as Geordie drove off, wheels spinning, throwing the lad out of the car and onto his back, sliding him into the snow bank.

Rosalind bent over her mother, trying to shelter her from the wind and snow, lifting her head and cradling her in her arms as she tried to revive her. She had not seen Davy fall from the car but looking up saw her dazed brother crawling toward them as he battled against the wind and snow. Holding a hand out to him, she shouted 'Come on Davy, come on.'

Disorientated and suffering from shock but uninjured, Davy reached his sister and grabbing her hand, pulled himself next to his mother whose eyes flickered open as she began to regain consciousness.

Looking frantically around her, Rosalind searched for sanctuary but could only see a few yards through the snowstorm. Seeing the tail lights of Geordie's abandoned car twenty yards further along the road, she shouted over the storm, 'Come on Davy, we have to get Mam out of the storm, we have to get into that car.'

With her back to the wind, she crouched over her mother and lifted her into a sitting position, both of them now with their backs to the wind with Davy holding his mother from the front.

Wrapping her arms around her mother, she shouted, 'Can you stand up Mam?' Sarah nodded and her two children tried to help her to her feet but she was still too groggy and the three of them fell in a heap as wind-driven snow clung to their clothes.

Afraid that a vehicle could come along and run over them, Rosalind grasped her mother tighter and began to drag her against the wind, toward the car. Davy did not need prompting; struggling to his sister's side, he grabbed his mother's coat and helped his sister in her fight with the elements. The wind knocked them down, collapsing them into a heap several times but after each fall, they picked themselves up, took hold of their mother again, and began their strenuous battle against the wind, dragging her toward the Vauxhall.

After a herculean effort, the exhausted pair paused when they were in the shelter of the car, where Rosalind, still holding her mother tightly, shouted, 'Open the back door, Davy.'

As Davy, pulled open the door and climbed inside, Rosalind began lifting her mother, who was at last able to help herself a little. With her son, pulling her from inside the car and her daughter steadying her from behind, Sarah was able to climb onto the backseat, Rosalind sliding in next to her, pulling the door shut.

Snow had already covered driver's side of the car and most of the windscreen and rear window, leaving only the passenger side windows clear but they soon misted up as the family clung to each other in the already cold interior of the car as the temperature inside dropped even more.

Rosalind looked at her mother's blood-streaked face; worried that she probably needed stitches to the cut on her cheek, she said, 'Mam we need to get you to a doctor or hospital.'

Her head throbbing and the cut to her face smarting, Sarah shook her head and said, 'I'm okay Pet, I just need a few minutes to pull myself together, what we need now is warmth, reach over and check that the gearstick is in neutral and try starting the engine.'

Squeezing halfway through the gap in between the front seats, Rosalind shook the gear lever to and fro and shouted above the noise of the howling wind, it's free,' and reaching for the ignition, turned as far as it would go. She heard a few clicks and grunts but nothing else. After trying several more times with the same result, she sat back down next to her mother and snuggled up to her. 'We'll just have to wait until a car comes along,' she said as she wondered how long they could survive inside a frozen car.

When the two constables from Hexham arrived at the turn off the A68 into Redesdale camp at ten minutes to nine-o-clock, two soldiers had already stopped four cars and a large, flatbed lorry. Driving to the front of the queue, gaunt and dour, PC Colin Wilson parked the police car at an angle on the road where PC Carlisle climbed out, buttoning up his heavy police greatcoat and walking over to the soldiers.

Turning his back to the wind and pulling up his collar he shouted, 'Hello lads, how long have you had the road shut?'

The soldiers, both wearing green, sheepskin-lined parkas, with the wire-edged hoods pulled up over their heads, leaned toward the PC, who towered over them both.

One of them yelled up at him, 'Just ten minutes.'

'Have you let any cars through since you've been here?'

'No, and there hasn't been any coming the other way,' and pointing to an Austin-Champ jeep parked on the road into the camp, shouted, Major Graham, our QM, is sat in the front of that Champ, he can tell you what's happening.'

The PC smiled at the young soldier and gave him thumbs up before hurrying across to the jeep where the QM, waved him into the passenger side of the vehicle that sported a canvas top, and sides with Perspex windows.

Once he had squeezed in and pulled the door shut against the wind he said, 'Good Morning sir, a bliddy awful day.'

The forty-six-year-old Major said in a raised voice, 'It certainly is Constable, I'm glad you made it.'

'Only just, the A68 from Otterburn south is closed to traffic now. As you probably know, I have to close it here. It is already closed on the Scottish side; I believe our Police HQ has spoken to you?'

The QM pulled his parka tight around his shoulders and answered, 'Yes, the Camp Commandant at Otterburn spoke to them first then passed them to me. I only arrived yesterday with a few vehicles and the advance party of my regiment, the main body of the regiment is due to arrive tomorrow, but that is obviously unlikely now, they should have left Essex this morning but have been held back. I have liaised with the civilian permanent staff here and we are making accommodation available for anyone stranded by the storm, it is basic ten-man rooms but they are heated and there is plenty of bedding.

Carlisle interrupted, 'That's good sir, and it looks as if we already have some customers, what about feeding them?'

'Not a problem, I have two cooks with me and a truck full of fresh and tinned rations, the cooks have already opened the kitchen and one of my staff-sergeants is organizing the dining hall. We'll make sure there is a bed for you and the other PC in the Sergeants' Mess accommodation because I don't think you will be going anywhere, anytime soon.'

The PC rubbed his gloved hands together and readied himself to leave the shelter of the inside of the jeep, saying, 'That all sounds great sir, what about parking? I would like to get the vehicles of this road while I can; I want to keep it clear for snow ploughs and diggers.'

The QM replied, 'There is parking outside the dining hall but I don't have anything to keep the camp roads clear with, there is an army snowplough at Otterburn but that is busy trying to keep the roads there open.'

Grasping the handle of the door, Carlisle said, 'Right, I'll get along and talk to the folk already here and see how many will be staying, I see my mate has already started,' and pushing the door open he stepped out into the storm, just as Jake drove the one-ton Austin into the camp.

The QM jumped out of the Champ and flagged the Austin down, then pointing to Jake; he pointed to the Champ indicating, 'Come and join me'.

Jake pulled on the handbrake, leaving the engine running as he climbed out, he said over his shoulder to Ian, 'Aah wonder what the owld bugga wants, we're probably in the shit again.'

PC Wilson was still speaking to the family of the first car in the front of the short queue when PC Carlisle joined him and took him to one side.

'The road beyond Otterburn is closed south and it won't stay open to here long unless there is a snowplough available but even they are going to struggle, look how deep it is already. The army can accommodate and feed anybody who is stuck, so I think we need to get the cars that are not going back to Otterburn, into the camp, we need to keep the road clear for snowploughs.'

Wilson nodded and shouted back, 'That's frigging marvellous, how are two of us going to control this and how long will we be here?'

Carlisle glared down at the complaining Wilson and replied angrily, 'Yor always bitching about something, you miserable sod, we've got a job to do here and we'll be here as long as it takes...'

Wilson stopped him, pointing vigorously at something behind him.

Turning around, Carlisle saw a large van being driving toward them. He stepped forward as the vehicle approached and the driver stopped next to him and wound his window down.

Carlisle shouted up, 'Where have you come from?' .

The driver leaned out, 'I tried to get ower te Kelso but there's a snow-drift blocking the road halfway up the hill te Carter Bar and Aah think the whole road will be closed soon.'

'Where are you going to?

The driver looked worried and shouted, 'Back te Newcastle and see what the boss says.'

Carlisle shook his head, 'The roads south are closed from Otterburn and the road to Otterburn is probably closed by now, the army is making accommodation and food available for folk so please drive into the camp and park up. Did you pass any cars on your way back?

'Yes, at the reservoir, a woman and two kids in a red car, a Ford Aah think, anyway I flagged hor doon and she said she was ganna torn aroond and come back. Then some bliddy idiot drove past me in a blue car ganning far too fast, he didn't stop, so bugga knas waat's happened to him cos Aah've only just managed to get te here, the snow is getting deeper aall the time.'

Carlisle thanked the man and then directed the driver into the camp before walking over to the jeep again to speak to the QM.

The QM opened his door in the lee of the wind as the constable approached, giving him a questioning look.

Leaning close to the QM, Carlisle said loudly, 'Sir, there are at least two cars on the road between here and Carter Bar,' and looking at Jake's Austin, asked, 'have you got a four-wheel drive vehicle with good ground clearance that can drive up as far as the reservoir and check that they are okay or on their way back. A red Ford should be here now or on its way along here, there is a woman driving it and she has two kids with her?'

The QM smiled and held up his thumb and turning to Jake said, 'Right Bombardier Grundy, have you and Trevelyan got parkas?'

'In the cab Sir,' Jake replied.

'OK, you heard what the constable said, I want you to drive up the road as far as the end of the reservoir and no further, if there are any vehicles along there that are stuck or in trouble, get the occupants into the back of your vehicle and bring them back here, got that?'

'Yes, Sir.'

The QM continued, 'You should be able to turn around at the farm at the end of the reservoir. Under no circumstance are you to try and recover any vehicles, and, if you think you may get into problems or the road is blocked, then you are to turn around and drive back here. You are not to take any unnecessary risks, is that understood?'

With mounting excitement, Jake replied, 'Yes Sir, understood.'

'Okay, I cannot spare anyone else to go with you, everyone else is already working flat out; now remember, take your time but don't linger; the snow is only going to get worse. If you think, it is going to be too deep, then turn around and come back,' and pointing into the back of the jeep he continued, 'take a dozen of these blankets with you. Now off you go and good luck.'

PC Carlisle thanked the QM and walked back to join Wilson, who, along with the two soldiers, was pushing a car that the driver was having difficulty trying to get through the ever-deepening snow.

Throwing the blankets he had taken from the jeep into the back of his truck, then battling the wind, Jake walked around to the cab.

Climbing in he grinned at Ian and said, 'We're ganning for a little drive and a wee bit of excitement.'

Puzzled, Ian asked, 'Where?'

He did not answer immediately as he concentrated on turning the truck around, driving it back onto the A68 and heading north, the windscreen wipers battling to keep the screen clear of snow.

Driving slowly northwest, he told Ian everything the QM and PC had said and added, 'We need to keep wor eyes peeled for the red Ford coming this way, Aah think she should have been here by noo.'

Staring intently through the cleared part of the windscreen, Ian replied, 'Got that, the snows about ten-inches deep now and the wind is building some big drifts across parts of the road – I doubt if a car can still get through this.'

Jake nodded, trying to control his nervous excitement as he imagined them rescue hordes of stranded travellers. However, after a few minutes of driving into the blizzard, he had stopped thinking about rescuing anyone; he needed all his concentration to keep the truck on the road that was hard to define in the almost whiteout conditions.

Ten minutes later, Ian said, I wonder where the red Ford is?'

'I hope they are OK, 'Jake replied as they drove slowly past the turnoff to Byrness, hidden by a fresh snowdrift and the whiteout.

With Jake concentrating on the road directly in front of them, it was Ian who saw the taillight of the Vauxhall first – 'Look, a light on the bank to the right.'

Jake leaned forward and squinted for a second or two then said, 'I see it, it's the back of a car,' and carefully pulled to a stop next to the half-buried Vauxhall.

The wind blasted snow against his door, as he shouted, 'Aah'll hev to climb oot your door,' and after they both pulled on their parkas, he followed Ian out of the shelter of the cab into the raging blizzard.

Stepping around the front of the truck and into the full force of the storm, the two young soldiers leant into the wind, and groped their way to the side of the car, crouching below it for shelter. Pulling himself up, Ian looked into the misted up window of the rear door as a hand wiped away ice and mist that had formed on the inside, and then, the frightened face of a red-haired girl appeared, staring back at him.

CHAPTER 8

Friday 8th February – 9:15 am
Ashington

Parking outside the red-bricked, late-Victorian Police Station in Ashington, DI Norman stepped carefully onto the icy pavement bracing himself against the blizzard and waited while his overweight DS climbed out the passenger side, and gingerly made his way around to join him.

Hurrying into the small foyer, Dodson slammed the huge blue door behind them as Jamie stomped snow off his shoes and said, 'Find out what you can about the Robertsons and Weedons and I'll brief the Inspector.'

Dodson nodded and tapped on the glass of the hatch in the dimpled, opaque window, and waited. It slid open half a minute later, the Duty Sergeant peering through at them, saying, 'Hang on, sir and I'll let you in, we have got some news for you.'

Inside the long, blue-painted corridor, he said, 'We have another body sir, Harold Weedon.'

Jamie Norman's eyes widened in surprise, 'Harry Weedon – we were just going to ask if you had anything on him, where and when did this happen?'

'We have a fair bit on Weedon, he and his son have been in here a few times; he's underground sir, that is 'doon the pit', DC Cotton is at the Colliery Manager's Office, he is waiting to brief you, I have the number here.'

'So do we have a crime scene underground?'

'Yes, sir, I have a constable going underground at the moment and DC Cotton is waiting for you, he has overalls and helmets for you both. The Manager has closed off the area for four hours and is keeping all the men bar one who was working there in the pit canteen.'

DS Dodson, snorted, four hours, he'll be lucky if we get finished doon there teday.'

Having dropped the two Grundy boys and Tommy off at Wansbeck School earlier, Edward Thompson looked out of his office window as the snow that arrived as a few wayward flurries minutes before, turned into a blizzard, blocking out his view over the yard of his office and workshop on Ashington's Jubilee Trading Estate.

Picking up the telephone on his desk, he dialled Kirkup's the Bakers in Highmarket and asked to speak to Jane, who said, 'Hello Edward, this storm is terrible.'

'It certainly is Pet, it is a lot earlier than forecast, hopefully, Ian and Jake are safe at Redesdale. I'll pick up the boys at lunchtime, it would be a struggle for them walking home in this, but knowing them they would probably enjoy it.'

'They probably would but would end up soaked to the skin, I am glad you can pick them up, we will have to go to the Grundy's house and speak to that awful woman to tell her that we have the boys.'

Rubbing the back of his head, Edward said, 'I hope Ronnie manages to get through before then and he can deal with her.'

An hour earlier, having kissed Mary and their four-year-old daughter Florence, goodbye, Ronnie Grundy climbed into his red, ten-year-old, Riley one-point-five saloon and drove off, hoping to be in Ashington just after ten o'clock. He was driving through Chester-le-Street when the blizzard swept across the A1 trunk road, slowing the heavy traffic down to a crawl as drivers struggled to see the road ahead.

Back in Ashington police station, Jamie North sat in the office of the immaculate, Inspector Brian Smith, who used his right, forefinger to smooth his moustache, modelled after his hero, Clark Gable. He briefed him on the interview he had with Mrs Robertson at the hospital and, the information DC Cotton had given him over the telephone a couple of minutes earlier.

Rubbing his hands, Jamie said in his quiet Scottish lilt, 'The overman at the colliery has told my DC that George Robertson worked for Harry Weedon on the same coalface.

He also said that according to the man at the shaft bottom, Robertson came up out of the pit around six am; two and a half hours before he was due to finish, and that he also left his pony tied to a girder and had apparently left in a hurry. This makes him our prime suspect and also explains why he was at home at the time of the murder of his father.'

Inspector Smith said, 'Well it looks as if you have just the one suspect who at the moment has managed to elude our patrol cars, mind he did have a good thirty minutes start on us. He could have gone anywhere.'

Jamie nodded in agreement and added, 'We'll speak to Mrs Robertson again later and see if she has any thoughts as to where he might go – relatives, friends etc. What we don't have, is motive. Why did he kill Weedon and then go on to kill his father? Having murdered Weedon - if indeed, he did - it looks as though he had gone home to take his father's money and flee but his father caught him in the act, tried to stop him, and was shot for his troubles. But why Weedon?'

Leaning forward, the Inspector said, 'We sent an officer round to inform Mrs Weedon of the death of her husband but there was no one in, he spoke to a next-door neighbour, who interestingly, said that Mrs Weedon had left Harry over two years ago. She also said that the son, Stuart Weedon, lives at home with his father, he is twenty-two and works nights at the Comrades Club. The neighbour thought he would have been home at that time of the morning but there was no answer.'

Jamie thanked the Inspector and said, 'I am going off to the colliery to visit the crime scene, which will be interesting;

I haven't been underground before; I'll just see what my DS has found out about the Robertsons and Weedons.

The small, one bedroomed flat above a shop in Station Road was not welcoming, especially on a freezing winter's morning. A cheap, red leatherette sofa with a Formica, topped, coffee-table in front, dominated the square-shaped, main room. A wooden-boxed fourteen-inch television sat on top of chipped occasional table standing next to the red-curtained window overlooking the busy shopping street. At the back of the room, a yellow kitchen cabinet, Belfast sink with a worn wooden drainer, and small grease-stained, electric cooker made up the kitchen with two steel-legged, plastic cushioned chairs and a small oilcloth-covered table, providing a dining area. The air was thick with the stench from cigarette smoke, an overflowing ashtray, greasy food, and dirty dishes piled up in the sink, the staleness of body odour adding to the unpleasantness.

Stuart Weedon walked out of the bedroom fastening his flies and stood next to the seventeen-year-old girl, sitting on the sofa, with her feet curled up and a mug of coffee clutched between her hands.

Leering at the girl he sneered, 'Whey, that's my morning constitutional, your turn the morn, Yvonne Pet.'

She looked up at him with deep-blue, sad eyes and feigned a smile that for a second or two, lit up her pretty but washed-out face, and shuddered, both from the cold and from revulsion. Wearing only a thin cotton housecoat over a cheap, red nylon negligee, she had a grubby, cream, woollen blanket pulled around her, the heat from the electric fire failing to warm her or the room, especially during the current bitter weather.

Weedon took a pack of cigarettes from his jacket that he earlier draped over the back of one of the dining chairs and offered one to Yvonne, who shook her head.

'I'll have one please, Stuart,' nineteen-year-old, Sandra said as she followed him out of the bedroom, wrapping a winceyette dressing gown around her slender figure. Pushing her dishevelled, dyed-blonde hair back from her emaciated face that made her mascaraed brown-eyes look huge, she sat down on the sofa and cuddled up next to Yvonne

The cigarette dangling from his bottom lip, Weedon, picked up the pound notes the girls had left on the dining table, 'Is that it, you weren't busy last night wor ye?

Sandra took a quick drag from her cigarette, 'Thorsday is niva busy, ye kna that. Teday's the best day – payday. Ye shud be ganning as we alwas get one two from foreshift and tha'll be more tonight before the dayshift men gan home te tha wives and then there'll be the drunks tonight who still have a few bob in tha pockets.'

Glaring at the two girls, he pulled on his jacket and took his overcoat from the peg behind the entrance-door of the flat and said, 'Aye, whey ye need te be busy if yer ganning te pay of the money ye owe me fatha. Aah'll caall in later tonight te see how yer deeing.'

Sandra stood up and holding her arms around her skinny frame, asked, 'Can we hev another heater, it's freezing in here and we've nee fags left.'

'I'll tell you what, he sneered, 'Aah'll get ye another heater when ye clean this shithole up, ye live like a pair of frigging pigs, it's enough te put any bugga off.' He threw the packet of cigarettes onto the coffee table where they bounced off and on to the floor, saying, 'Ye can have waat's left in here, Aah'll bring some more later; noo get this place cleaned up.'

Yvonne spat, 'The mess didn't put you off did it?'

He walked up to her and raised his hand as if to strike, warning, 'Less of ya lip or ye'll get another clip, ye cheeky bitch, this place was nipping clean when Edna worked here. Ye better get it cleaned up or Aah'll be teking more off ye both,' and fastening his overcoat, left the flat saying over his shoulder, 'Get cleaning ye dorty buggas ye.'

CHAPTER 9

Friday 8th February – 9:15 am
Redesdale – Treshinish House

'This is what it must be like to be inside a refrigerator,' Rosalind thought, shivering as she cuddled her mother, with young Davy sandwiched between them. The snow had almost completely covered the car, only the side next to the road and in the lee of the wind remained visible as the blizzard raged outside. She noticed the condensation on the inside of the windows had frozen as she struggled to keep her mother and brother warm.

When they had first climbed into the car, she had concentrated on tending her mother who was still groggy from her battering by Geordie Robertson. The cut on her cheek was the biggest worry, two inches long and open, it looked raw and painful, blood still seeping down her face, staining the collar of her coat.

In an attempt to stop the bleeding, Rosalind had placed her handkerchief on the wound and wrapped her mother's own scarf tightly around her head to keep it in place. Her mother had winced as Rosalind tightened the scarf but did not complain but she still looked dazed and shocked.

After forty minutes sheltering inside the freezing car, Rosalind realised that they were likely to freeze to death if they remained there much longer and with no sign of the blizzard easing, she was beginning to despair. In desperation, she was mentally preparing herself to leave her mother and brother in the car and seek help – but where. She remembered seeing a turn off for a village but she could not remember how far back it was and had no idea how far off the road to the village was – it could be miles away.

Muffled rumbling just audible above the sound of the wind interrupted her thoughts. Not sure, what the noise was she let go of her mother and turning to the side window, rubbed the ice and condensation off, leaning close to the glass to look out. She saw the wide-eyed face of a young man wearing a beret, complete with a topping of snow.

'Mam, someone's here,' she shouted with excited relief as Ian opened the door and leaned in.

'Are ye's alright, we've come to tek ye back te camp,' he shouted.

A flicker of a smile showed the relief Rosalind felt as she said, 'My Mam's hurt, she has a cut on her face.'

Looking at Sarah, who looked very pale and shocked, Ian could see the bloody handkerchief below the tartan scarf and turned to shout at Jake, 'We need the first-aid kit out of the cab.'

Jake gave a 'thumbs up' and disappeared into the storm.

'Did your Mam cut her face in the crash?'

'No – we didn't crash, this is not our car, the man who crashed this car hit my Mam and took ours, and he has a gun.'

Ian thought for a second before asking, 'Is your car a red Ford?'

Sarah stirred and answered, 'Yes, why?'

'Because we have been looking for you and your car; we'll put a bandage on your face then get you out.'

Jake returned and handed the black, metal, first-aid box to Ian who shouted, 'Take the lass and lad and put them in the back with some blankets, I'll put a field dressing on the woman.'

Ian helped Rosalind out of the protection of the car where Jake wrapped his arms around her shoulder and shouted, 'I'll come back for the lad,' and holding onto Rosalind, he helped her around the front of his truck and into the lee side shouting, 'Hang on a second.'

Leaving her there, he stepped around to the rear of the truck, unfastened the tailgate, and lowered it before going back for the shivering girl, helping her climb into the rear. Picking up a couple of blankets, he shook them open and wrapped them round Rosalind who pulled them tight around her as Jake sat her down on the wooden bench seat, just behind the cab.

Jake knelt down, noticing her red hair and bright hazel eyes and caught off guard by the intensity of her eyes, he stammered, 'Hang on, am ganning for your brother.'

Having taken off his woollen gloves, Ian had carefully removed the blood-soaked handkerchief from Sarah's face, replacing it with a large, sterilized 'First-Field-Dressing', when Jake returned and took Davy out into the storm to join his sister.

A couple of minutes later, when Jake came back, Ian asked Sarah, 'Are you ready?'

Looking determined, she nodded, 'Yes,' and between them the two lads helped her out the car, and held onto her as they guided her through the blizzard to the rear of the truck and up inside, making the traumatised family as comfortable as possible with blankets.

Jake shouted, 'Right, we'll put the tailboard up and fasten the flap te keep the wind oot, Aa'm going to have to drive to the end of the reservoir before I can turn aroond as the road is too tight to risk it here, hang on te each other cos it might be a bit bumpy.'

Back in the cab as Jake battled with keeping the truck moving through drifting snow, Ian shouted, 'That wasn't their car it belonged to some big bloke who punched the woman and hit her with a revolver and stole their car – we'll have to watch out for him, he's in their red Ford.'

Concentrating on the road and becoming increasingly worried that they would not find anywhere to turn around, Jake shouted back, 'What a bastard, Aah hope the bugga gets caught in a drift.'

The width of road that was useable, continued to shrink, drifting snow building the banks ever wider and deeper as Jake battled to keep the Austin moving. Twice he came to a shuddering halt in deep drifts that had formed across the road where the forest was thinnest. Both times, he had remained calm and, remembering his training, reversed a few yards, before driving at the drift a little faster and breaking through. The second drift took him three attempts before he cleared it.

As they continued on, Ian grew concerned that they would not be able to carry on and could become stranded with the family in the unheated and almost freezing back of the truck. He looked at Jake and shouted, 'I don't think we are going to get back, the snow is not letting up.'

The concentration on Jake's young face, masked his fears as he too realized they were unlikely to be able to drive back to Redesdale through the raging storm.

'We need to find shelter,' Jake said, 'the QM said we could torn roond at a farm just past the reservoir, Aah think we've been driving alongside it for a good while, so we must be nearly there noo. We'll see if tha's any bugga there and if they'll tek us in.'

The full force of the wind tore into them when they left the shelter of the trees at the end of the reservoir, the truck swaying, almost to its tipping point, as Jake fought to keep it straight.

Unheard by the lads in the cab, Rosalind screamed when the wild rocking of the truck threw the three of them from the bench seat onto the hard, metal striped wooden floor. A mother's instincts drove Sarah to grab her two children and cling on tightly to them as Jake drove on.

'*THERE - ON THE LEFT,*' shouted Ian pointing at buildings a few yards back from the road, ten-yards ahead.

Not wanting to lose traction, Jake kept his foot on the accelerator and swung the truck hard to the left, blasting up a cloud of snow as he ploughed the Austin through a three-foot high drift, before braking to a sliding halt in front of the huge oak door of Treshinish House.

Leaning forward, he rested his forearms and hands on the top of the steering wheel and turned to Ian, smiled and said, 'Whey that was a canny bliddy drive.'

Grinning, Ian replied, 'It certainly was, well done Jake lad, not bad for a novice driver.'

With the driver's side of the truck in the lee of the wind, Jake opened his door, jumped out into two-feet of snow, and waded his way through to the oak door, pulling the hood of his parka up to protect himself from the gale force wind. Grabbing the heavy ring held in the mouth of a black, cast iron lion's head, doorknocker, he banged it several times.

Ian joined Jake just before the door swung open and Maggie Gray reached forward and grabbed both lads, pulling them inside before trying to close the door against the wind. Both lads turned and helped her push the heavy door closed.

Smoothing her greying, blonde hair, back from her face, she smiled at them and said, 'I was watching for my son, and saw you bash your way through the snowdrift, are you both all right, ye'll niva get back to camp through that.'

Pulling his hood back off his head, Jake replied, 'We are both okay missus but we have a woman and two kids in the back, the woman's been hort and like ye say we're not ganna get back te camp in this storm, can we bring them in here?

Pulling up her shawl-collared, woollen cardigan that she had pulled on over her jumper, Maggie ordered, 'Get them in out the cold now, go on hurry up.'

A couple of minutes later, she opened the door again, Jake and Ian's' studded boots, clattering onto the stone floor of the porch as they helped the Dawsons inside.

After pushing the door shut, Maggie opened the inner, half-glazed door into the hall that smelled of cooked bacon, 'This way, into the parlour,' she said, leading them into the large, comfortable room with the door of a wood-burning stove open, displaying a welcoming roaring fire. Bookcases loaded to overflowing with books of every size and colour, flanked the huge fireplace that contained split logs stacked on either side of the stove. A huge ornate, gold-painted mirror hung above the oak mantel, reflecting light back into the room and a wooden boxed radiogram took pride of place in front of the right-hand bookcase.

Maggie had half-closed the internal Georgian wooden-shutters on both windows leaving only a narrow opening in order to retain heat but also to allow natural light into the room.

Bring them roond and sit them doon on here,' she said, pointing to the six-foot-long, red velvet sofa that stretched across a multi-coloured, Turkish rug in front of the fire and, plumped up a couple of the half-dozen cushions spread along the sofa.

Helped by Ian and, still wrapped in a blanket, Sarah Dawson sat down and sighed with relief as she looked at the fire burning fiercely in the stove. Shivering from the cold journey in the back of the truck, Davy sat close to her as Rosalind sat down next to him, wrapping her arm protectively around him.

Standing in front of the stove, Maggie pointed to one of the two matching, red velvet armchairs on either side of the fireplace, saying to the two pals, 'Sit yorsells doon lads and I'll get the kettle on. I've already got a lad in the kitchen who got stuck earlier.'

Raising his eyebrows, Ian looked across at Jake who was staring toward the door. Following Jake's look, Ian saw the intimidating, greatcoat-clad figure of Geordie Robertson standing threateningly in the doorway. An Elastoplast on the cut over his nose that Maggie had seen too and a purple bruise under his right eye; he held a half-eaten bacon sandwich in his left hand, his right hand gripping the revolver, by his side.

'Fuck me,' he snarled, look who we've got here, Shepherd and Grundy!'

Rosalind turned around and clutching her hands to her face, yelled, '*THAT'S HIM!*'

No one moved for the few seconds during the shocked silence that followed Rosalind's shout-until Jake made his move. As impulsive as ever, he ran at Robertson, determined to knock the huge youth over, but the heavy sheepskin-lined parka he was wearing hampered his rush. Robertson was no slouch, lifting the revolver; he pointed and shot Jake at point blank range, just as he leapt at him.

The bark of the revolver was deafening in the room, the power from the blow of the bullet striking Jake, spinning him in mid-flight, crashing him into a heavy oak bureau to the left of the door. He collapsed, onto the polished pine floorboards, lying face down and motionless.

Rosalind screamed in shock, Davy clung to his mother and Maggie reached behind her for the heavy-steel poker that leant against the fireplace, as Ian rushed around the sofa to attack Robertson but stopped suddenly.

Staring into the muzzle of the revolver that was pointed at his face; he knew the man in front was ready to fire and said, 'You mad bastard, what the hell do you think you are doing?'

An insane grin bared Robertson's uneven teeth, his eyes burning with rage, he fumed, 'Aah'll kill the fucking lot of ye if any fucka moves, Aah've already killed two bastards this morning as well this useless tossa, so Aah've fuck all to lose. But ye, Ian fucking Shepherd, I owe you a good hiding from our last fight in the Third Ra, noo let's see hoo fucking hard ye are.'

Keeping the revolver pointed at Ian's face, he pulled back the cocking hammer with his thumb and carefully swapped the revolver to his left hand. Expecting to him to fire, Ian lunged forward straight into Robertson's meaty, right fist that, combined with his own rush forward, was powerful enough to knock him onto his back. Scrambling to get up, a powerful kick to his head, bowled him onto his back, curling into a ball as Robertson unleashed more savage kicks to Ian's head and ribs.

'Die you little fucking shit,' Robertson snarled as he vented his anger and frustration, bending down to rain punches on Ian's head, only stopping when Maggie threw the poker at him, striking him on his right shoulder before clattering to the floor. Turning, he stood up, pointed the revolver in Maggie's direction, and fired wildly, the bullet shattering the large mirror over the fireplace, showering Maggie in flying glass.

Sarah had wrapped her arms around her two children and pulled them down onto the sofa, trying to cover them with her own body as Maggie dropped to her knees in shock and pain from several small cuts to her head and neck from flying glass.

Robertson stepped over Jake to stand behind the sofa, pointing the revolver at Maggie, bellowing, 'Ya fucking bitch, Aah'll blow yor fucking heed off,' but did not fire when he heard movement behind him.

Turning, he saw Jake roll over onto his back, blood trickling from a cut on his right temple and a small bloodstain on his parka just above his right-hand hip pocket. Moaning, Jake clutched his side and curled up in pain as Ian tried to kneel. Robertson moved quickly, smacking Ian on the side of his head with the revolver, knocking him onto his back before turning to Jake, kicking him savagely in the ribs.

A demented look on his face, he ignored Jake's yell of pain and spat, 'Aah've got ye bastards where Aah want ye, and am ganning te enjoy this.' Then taking out the four lose rounds of ammunition from his greatcoat pocket, he broke the revolver open, and slid them into the chambers to join the other two before snapping it shut.

The drive from Bellingham to the A68 at Otterburn had been difficult for Jack Gray, the road often, almost disappearing under shallow snowdrifts. However, the low-revving, 8.4-litre diesel engine, powered his mighty

Scammell Pioneer recovery-truck through the drifts, his vantage point high in the cab, providing him with a good view of the road ahead as he drove slowly on.

By the time he reached the A68 the blizzard had become ferocious and felt as though it was trying to blow the truck off the road as it tore at the canvas and Perspex driver's door window. Used to driving in all kinds of weather, Jack was confident that he could still make it home to his mother, alone at Treshinish House but, in acknowledgement of the ferocity of the blizzard he pulled on his WW2 Russian, ex-army, fur-hat.

A snowplough with a truck spreading rock salt was attempting to keep the road clear from the A68 to Otterburn but it looked as if they were fighting a losing battle.

It was nine-thirty before he brought the Scammell to a halt at the turn-in to Redesdale Camp where, PC John Carlisle; wrapped in his dark-blue overcoat, with his 'Bobby's helmet secured in place by its chin strap, leaned into the gale at almost at 40°. Both his overcoat and helmet were plastered white down the windward side from gale blasted snow.

Jack climbed down from his truck as an army; three-ton Bedford towed the last of the stranded vehicles, a delivery van, into the camp.

PC Carlisle took Jack's arm and struggling through the snow, led him around to the sheltered side of the Scammell.

Once out of the worst of the gale, and trying not to stare at the scars on Jacks' face that looked livid from the effects of the cold, he shouted, 'We could have done with your help earlier, we've had to take more than a dozen stranded vehicles into the camp and it was a bit of a struggle. We've also closed the road, so you'll have to park up there as well.'

Shaking his head, Jack shouted back, 'No, I'm going on, my mother is on her own in wor farm at the other end of Catcleugh Reservoir, and I'm not leaving her on her own in this.'

'We sent a small army truck along there to look for stranded vehicles, forty-minutes ago and it hasn't come back yet, there are at least two cars along there, one of them with a woman and two kids in.'

'Even More, reason to let me through and see what help I can give them.'

Carlisle nodded and shouted, 'My mate is up in the camp at the moment, on the telephone to our HQ trying to get an update on the storm and road closures, do you want to wait to hear what he has to say?'

'No thanks,' Jack said as he climbed up into the cab through the passenger door and clambering over to his seat, started up the huge engine before waving to the PC as he drove off into the blizzard.

John Carlisle shuffled across to the police car and took off his helmet before climbing into the front seat, glad to be out of the storm as PC Colin Wilson opened the driver's door and slid in to join him.

'Start the engine up and let's get some heat in here,' Carlisle said.

Wilson started the engine and checked that the heater was on full before turning to his tall partner, 'Bloody weather is going to be like this until at least tomorrow morning, so we'll be spending the night in this back of beyond shithole,' he complained.

'It could be worse, Carlisle replied,' we could be stuck in the car till then but at least we have shelter and food here, anyway, did Hexham have owt more to say?'

Rubbing his arms, Wilson continued, 'Aye, there's been a double morder at Ashington, the suspect buggared off in a two-tone, Blue, Vauxhall Cresta, they have iviry bugga oot looking for him. A nineteen-year-old, six-foot-three, big frigging, trouble-maker with black hair; he soonds like bother.'

Carlisle, sat quietly for a moment, rubbing his chin as he sought to remember what the driver of the van that came back from Carter Bar had said.

Sitting up straight, he said, 'Listen, the fella driving the van that failed to get up to Carter Bar, mentioned seeing a blue Vauxhall driving recklessly, I'm going up to the cookhouse to see him, I'll be back as soon as I can.'

'Aye okay – champion,' Wilson muttered, pulling his collar up and hunkering down into his seat.

CHAPTER 10

Friday 8th February – 9:40 am
Ashington

Standing in front of the mirror over the fireplace in the sitting room of the Grundy house, Edna applied scarlet lipstick to her thin, tight lips, then rubbing them together she dropped the lipstick into her handbag.

Turning from the mirror, she looked down at Howard sitting on the sofa, reading a tattered copy of the Beano and said, 'Right Pet, am off te school te fetch them two little buggas back here so I can find oot what they've been saying te, Jake. I divin't want them spoiling things here, becos if Albert finds oot what Aa've done, he'll hoy us oot and ye might hev te gan and live with yor Aunty Patsy in Pegswood again.'

Howard wrinkled his pudgy face and tried to look upset but the thought of going back to live with his aunt and uncle delighted him.

'They knew how to spoil a growing lad,' he thought, guessing it may have something to do with them not having any kids of their own.

Edna had purposely kept her son at home while she thought through her options and, having seen the blizzard raging outside, she was glad she had. Blizzard or not, she had to get Albert's boys out of school and find out what they knew. Walking through the kitchen into the hall, she took a pair of fur-lined, suede booties from the stairs and pulled them on over her nylon stockings. Wrapping a plaid scarf around her head, she pulled on her thick, grey, winter coat over her cardigan and black skirt, and after fastening the buttons right up to the neck, stepped out into the blizzard.

The five-hundred-yard walk to Wansbeck School was exhausting, the snow on the un-cleared pavements was several inches deep and the gale force wind blowing from behind her, kept trying to bowl her over, causing her to hang on to railings or lampposts several times to regain her composure. Traffic on the main road was very light but she did note that the buses were still running; ploughing through the grey slush created by rock salt and traffic.

Arriving at the school, dishevelled and cold and, expecting problems taking the boys out of their classes, she found that, because of the blizzard, a few other parents were doing the same. The boy's teachers made sure the boys were dressed in their duffle coats before handing them over.

Thanking the teachers, Edna, gave them a sickeningly sweet smile and grabbing the boys hands tightly, hurried them out into the storm, Billy protesting, 'Mr Thomsin was ganning to pick us up.

'Aye, whey he's not noo,' she said as she dragged them into the full force of the wind that plastered the front of their coats and hoods with snow. They struggled past the Holy Sepulchre Church and on into the small plantation where she pulled them into the seating shelter and, without releasing her grip on them demanded, 'Right ye little buggas, what hev ye been telling yor Jake?'

The two brothers were so intimidated by her that neither of them tried to escape her clutch as Billy shouted, 'We've telt him iviry thing aboot ye, hoo ye nip and slap us when Dad's not there and hoo yer just efter his money and ye keep on telling us ye'll hev us sent te borstal if we say owt.'

'Is that aall?' she sneered.

'Aye,' Billy answered quietly.

Unable to control his fear and anger, Roger found his voice and shouted, 'Nur, we telt him that we hurd Mr Hindmarsh telling Mrs Hindmarsh that ye're prosytitoot and shud be locked up and that if my Dad knew he would hoy ye oot.'

Trying to control her rapidly mounting anger, Edna snapped, 'De ye kna what a prostitute is Roger?'

'Nur but Aah kna it's summat bad becos Mrs Hindmarsh said yer wor a dorty bugga and wanted te kna hoo Mr Hindmarsh knew.'

Billy butt in, 'Aah kna what a prossy is and when my Dad finds oot he'll kick ye oot of wor hoose.'

Without replying, she tightencd her grip and marched off into the storm, dragging the two terrified lads with her, realising her plans for Albert were going to come to nothing as she thought through her options.

Thinking back to how their marriage had all but failed, her weak and idle husband often taking days at a time off work, leaving them always short of money, she had lost all respect for him and nagged him constantly; eventually become violent, often striking him with whatever was at hand during their many one-sided arguments.

It was no wonder she was attracted to the flash, money spending Harry Weedon when she first met him at Bingo at the Piv, where he preyed upon younger women. Despite his weasel-like features, she allowed him and his money, to seduce her, resulting in her accommodating him in the back of his flash car when he drove her back to Pegswood.

Foolishly, she took £30 from him and thinking it was a gift; squandered the money on Bingo and booze. When that was gone, he gave her another £20, saying, 'Enjoy it Pet, there's plenty more where that came from.'

However, two weeks later, she was taken aback, when, after another session in the back of his car, he casually asked, 'When are you ganning te pay me money back?

Thinking he was joking, she replied, 'Divin't be daft, Aah hevn't the money to pay you back but Aah hev the body te keep ye satisfied.'

He slapped her hard, knocking her head back against the window of the car and grasping her by the throat, growled, 'Listen, ye fucking slut, Aah can get a shag anytime Aah want. Ye better work oot hoo yor ganna pay me back or that soft fucking husband of yors will find oot what a whore ye are, and Aah can alwas send somebody roond te yor hoose te fettle him and yor bairn.'

Terrified by his threat to Howard she pleaded, 'Leave me bairn alone, Aah'll get the money for ye somehow.'

Without releasing his grip, he sneered, 'Noo just hoo are ye ganna dee that Pet? Yor fella isn't ganna giv it te ye is he and Aah divin't really want te see yor bonny face carved up.'

Four weeks later, her husband was found dead in his ancient car, the engine still running with a hosepipe attached to the exhaust, pushed through the small quarter-light in the front window. Shortly afterwards, Howard moved in with his aunt and uncle in their colliery house in Pegswood and Edna began working for Weedon in the flat in Station Road.

Staggering through the storm the last fifty yards up the narrow back lane, she decided on a new plan of action.

Instead of taking the boys into the house, she dragged them across the road to Albert's, stout, green wooden shed. Releasing Roger's hand, she leant on him, pinning him to the shed, while she unhooked the broken padlock from its hasp and allowed the door to swing inwards. Pushing Billy inside, she grabbed Roger and pushed him in after his brother.

After the ice cold air of the blizzard, the heavy smell of oil, grease, and paraffin was a cloying attack on their nose and senses, as they stood afraid in the middle of the cramped shed.

Backing up to a bench laden with tools and moped engine parts, they wondered what she was going to do, 'Why have you put us in here?' shouted Billy, afraid of what she might to do to them.

'Ye can bide in here until Aah sort things oot in the hoose,' she spat in a raised voice.

Billy tried to get past her shouting against the noise of the wind blowing through the door, 'Ye canna leave us in here, we'll freeze te death.'

Edna smacked the side of his face so hard that he fell back against the wooden spindle-backed chair that his father sat in to smoke his cigarettes.

'Ye can light the paraffin heater, tha's matches on the shelves at the end there.'

Stepping out, she pulled the door closed, flipping the hasp over, and sliding the padlock in to stop it opening. Looking up and down the street, she checked to see if anyone was about. She need not have worried, no one was venturing out into the blizzard that made it almost impossible to see across the narrow back lane.

Roger threw back his hood and wiped the dewdrop from his nose before taking off his glasses to wipe the condensation from them with a grubby handkerchief he pulled from his pocket. Replacing his glasses, he looked up at the kaleidoscopic ice patterns on the multi, small-paned window and said, 'Can we get oot the window, Billy?'

Reaching up for the cellophane-wrapped, box of Swan Vestas matches lying on a shelf and opening them, Billy replied, 'Nur, it doesn't open, and anyway, Dad had got that steel grid thingy ower the outside te stop anybody breaking in.'

Roger turned to watch his brother who, lifted the locking clasp on the Aladdin, Blue-Flame, paraffin heater and tipped the top-half to one-side, exposing the blackened wick, 'De ye kna hoo te light it?'

With a contemptuous look, Billy answered, 'Aye of course man, Aah've watched Dad de it a thoosand times.'

He struck a match and, held it against the wick until a dark-yellow, uneven flame spread half way around and then carefully tipped the funnel back over the top of the flame that turned a pale blue. Turning his back to the heater, he did not see the flame change slowly back to yellow, giving off a thin wisp of dark-grey smoke.

Stamping his sodden leather shoes, Roger moaned, 'My feet are frozen, and am caad.'

'Whey, keep on dancing and ye'll waarm up,' Billy said as he sat down on the chair, holding his feet toward the stove as his brother danced a little jig by the door.

Edna hit the house like a tornado, ordering Howard, 'Get upstairs and pack ye clothes inte yor holdall,' and then hurrying into the sitting room, she began rummaging through the drawers and cupboards behind the sofa, casting most of the contents across the floor. Not finding what she was looking for she threw the cushions from the sofa and two armchairs onto the floor and tipped them up to look underneath. The understairs cupboard was next; dragging the contents out one by one, she examined them carefully before dumping them on the kitchen floor.

On through the remainder of the kitchen she tore, then the pantry leaving food and crockery strewn haphazardly, across the room. Having searched the downstairs, she cast off her coat and charged upstairs where she continued to wreak havoc as she searched every nook and cranny, finally collapsing in a breathless, sweating heap on Albert's bed.

'Where the buggary does he keep his bliddy money,' she yelled.

Looking concerned, Howard walked into the bedroom and said, 'Billy telt me he keeps it in a bank, he's got ower eight hundred punds.'

Edna sat upright and yelled, 'How de ye kna hoo much he's got?'

'Cos Billy showed me his dad's banking book.'

Taking a deep breath, she lowered her voice and asked, 'Where did he get the bank book from Pet?'

Howard smiled, pleased that the information his mother wanted, 'Under the carpet on the top stair,' barely finishing his sentence before his mother charged past him and out onto the landing, where she knelt down, clawing at the edge of the stair carpet.

Howard walked up behind her and casually said, 'Unclip that brass thingy Mam, then ye can lift that wooden rod and the carpet comes up.'

Muttering obscenities under her breath, she undid the carpet rod, slid her hand under the now loose carpet, and grabbed the small, thin, navy-blue bankbook, shouting, 'Got the bugga!' Flicking through the pages, she checked the amount and beamed a greedy smile before saying, 'Barclays Bank, reet ye bugga.'

Smiling at Howard, she said, 'Get yersell doon stairs and get yer wellies and coat on, am ganna put ye on the bus te yer Aunty Patsy's, ye kna which stop te get off divin't ye?'

Delighted, he replied, 'Yes Mam,' and hurried downstairs as Edna stepped into their bedroom and began stuffing her meagre collection of clothes into a small, brown leather suitcase.

Without a thought for Billy and Roger, a few minutes later, dragging her bewildered son with his holdall behind her, she struggled to the bus stop in Highmarket, the blizzard blowing into her back, hurrying them recklessly along.

'Come on she yelled, Ye'll catch the ten-past-ten bus.'

The bus was fifteen minutes late and with both of them frozen despite sheltering in Billy Scott's shop doorway, she handed him sixpence for his fair and helped him up into the bus.

'Fucking useless bit of junk,' Stuart Weedon yelled, thumping the steering wheel of his eight-month-old, red MGA Roadster, venting his frustration after his sports car slid sideways in the slush of the Avenue that led to the terrace of Sycamore Street. With the soft top up and the blizzard raging, his vision was limited through the small area of the windscreen that the wipers battled to keep clear, making driving extremely hazardous.

Having already been temporarily stuck three times, and having to wait to be pushed out by passers-by that were few and far between in the blizzard, it was just before ten-o'clock when he eventually pulled up behind the blue and white, Police Panda Car parked outside his home.

Glaring at the police car he swore, 'What the fuck are they after?' He wondered if they were inquiring about one of his or his father's dodgy dealings.

Climbing out the MG, he slammed the door and bent to lock it as the grey-haired police sergeant climbed out of the Panda, pulled on his helmet and leaning close to Weedon so that he could be heard over the howling of the blizzard, asked, 'Mr Stuart Weedon?'

'Yes, that's me waat de ye want?'

'I am Sergeant David Malcolm, can we go inside - sir?'

Leaning a hand against the railings in front of the small yard to steady himself, Weedon spat, 'Why, what am Aah supposed te hev done?'

The sergeant stepped closer, 'Nothing – that I am aware off, Aah need te talk te ye aboot yer father lad.'

Walking past the sergeant to his front door, Weedon fumbled with his bunch of keys, before finding the right one to open the door. Stepping inside he held it open until the sergeant walked in past him, into the small hallway. Closing the door to the noise of the blizzard, he unfastened his overcoat and shook snow off before leading the way into the living room where he leant over the fire to warm his hands and asked over his shoulder, 'Whey waat de ye want me Fatha for?'

'Perhaps ye better sit doon Mr Weedon; I have bad news for ye.'

Standing up straight, Weedon turned to look up at Malcolm, who was taking his helmet off, 'Bad news – waat bad news?'

Without feeling any sympathy for the weasel-faced runt in front him, the Sergeant said, 'I am sorry Mr Weedon, but a body was found doon the pit this morning and is believed to be your father, Mr Harold Weedon, several of his workmates identified the deceased as being your father.'

'Deed – me Fatha – doon the pit, hoo did that happen, did sumat faall in on him?'

'No Mr Weedon, not an accident, we are treating his death as suspicious.'

Shocked, he took off his overcoat and threw it over the back of the armchair sitting next to the fire, 'Ye mean mordered, some buggas mordered me Fatha?'

'It looks that way but until the post-mortem, we cannot say for sure but we are looking for someone in connection with yer father's death.'

'Who?'

Taking out his notebook, the sergeant asked, 'Do you know George Robertson, Mr Weedon?'

'Geordie, aye Aah kna him, why has that big bastard killed me Fatha?'

'Would you know of his whereabouts?'

Without concealing his anger, Weedon snapped, 'Nur I divin't fucking kna where the bastard is, if Aah did Aah would tell ye.'

Sergeant Malcolm scribbled in his notebook and asked, 'What was the relationship between Robertson and your father?'

Thrusting his hands into the trouser pockets of his dark-blue, Italian-style suit, Weedon, snapped, 'What fucking relationship, he worked for me Fatha in the pit and helped oot at the betting office, tha was nee relationship.'

Rubbing his chin, Malcolm asked, 'Do you know William Robertson, George Robertson's father?'

Weedon, wrinkled his brow and paused for a second or two before answering, 'Big Bill – aye Aah kna him, him and me Fatha own the betting shop, he's on night shift this week so he'll be opening it up at eleven this morning, why, has he got something te de we me Fatha's morder as weell?'

Shaking his head, Malcolm replied, 'No lad, we don't think he had anything to do with your father's death and - he won't be opening the betting shop this morning.'

'Why not, is it becos Geordie had something te de we me Fatha's death then?'

'No not that, Mr William Robertson *has* been murdered,' replied the Sergeant matter of factually.

'*WHAT!*' yelled Weedon, 'who the fuck mordered him, why would anyone want te kill him or me Fatha,' he said, knowing that many people in Ashington will be delighted to hear of their demise.

'Perhaps you could help us there, do you know of anyone who had a grudge or disagreement with either your father or Mr Robertson?'

'For fuck's sake man, nur Aah divin't anyway, enough with yer fucking questions, where's me Fatha, I want te gan and see him.'

Nodding, the sergeant replied, 'I am not sure they have got him out of the pit yet, they will be taking him to the

Coroner's mortuary at the RVI. We need to inform Mrs Weedon, where is your mother?'

'Mam? She buggared off a couple of years ago.'

A puzzled frown on his face, the Sergeant said, 'Two years ago? Where did she go, have you a forwarding address for her?'

Flustered, Weedon stammered, 'F, f, forwarding address – nur, Aah hevn't, she went doon Sooth, Aah think.'

'Where doon Sooth?'

'Aah've telt ye Aah divin't kna, just doon Sooth somewhere.'

Sergeant Malcolm did not let up, 'How far doon Sooth, lad? Durham? Leeds? London? Lands End?

'Aah' divin't kna man.'

Writing in his notebook, the Sergeant continued, mimicking some of Weedon's words, 'So your mother buggared off a couple of years ago, for somewhere doon Sooth but you divin't kna where; did your father have an address?'

'Aah divint kna man,' replied Weedon, his face turning bright red.

'Okay Mr Weedon, why did your mother leave?'

'Cos they wor alwas bliddy arguing and screaming at each other.'

Malcolm shook his head and tightened his lips in mock disapproval before asking, 'And what did they argue about?'

'For fuck's sake man, ye've just telt me, me Fatha's been mordered and yer asking me all these fucking questions, can ye not just leave me alone?'

'Yes of course Mr Weedon but we do have to inform his next of kin - yor mother so I will be off in a minute, we would appreciate it if you could look through any papers your father may have to see if you can find a contact address.'

Desperate to clear his thoughts, Weedon walked to the back door, waiting for the Sergeant, 'Aye Aah will, am not fucking sackless or donard, Aah'll hev a look shortly.'

Putting his helmet back on, Macintyre walked slowly to the door, stopping next to Weedon, he looked down at him, smiled, and asked, 'Where do you work Mr Weedon?'

'Waat the fuck dee ye want te kna that for?'

'Oh just wondering, where ever it is, it must pay well, judging by your smart car,' he said, and touching his helmet with his finger in a mock salute, opened the door and stepped out into the blizzard, saying over his shoulder, 'We'll be in touch, oh, and sorry about your father.'

Weedon slammed the door and stepping over to the window watched the Sergeant climb into his car and drive off. He waited a few seconds then hurried across to the large airing cupboard next to the fire. Kneeling down, he opened it up and slid an inner door to one side revealing a small safe with a dial combination lock in the centre, a sturdy brass handle next to it.

Trying the handle several times, he sat back and said, 'Fucking, fucking – fuck, ye stupid owld bastard, hoo many fucking times did Aah tell ye that ye should let me kna the fucking numbers.'

Angry, frustrated and worried, he rocked back and forwards on his knees for a minute or two, wondering how he was going to get it open.

Not wanting alert the taxman, his father did not have a bank account. He kept all of the cash they earned from loan sharking and prostitution in the safe.

A few minutes later, with his overcoat pulled over his shoulder's Weedon knocked on the door of his neighbour, Betty Turnbull. The door opened almost immediately and the buxom, fifty-something Betty squinted through the wind-driven snow at Weedon

Then taking him by the arm, she said, 'Eeee, come on in Pet, whativa's happened, the polis knocked on me door urlier asking where ye or yer Mam was. Aah telt them aboot yer Mam leaving and me cooking yer dinnas for ye both...'

'Aye Betty, ta, Weedon interrupted, 'Look me Fathas been killed doon the pit, so tha's a few things Aah hev te sort oot, if anybody wants me, 'Aah'll be doon at the betting shop.'

Wrapping a pudding-like hand around her chin, Betty, who disliked father and son immensely but was happy to cook one main meal a day for them in exchange for a few pounds, said sympathetically, 'Eeee, that's aaful bonny lad, ye must be mortified, so will ye be wanting yer dinna tonight?

Turning to leave hc answered, 'Aye later on, Aah'll let ye kna when, after Aah get back,' and opening the door, hurried back to his own front door, locking it before climbing into his car and driving off to the betting shop

CHAPTER 11

Friday 8th February – 10 am
Redesdale

The blizzard propelled PC John Carlisle back to the Sunbeam Rapier police car parked next to the entrance to Redesdale Camp, slamming him into the side of the vehicle. Steadying himself, it required all his considerable strength to pull the car door open and hold it against the howling wind while he climbed into the almost oven-like interior, banging his helmeted head as he did so.

Relaxing in the driving seat, enjoying the warmth provided by the heating on full blast, PC Wilson watched Carlisle slam into the car, before opening the door, allowing a blast of ice-cold, snow-laden air inside. He shouted, 'Bliddy Hell man John, forst ye try te knock the car ower and then ye let aall the bliddy heat oot, look at ye, ye've brought haf the bliddy snow in with ye.'

Taking his helmet off, Carlisle dusted snow from the front of his greatcoat and undid the top three buttons before snapping, 'Good God man, it's like an oven in here, torn the blower off.'

Reaching forward, Wilson reluctantly turned the heater fan down a couple of clicks and asked, 'Whey, did you speak to anyone back at Hexham – all snug in tha nice warm bliddy offices?'

'Yes, I spoke to the duty sergeant and told him about the possibility of there being a blue Vauxhall stuck up ahead somewhere. He informed the Super. They are going to try and get another car up here with two or three more guys and a couple of Lee-Enfields.'

Wilson sat up, 'Bugga me, they must think this bloke is dangerous if they're arming them.'

Carlisle nodded vigorously and added, 'Yep they say very dangerous – that is if it was him, they are still searching the local area in case he went to a mate's house or a relative – if he has any locally. The Super said they are not sure when they can get assistance up here but the snowploughs are working flat out trying to clear the road. Hexham are also arranging for the snowplough from the Ranges and a farmer's tractor with a front-bucket to help the Otterburn snow plough clear the road. There's a stockpile of rock salt at Otterburn that they are using, they're determined to try and get the road open as soon as possible.'

Wilson looked sceptical, 'That's aall very weell but tha's nee sign of this bliddy blizzard stopping is tha?'

'The latest forecast is tomorrow morning – clear skies and the wind dropping.'

The smell of bacon and eggs welcomed the assorted group of stranded travellers as they gathered in the wooden cookhouse up in the camp. The QM, Major Trevor Graham watched them arrive; leaving when his Regimental Quartermaster Sergeant, (RQMS) began briefing them on how they were to be looked after.

Commissioned from the ranks, the QM served with 7 Armoured Division throughout WW2, and later, in Korea with the Commonwealth Brigade. As a result, he took events in his stride, he was not prone to panic, or worry, but he cared about the soldiers in the regiment.

'Soldiers first, officers and SNCOs second,' was how he was brought up and how he carried out his role as QM. Wanting to know what had become of the two young soldiers, he sent looking for stranded vehicles; he climbed into his Champ and drove down to the road junction, sliding to a halt alongside the police car.

Seeing the Champ pull up, PC Carlisle said to Wilson, 'I best go and tell the Major what's happening, he must be worried about his two lads.'

Inside the Champ, the QM asked him, 'Any news? Any sign of my lads?'

'We haven't seen or heard anything of them yet sir but the fella who lives at the far end of the reservoir drove through half-an-hour ago in a big, ex-army recovery truck, he reckoned he would get through no problem. However, there is a very remote possibility that one of the cars that your lads went looking for may have been driven by a lad who is wanted in connection with a murder.'

The QM gave Carlisle an incredulous look and asked, 'When did you find this out?'

'Just fifteen minutes ago; I've just got back from talking to our HQ, they are sending another car with armed officers to join us.'

'Armed officers? Does that mean the wanted man is armed?'

Nodding, Carlisle replied, 'Possibly - sir, with a revolver but we have no confirmation on that or that he was in the car up the road?

The QM gave the PC a sideways look and growled, 'My lads better be okay.'

Jack's arms were beginning to feel the strain of fighting the massive steering wheel of the Scammell every time he ploughed into a drift. No power steering meant it took a fair amount of strength to turn the wheel at the low speed the blizzard forced him to drive, the deep snow making it even harder to turn. On several occasions, he stood to apply greater leverage to turn the huge tyres in the snow.

The blizzard that continued to reduce visibility to a few yards meant he almost missed the half-buried, blue Vauxhall. Seeing it at the last moment, he stopped and climbed down to check that the vehicle was empty and, saw the broken telegraph pole with the snapped line. Satisfied that there was no one about, he continued his battle with the blizzard, eventually ploughing through a large drift at the end of the forest a hundred yards from Treshinish House.

Once out of the shelter of the trees, the wind tore at the canvas and Perspex side window creating a gap that the wind took advantage of to blast Jack with snow, limiting his vision even more. Approaching the turn in to his home, he saw where the army truck had smashed its way through the snowdrift and parked directly in front of the front door to the house.

'At least they are safe,' he thought, I wonder if they picked up the driver of the Vauxhall?'

Straining hard, he turned the driving wheel and keeping the engine revs steady drove over the drift and brought the Scammell to a halt alongside the much smaller Austin.

Stretching the stiffness out of his weary shoulders, he climbed out the cab and stepped down into the gap between the two vehicles that provided some shelter from the worst of the Blizzard. Keen to check on his mother, and enjoy a large mug of tea, he hurried round to the heavy oak door, holding onto the handle to prevent it flying inwards as he opened it and stepped into the porch, forcing the door shut behind him.

Stamping snow off his boots onto an old coir-mat, he undid the top two buttons of his stockman coat and smiled, acknowledging how much quieter it was out of the blizzard even though the wind still howled outside.

Opening the inner-hall door, he walked through, and shouted, 'I am home Mam.'

There was no answer from his mother, just the welcoming bark of his collie, 'Jess' from the scullery at the back of the house. Stepping into the parlour, he stopped, trying to make sense of what he was seeing.

A few minutes earlier, ignoring the intimidating figure of the raging Geordie Robertson as he reloaded his revolver,

Rosalind Dawson rushed over to Jake, kneeling next to him to see how badly wounded he was, asking, 'Where did he shoot you?'

With his right hand pressed to the cut on his temple, Jake touched his left side and winced, 'Here in my side.'

Robertson cut in, 'He'll get another in the fucking heed if he tries owt, noo Grundy ye useless twat, hand ower the keys te yer truck.'

Rising from the sofa, Sarah helped Maggie to her feet, noting that none of the cuts and scratches to her neck and head appeared to be serious.

Maggie stood up, gripping Sarah's arm to steady herself, when something outside caught her attention, looking out of the window, she saw the big Scammell and without thinking, said loudly, 'Jack!'

Rushing round to the window, Robertson watched as the Scammell drove slowly into the yard, 'Noo that's waat Aah need te get oot of here he snarled, and walking across to the two women, he pushed Sarah onto the sofa next to Davy, then grabbed Maggie by the back of her hair, holding the revolver to her head.

Jack stood motionless, only his eyes moving, taking in the disturbing scene before him. On his immediate left he saw a pretty, auburn-haired, teenage girl bent over a young soldier who was bleeding from his temple and clutching his left side, behind them, below the first window, another young soldier lay curled up, blood trickling from his nose and although both eyes looked swollen and red, Jack noted a steely glint. A very attractive middle-aged woman with the same colour hair as the teenager sat on the sofa with her arms around a young boy; but what held his searching eyes, was the figures in front of the fire. He could see blood on his mother's neck; her head pulled back by the huge hand of an enormous youth who held a revolver in his other, the muzzle digging into Maggie's ashen coloured face.

Jack forced himself to remain calm while he assessed the situation while glaring at Robertson; knowing he needed to get him out of the house, he said nothing, waiting for the monster to say something.

He did not have to wait long, Robertson snarling, 'Will that truck get me over Carter Bar?'

Without hesitating, Jack replied, 'Aye, no problem at all, Aah've been ower the top in a lot worse than this,' he lied.

Knowing her son to be lying, Maggie kept quiet, wondering what he was going to do, praying he would not risk his life unnecessarily.

Sarah sat back down next to Davy, her eyes glued to the imposing figure at the door, his striking blue-eyes diverting her attention from the scars running down his cheek.

Jake pulled Rosalind's arm, gently moving her away from the door as Robertson pushed Maggie forward, saying, 'Right, back-up, do owt daft and Aah will shoot yer fucking mother.'

Jack didn't move, 'Listen, Aah don't know what bother ye've got yourself into, or what's happened here, but leave my mother here, Aah'll take you ower the Bar.'

'Nur she's ganning we me te mek sure ye divin't try owt, noo back up.'

Jack stepped back into the hall and stopped, 'There are only two seats in the cab, she'd just get in the way, I promise you, I won't try owt.'

Pushing Maggie out of the way, Robertson swung the revolver up, aiming it at Jack's face, fighting the nausea of mounting panic once again.

Struggling to compose himself, he breathed deeply before saying, 'Right, this is what's ganna happen, am ganna stay a yard away from ye and you will move very slowly, ye will open the forst door wide and then the second, got that?'

Jack nodded, 'But the wind and snow will blow in.'

'Aah kna that for fuck's sake. Once the doors opened ye will waalk roond te the passenger door and climb in very slowly and once yor seated, Aah will climb up after ye.' Then pulling the cocking hammer back with his thumb, he warned, 'Aah'll blow yer fucking heed off if ye as much as twitch, Aah've already killed two bastards teday so a thord winnit mek any difference.'

Not showing any emotion despite being shocked by the lad's confession, Jack turned very slowly and pulled open the inner door, pushing it all the way back until it rested against the wall. Stepping forward, he put his left hand up against the oak door, twisted the big handle open with his right hand, and immediately fought to stop the door smashing him off his feet as the blizzard blasted into the hallway.

Robertson leant into the gale and followed Jack slowly outside and into the lee of the Austin where they both steadied themselves. Robertson waved the revolver at Jack motioning him to go on.

Inside the parlour, Ian sprang to his feet and staggered into the hall where, Maggie grabbed his arm to stop him rushing outside, and shouted, 'Come with me.'

Trotting to the end of the hall, she opened the door to the back passage and stepping inside, twisted open the steel handle of a large grey metal cabinet. Reaching inside she pulled out a 12 gauge, double-barrel shotgun, calmly snapping it open before reaching inside the cabinet again and pulling two cartridges from a box, sliding them into the chambers, and snapping the gun shut.

She handed Ian the gun, saying, 'Mind ye don't hit my lad with it.'

Lifting the butt to his shoulder, Ian moved swiftly to the front door; fighting the wind, he moved out into the lee of the truck. There he took a deep breath and readied himself, walking quickly around the front of the Austin into the full force of the blizzard and along to and around the front of the Scammell.

Jack, having climbed slowly up, was in the cab on the passenger side while Robertson stood a yard from the truck with the revolver pointing up at him.

Ian's stomach tied itself in a knot and he gulped in a mouthful of wind-driven snow before shouting, '*ROBERTSON!*'

Geordie turned, instinctively pointing and firing the revolver at Ian - the shot was wild, missing Ian by several feet, and now he was looking at the twin muzzles of the shotgun. He fired another wild shot and turned, running into the blizzard as Ian aimed, lifting the barrel high at the last moment before firing, his training, and conscience, stopping him from shooting Robertson in the back.

It was the first time Ian had fired a shotgun, let alone both barrels at once, the kick and noise catching him off guard as he watched Robertson disappear into the snow.

Jack jumped down next to him, shouting above the blizzard, 'Have you any more cartridges'?

Ian shook his head and Jack grabbed his arm, motioning him to go back into the house. Ian turned bracing himself against the truck as a worried looking Maggie stepped around the front of the truck, shielding her face with her forearm. Jack stepped around Ian and putting his arm around his mother helped her back inside the house where he and Ian pushed the big oak door shut, sliding a large black iron bolt home.

Once in the hall He said, 'Okay, let's lock the place up Mam then we'll see who we need to patch up first, that bugga oot there can wait.'

CHAPTER 12

Friday 8th February – 10:05 am
Ashington

Storming out of Barclays Bank, Edna was spitting mad. Having caught a bus from Highmarket to the bus station in the centre of town, she fought through the blizzard, past the Grand Corner and into Barclays. The only customer in the bank, she presented Albert's bankbook to the teller, saying that he had asked her to draw out his money, as he was unable to get to the bank during working hours. A short and heated argument followed after the teller informed her that only Albert could draw money from his account.

Sheltering from the blizzard in the entrance to the bank, she thought through her options for a second or two, deciding to go to Weedon for help, thinking, 'After all, he was responsible for me being homeless.'

Cursing the weight of her small suitcase and the blizzard that now propelled her across the street, past Shepherds store, down North Seaton Road, into Milburn Road, and along

Third Avenue. Finally, feeling cold, weary, and hungry, she turned into Sycamore Street, staggering fifty yards down to Weedon's house where she banged on the door.

There was no answer, and when her frantic banging and kicking, also went unanswered, she swore loudly and struggled next door banging on Betty Turnbull's door.

Opening her door, Betty held it against the wind, squinting at the bedraggled figure in front of her, 'Can Aah help ye Pet?'

Bracing herself against the wind that was trying to push her into Betty, Edna shouted, 'De ye kna where Harry Weedon is?'

A satisfied smile spread across Betty's face that she replaced with a look of concern before taking Edna's arm, saying, 'Eeee, come on in flower, Aah've some bad news for ye,' and leading her into the living room heated by the roaring fire in the black-leaded range, continued, 'Are ye a friend of Harry's pet?

Edna dropped her case and stood in front of the fire warming herself as the snow on her coat melted and began to steam, 'Yes me and Harry are owld friends, Aah need te see him as soon as Aah can, where is he?

Betty hitched up her plump breasts with crossed arms, trying to look concerned while delighting in the juicy gossip she was keen to divulge, she replied, 'Am very sorry te tell ye this but Harry was killed doon the pit last neet, his son has been in te tell me.'

'Killed?' 'What – in an accident?'

'Eeee, noo aah divin't kna the details Pet, just that he's deed, ye look aall in, dee ye want a cup of tea?'

Shocked at the news, she tried to make sense of where Weedon's death left her as she replied, 'Oooh, yes please, Aah'd love one but canna use your lavvy forst.'

'Whey aye, pet, ower the road, the one we the green door, 'Aah'll get the kettle on.'

Edna struggled across to the freezing outside toilet, where she thought what implications Weedon's death might have for her as she quickly used the toilet and hurried back to the warmth of Betty's house, having decided what she was going to do.

Sitting in front of the fire, she sipped the large mug of hot, sweet tea, savouring the taste and heat, taking scant notice of Betty's incessant chatter, as she planned her next move; deciding that she was going to go to the flat.

Handing Betty the empty mug, she stood up fastening her coat and picking up her suitcase, said, 'Thanks very much for the tea Petal, am off te catch a bus back up te Station Road.'

Inside Albert's shed, the thin wisps of grey smoke turned black and were gathering in the apex of the shed like a black, boiling thundercloud as the fuel in the Aladdin heater ran dry and the wick itself burned. Sitting with his hood over his head and his arms wrapped around himself, Billy slept while Roger leant against the door, stamping his frozen feet and pulling his duffle coat tight around him with his hood pulled low over his bespectacled eyes.

Driving at just over ten-miles-per-hour behind a 'United' bus, their older brother, Ronnie, reached Bedlington. As he drove slowly on he thought about his beautiful Chinese wife, Mary, and how they met when he was serving in Singapore and how proud he was and how incredibly lucky he felt when her brother agreed to their marriage. Concerned that he left them just before the blizzard struck he hoped that he would be able to resolve problems at home and be on his way back to Mary and their daughter either tonight or tomorrow morning.

The tragic death of his mother flo, when an RAF jet smashed into the terraced row of colliery houses that the family lived in, marred their wedding and return to the UK. Now the terrible Edna was manipulating his gullible father, blinding him to her mistreatment of the two boys and hiding her real reasons for moving in with him.

Down below Ashington Colliery, accompanied by the Colliery Manager, DI Norman and DS Dodson after a long and tiring walk finally arrived at the Mothergate in the Duke Pit, where Harry Weedon's body lay. The Foreshift Overman waited for them, the Davy lamp hanging from his belt and the yardstick he leant on, indicating his position in the pit hierarchy.

Sweating, panting heavily, and unable to conceal his fear and dislike at being so far underground, DS Dodson muttered, 'Thank Christ we're here, let's hope we get this ower quickly and get oot of here.'

Two other headlamps shining next to the overman belonged to a PC sent down to secure the area and a very unhappy Bill Carter.

Striding up to the overman, the manager said, 'Aye Geordie, this is a bit of a bugger, have ye got the other faces working?'

Pushing his helmet back, the overman replied, 'Yes, aall working and Aah've got the drillers on these two but Aah've telt them not to come oot the Mothergate.'

'Right,' the Manager said, 'this is Inspector Norman, and Sergeant Dodson, show them where the body is.'

Norman stepped forward asking, 'Who found the body?'

'Aah did,' said Bill Carter, pushing himself up from the chocks he was sitting on.

'And you are?'

'Bill – William Carter, Aah work on the face here, we wor riding oot –bye on the belt when Aah saw him.'

'Okay, then I want you to show me where it is and tell me what you know,' then turning back to the Manager and Overman, he said, 'Thanks very much for all your help but can I ask you both to stay here while the DS and me examine the crime scene. When the doctor arrives with your rescue blokes, can you send him in here but keep your guys back, until we call them forward.'

Sounding put out, the manager replied, 'Fine, I'm off, I have a pit to run, if you can check in with me before you leave please, Geordie will bide hear until you're finished.'

DI Norman replied 'Got that thanks, just one last thing, who confirmed that Mr Weedon is actually deceased?'

Bill coughed up coal dust, spitting on the ground in front of him and replied, 'Me, I climbed ower the belt and saw his heed had been smashed in, and Aah checked to see if he was breathing, he's deed alright.'

Norman nodded, 'Okay, Mr Carter, please show us the body and tell us how you found it; you will have to come into Ashington Police Station this afternoon so we can take a full statement from you.'

Struggling to control his anger, Bill snapped, 'Bliddy hell man, Aah've just finished a full shift and need a shower, food, and bed.'

His prickly nature increased by his fear of being underground, DS Dodson snapped, 'Aye, well you will be able to enjoy the forst two but ye'll hev to wait a bit before ye get to your bed. Tha's been a morder here, Mr Carter and we need statements from iviry body involved, including establishing time of death and where you wor when it happened.'

'How,' Bill replied angrily, 'Aah didn't have owt te de with this, Aah, was on the coal face aall shift apart from twenty minutes heving me bait we me marras, and Weedon was alive then, we aall saw him. Aah didn't like the bugga but Aah wouldn't waste me energy on the swine either.'

DI Norman, stepped in, 'Why did you not like him, Mr Carter?'

'Whey man iviry bugga knas he's a nasty sod, he's up te all sorts of shite.'

'Such as?'

'Loaning folk money they cannit payback for a start, and ye need to check oot how they pay him back.'

'We will, Mr Carter but first show us the body and talk us through how you found it.'

A few minutes later, the Doctor arrived, DI Norman showing him the body saying, 'We have a possible weapon,' and held up an evidence bag containing the fishplate.

After scrambling over the conveyor and spending five minutes examining Weedon's body, the Doctor climbed back, 'Likely cause of death is blunt trauma to his head, he's been dead a few hours and more than that you will have to wait until I can carry out an autopsy and I can see him properly.'

Before going underground, Norman left DC Cotton and a uniformed officer in the pit canteen, taking statements from the men who were working on the coalface for the shift. Several wives braved the weather to walk to the colliery, worried about their husbands not arriving home from foreshift. Having been to the colliery offices to inquire about them, they sat alongside their husbands in the canteen, chatting, and enjoying cups of canteen tea but above all, relieved that their husbands were safe.

Earlier, word of the murder spread quickly around the canteen and pit baths and now, was spreading rapidly around Ashington as miners returned home with the news.

It was nearly eleven-thirty when Edna wearily climbed the steep backstairs to the flat in Station Road, ready for a confrontation, determined to take back the flat. She waited almost a minute before Yvonne, still wrapped in her housecoat, opened the door, allowing cigarette smoke and stale air to sweep over her.

Pushing past Yvonne, she stormed into the tiny flat, stopping by the sofa where she cast her eye around, wrinkling her nose and mouth in disgust at what she saw and smelt.

Glaring at Sandra who was curled up on the sofa, fag in one hand and magazine in the other she spat, 'Ye filthy pigs, look at the state of this place and the stink, it's enough te mek ye vomit. Aah had this place spotless, noo look at it, yer cannit be bothered to clean up after yer bliddy sells, you dorty buggas ye.'

Sandra opened her mouth to speak but Edna stopped her, 'Divvin't say a bliddy word Hinny, am in nee mood for yer excuses or moans, noo listen up the pair of ye, ye've got fifteen minutes te get yorsells dressed and oot of this flat and ye winnit be coming back. Noo come on get sorted oot and bugga off ora'll bliddy wipe the floor wee the pair of ye.'

Sandra began to sniffle as Yvonne said, 'Ye cannit hoy us oot man, the Weedons will gan mad.'

Silencing her a withering look, Edna snapped, 'Harry is deed, killed doon the pit last night and Aah'll sort that bliddy little shit of a son of his oot, no come on, Aah winnit tell ye again, bugga off back te yer mothers.'

Yvonne whimpered, 'Me Dad winnit hev me back...'

'Am not interested Pet get moving,' snarled Edna, pushing her toward the bedroom.

While the two girls whispered to each other as they quickly sorted out their meagre belongings inside a small wardrobe, Edna shouted, 'Ye can tek them sheets off the bed with ye an' aall, Aah don't suppose ye two buggas hev iver had them washed!'

Edna took her coat off and hung it behind the door to the outside hall, then strode across to the sink, turning on the tap on the gas boiler, checking that the burner burst into flame before she started to sort out the crockery and cutlery ready for washing, yelling, 'Hurry up ye two, Aah want ye oot noo.'

The black smoke in the shed was growing deeper and ever lower, until Roger sniffed in the first wisps when they reached down to him. He coughed and pulling his hood back, saw that the top half of the shed was full of thick, black-smoke and more was flowing from the heater.

He coughed again and grabbed his sleeping brother by the shoulder, shouting, 'Billy.'

Sitting up with a start, Billy saw black smoke billowing out of the Aladdin and acting instinctively, he leant forward to unfasten the top and flip it open shouting at Roger, 'Smash the window open, quick.'

Grabbing a rag from the bench, he began rubbing the glowing wick, smothering the burning embers as Roger dithered, looking for something to use to break the window.

Having smothered the flame, Billy leapt up and grabbed a hammer from a rack above the bench, coughing when he swallowed a mouthful of acrid, black smoke.

Shouting, 'Oot me way ye sackless sod,' he attacked the window, smashing out all six panes of glass before turning his head away as a gust of wind-driven snow, smacked him in the face.

Grabbing Roger, he pulled him down onto the floor, 'We'll hev tee stay doon here until the smoke clears,' and wrapped his arm around his younger brother as the blizzard drove snow through the broken window, coating the grubby interior and boys in pristine white.

CHAPTER 13

Friday 8th February – 11 am
Upper Redesdale

Kneeling down next to Rosalind as she helped a grimacing Jake undo the large buttons on his parka before carefully pulling it open, Ian said, 'Look ye can see where the bullet's gone through his belt.'

Looking at the heavy, green webbing belt, Rosalind asked, 'How do you unfasten this?'

Grabbing the belt at either side of the buckle, Jake gritted his teeth and said, 'Like this,' pushing the two ends together and unclipping the belt, sighing deeply as the belt released its grip on his waist and wound.

Turning to Ian, Rosalind said, 'There doesn't seem to be a lot of blood and looking at your face, I think you are going have a lot of black and blue bruises.'

Before Ian could answer, Jake said, 'Me heed hurts more than that, I didn't half smack it on this cupboard.'

Ian tried to smile but the lumps and bruises on his face turned it into a grimace as he said, 'Whey if ye had engaged your brain before ye jumped at Geordie, you might not have been shot and might not have banged yor thick heed.'

Touching Jake on the arm, Rosalind smiled at him, 'I thought you were very brave – silly but brave.'

Looking into her hazel eyes, he tried to smile back but the pain he felt made it look more of a frown, 'Aye that's me.'

Having ensured the house was locked up; Jack walked into the hall with his mother and picked up the telephone handset, holding it to his ear, 'Just as I thought, it's dead; the Vauxhall smashed a pole and brought the lines down. We're on our own while this storm lasts.'

Replacing the handset, he took his mother's arm, saying, 'Howway and sit doon so we can see to the cuts on your neck.'

Tutting, Maggie replied, 'Am alright Jack, that laddie needs seeing te first, am ganning to get the first aid chest and then I'll have a look at that poor woman's face.'

Jack and Ian helped Jake to his feet and supported him as they walked him to the sofa. Standing in front of the fire, with Ian's help, Jake took off his jacket, wincing as Ian and Rosalind gently pulled his pullover up and over his head.

Sarah moved a tearful and shocked Davy to the opposite side of the long sofa, wrapping her arm around his shoulders; he snuggled into his mother.

Unbuttoning Jake's bloodstained khaki shirt, Rosalind lifted it away, bending slightly to examine the wound as her mother watched from the other end of the long sofa.

Holding the left side of his shirt up, Jake asked, 'How bad is it?'

Ian leant forward and took a close look at the wound, 'It hasn't bled very much, it looks as if the bullets not gone right in, just gouged two or three inches out of his side, I think his web-belt might have deflected or slowed the bullet down.'

Giving Ian a sideways look, Jake said, 'Still bliddy horts though.'

Stepping between Rosalind and Ian, Jack asked, 'Mind if I have a look?

Maggie sat down next to Sarah who was watching Jack intently, and whispered, 'He gets embarrassed when folk stare at his scars Pet.'

Blushing, Sarah whispered back, 'Sorry but I wasn't looking at his scar, I was looking at his eyes.'

After examining Jakes wound, Jack said, 'That's not to bad lad, ye wor lucky, we can bandage that up til ye get to a hospital,' and then looking at Jake's head, said, 'Ye might need a couple of stitches on your head as well.'

Jake grimaced, Whey, that pig Robertson failed to kill me, we'll have to get after him.'

'Not you lad,' Jack said, and then realising what Jake had just said, asked, 'Do you know him?'

'Aye, Ian and me went te school with him, he's a reet nasty bit of work and hoys his weight aroond Ashington; Ian had a hell'uv a fight with him at school and hammered him.'

Thinking back to his epic fight with the then, school bully, Ian said, 'Aye but he gave me a canny hammering then as well and Aah doubt I'd last a few seconds with him now, he's huge. But he said he'd shot two people this morning, I wonder who and why?'

Shaking her head in annoyance, Rosalind interrupted, 'That's all well and good but we need to bandage this wound and my Mam's face needs looking at,' and took Davy's hand, moving him to the armchair to the right of the fire as Maggie opened the first-aid chest.

Using a pair of medical scissors taken from the chest, she carefully snipped through the bandage that held the dressing over Sarah's right cheekbone.

Sarah stiffened, gritting her teeth as Maggie, gently eased the blood-soaked pad off the wound, revealing a three inch long, Y shape cut with congealed blood around the still raw centre.

Concerned, Maggie looked up at Jack who was wrapping a bandage around Jake's waist and said, 'This needs a couple of stitches to hold closed until she gets to see a doctors or hospital, whenever that might be.'

Jack glanced at Sarah's face and nodded, 'Yes so does the cut on this lad's head, and I need to check the other lad out, he looks as if he has had a helluva beating; are you doing them, or me?'

Standing behind her mother, Rosalind asked, 'Stitches, can you stitch cuts up?'

Maggie smiled up at her, 'Aye lass, I've stitched Jack up a couple of times, ye've got to be able to look after yourself up here Pet but Jack's better than me, he has a steadier hand. He made a grand job of young Bob Fenwick when he ripped his arm open on a broken bottle he fell on...' she paused and looking at Jack and unable to conceal the alarm in her voice, said, 'The Fenwicks Jack?'

'Aye Mam, I haven't forgotten them, I'm sure Young Tom can look after things there, I'm going along as soon as we are sorted out here.'

Concern etched on her face, Maggie asked, 'What with that lad running around with a pistol?'

I'll take my gun with me and the lad here, Ian is it?'

Ian nodded and Jack continued, 'Aye, Ian can have the other one in case the bugga tries to get back in here, keep Jess with you and she'll let you know if he is outside.'

Touching Maggie on the arm, Sarah said, 'Just clean my cut and put a bandage on it, I'm sure it doesn't need any stitches.'

Jack expertly finished tying a neat knot on Jakes bandage, helped him to lie back on the sofa and stepping over to Sarah, gently placed his hand on her chin, turning and lifting her face to examine the cut.

'It needs stitching, it could be a while before you get out of here and it could begin to heal over, I'll do it, I stitched up a lot worse than this in the war – I was a medic in the paras.'

When Jack let go of her chin, she turned to look up at him and smiled, He smiled back, then remembering, quickly turned his face to his left, trying to hide his scars.

Maggie picked up the first-aid box and taking hold of Ian's arm, led him into the kitchen, guiding him to a chair at the table, 'Right sit yer sell doon and I'll check your face and head.

Ian winced a few times as she applied TCP to small cuts and grazes on the side of his head, ears and cheekbones before sticking a plaster under his right eye and one on the bridge of his nose.

Leaning back she examined his face again saying,'Your nose doesn't seem to be broken so when the swelling goes doon, ye'll still be a bonny lad but I think yor going to look slit-eyed for a while, the way your eyes are starting to swell, and your left eye is bloodshot.'

Touching the side of his eyes, feeling the puffiness, he replied, 'He made a canny job of me, that's for sure, thanks Mrs...?

Maggie smiled at him, gently patting his cheek, 'Maggie, lad, everybody calls me, Maggie.'

Geordie Robertson expected to feel the blast of shotgun pellets in his back as he turned and fled after firing the two wild shots at Ian. Fear drove him into the storm, head down, he charged out of the courtyard and onto the snow-covered road, stumbling north, ploughing through the snow like charging bull.

Exhausted after several minutes of battling the blizzard, he stopped to suck in air and lean on Sarah's car that he abandoned earlier when the depth of the snow brought it to a shuddering halt. Squinting into the snow, he could see that storm had added several more inches to the drift in front of the Ford ensuring it would be hopeless to try to use it.

'Fuck he thought, how the fuck am I ganna get oot of here.' Still thinking that Ian and the tough-looking Jack would be after him, he leant into the wind and continued up the road, wading through the powder-snow that at times was up to his waist.

Four hundred yards further north, seventy-year-old, Tom Fenwick, took some of his considerable weight off his arthritic knees by leaning on the sill of the kitchen window at the rear of his farmhouse that was sheltered in a belt of pine trees, just off the east side of the road.

'Doesn't look like it's ganning te let up for a lang while yet,' he said to Ruby, his diminutive wife who was beating the air out of a cake mix in a bowl, clamped under her left arm.

Raising her head to peer at him through spectacles balanced on her nose, she answered in her rapid, sing-song voice that rose higher the more sherry she sipped, 'Eeee, and nee telephone te tell Young Tom that the roads closed, whaat are they ganna dee, spend the neet at Alnwick? I hope they are not trying te get home. Ye kna what he's like, he'll try to drive back in that silly car of theirs. He should hev teken the Thames truck shouldn't he?'

Tom turned and shuffled back to sit on cushions piled on the wooden spindle-back armchair sitting close to the wood burning stove in the corner of the long farmhouse kitchen, it was his favourite seat in his favourite room of the rambling, Northumbrian farmhouse.

'They couldn't torn up te a fancy do in a Thames truck, he had te tek the Austin, it's a canny car man.'

Placing the mixing bowl carefully on the table, Ruby, flicked flour from the immaculate white dust coat she was wearing and in short, quick steps, clip-clopped across the red-tiled floor in her black, court-shoes to the chipped and worn but efficient Rayburn oven. Opening door and reaching down with oven-gloved hands, she pulled out a tray of scones that filled the room with the smell of cinnamon.

'And here's me making cakes and scones for them coming back. I hope tha not ganning te be wasted, ye'll hev to eat them aall because I'm not watching them gan te waste.'

Tom chuckled, 'They'll keep for a couple of days and ye canna begrudge the pair of them ganning te her mam and dad's fiftieth anniversary, can ye?'

'No I suppose not,' she said as she carried the scones back to the large, pine, kitchen table, placing them on a wire rack to join two stotties she made earlier.

Looking at the snow building up on the outside of the two windows, Tom said, 'It's the sheep, I'm worried aboot, we need te go and see if any need digging oot and get some forage up te them, it's just as weell tha all in the in-bye fields; whaats left of them after this winter.'

Ruby tutted and snapped at Tom, 'You're not going out there that's for sure, or we'll end up having te dig ye oot. I'll feed the tups in the barn...' She stopped in mid-sentence, looking up like a startled pheasant when she heard loud banging at the front door that alarmed Nelson, the collie lying at Tom's feet, the dog running to the kitchen door, barking with excited expectation.

'I wonder who that is,' said Ruby, 'it cannit be one of ours.'

Tom grunted as he pushed himself up from his chair, years of farming in the bleak hills having taken their toll on his once powerful body, arthritis making movement slow, and painful, 'It could be Jack coming to see if we are alreet.'

'No, why would he, he doesn't know that Young Tom's not here.'

'Aye yer right as normal Pet, shall Aah gan te the door?'

Already heading into the hall, Ruby replied, 'By the time ye get there, whoever it is will hev died of cowld.'

Stepping into the hall, Ruby flicked the old brass and Bakelite switch by the door, lighting two pendant bulbs illuminating the otherwise dark, twenty-foot long hall that led to a vestibule door with a stained-glass upper half. Opening it, she stepped through and reached for the handle of the front door.

The front of the house was in the lee of the blizzard but the wind whipped the snow in swirls around the huge figure that towered over her when she pulled open the door. Shocked by the size of the stranger and the wild look on his face, Ruby stepped back, her composure gone as Nelson crouched behind her, growling, the sound seeming to come from deep within him.

Exhausted from his struggle through the storm, covered in snow, his face swollen from the crash, Robertson leant his elbow on the doorframe and gasped, 'Hello missus, me cars stuck in the snow, canna I come in oot the storm?'

Struggling to regain her composure, Ruby's kind heart won over her fright, 'Eee, of course, ye can lad, ye look done in, come on inte the kitchen and we'll get ye warmed up.'

Shuffling in, Robertson closed the door behind him and dusted off some of the snow clinging to his greatcoat, before following Ruby as Nelson slunk into the kitchen and hid behind Tom.

'Aye lad, what's happened to you?' asked Tom.

'I slid off the road and bashed my face, my cars well and truly stuck and divvint kna what te de.'

Tom eyed him suspiciously as Ruby pulled a chair back from the table, 'Here lad, put this ower by the stove and sit yersell doon, I'll mek ye a cup of tea and butter one of these scones for ye.'

Robertson lifted the heavy wooden chair with ease and placing it on the other side of the stove to Tom, sat down, pushing his sodden boots close to the stove. Leaning forward, he held his hand close to the fire as the remaining snow on his greatcoat melted and dripped onto the tiled floor.

Tom eased himself back into his chair, 'Hoo far doon the road is yer car?

Staring into the flames of the burning logs, Robertson paused for a second, 'Aboot half a mile, in a snow drift.'

'Would it not have been quicker te walk back to Treshinish?'

Raising his head, Robertson glared at Tom, 'What's Treshinish?'

Ignoring the malevolent look, Tom leant forward, staring back at him and said, 'The big Farm ye must have past just before ye got stuck, ye wud hev been closer to that than here.'

Robertson shook his head, 'Aah didn't notice it, so I just came this way.'

Pouring boiling water into a waiting teapot, Ruby chided her husband, 'Leave the lad alone Tom, can ye not see he's worn oot!'

Tom ignored the rebuke, 'Ye say ye bashed yer face, who put the plaster on yer nose?'

Feeling his anger building once again, Robertson snapped, 'Aah did, Aah had some in the car, why are ye asking me all these bloody questions?

Sitting back in his chair Tom continued to study Robertson as Maggie filled a mug of tea, scooping in two spoons of sugar and pouring in milk before stirring it, the spoon clattering loudly in the mug.

'Here ye are lad, get this inside ye, it'll warm ye up,' she said handing him the tea and a still warm scone.'

His suspicions growing, Tom asked, 'When did you get stuck, it must have been a while ago, judging by the snow outside?'

Swallowing a large mouthful of hot tea, Robertson, swore, 'Fuck that's hot,' and turning to Tom spat, 'Aah sat in the car for a while wondering what best te de.'

'Divint swear in here lad, it's not nice is it.'

Ignoring the remark, Robertson wolfed down the scone and took a careful sip of the tea before saying, 'Who else is here, it's a big hoose?'

Tom narrowed his eyes and asked, 'Noo why would ye ask that?'

Anger gripped Robertson again, leaping to his feet he snarled, 'Shut the fuck up ye stupid, fat owld bastard or Aah'll shut ye fucking up.'

Ruby almost dropped the cup of tea she was taking to Tom and stopping to stare in shock, could only manage to say, 'Eeeeeeeeee.'

Tom pushed himself up, 'Right that's enough from ye, ye can get yorsell oot this hoose noo, Aah' divin't kna what ye've been up te but you're a bad bugga, Aah'll not hev ye in this hoose, noo get yer sell away back te yer car.'

Robertson flung the mug at the fire and stepped forward, smacking Tom with a powerful backhander that knocked him back over his chair, blood spurting from a split lip as he fell heavily, just missing Nelson. The dog leapt at Geordie, grabbing the bottom of his great coat, worrying it and snarling as Ruby rushed to her husband.

Grabbing the front of his open greatcoat, Geordie swung it to one side, lifting Nelson off his feet and smashing him into the hot stove but the dog clung on dragging at the heavy coat until Geordie stamped his right foot down on the dog's hind legs. The dog let out a screech of pain, releasing his hold on the coat as Geordie kicked it in the ribs that crackled under the force of the blow, hurling it across the kitchen, smashing into the wall a few feet from Ruby and Tom.

Whimpering Nelson tried to stand but sunk down in pain as the now out of control Robertson strode across and unleashed two more powerful kicks at the defenceless animal, leaving it howling.

Ruby helped Tom to lift himself onto his knees and as he struggled to stand, and watched in helpless horror as Geordie kicked the dog for the third time.

Tom growled, 'You bloody swine, ye, 'I'll swing for ye if Aah get me hands on yer.'

'Tha's nee chance of that is tha ye fat twat,' Geordie snarled before swinging his right fist into Tom's face, knocking him sideways, taking a screeching Ruby with him as they both landed in a heap next to poor Nelson who was whining pitifully.

Standing over them, Robertson took the revolver from his pocket and pointed it at Tom's head, warning, 'Stay where ye are the both of ye or Aah'll blow yor frigging heeds off.'

Leaving Tom semi-conscious, lying half across a shocked and shaking Ruby, he strode over to the kitchen table and grabbed another scone, slapping butter on the outside before stuffing into his mouth.

A little earlier, back at Treshinish House, Jack cleaned the cut on Sarah's face with stinging antiseptic, bringing tears to her eyes before he carefully inserted six neat stitches into her wound while she gritted her teeth, never taking her eyes from him, as he concentrated on doing the best he could.

Finished he said, 'There lass, am sorry about the pain but it needed doing, they might replace them at hospital but I've done a canny job, even if I say so myself.'

Rosalind, who had cleaned up Maggie's cuts and covered them with four small plasters, looked across and said, 'Eee Mam that looks very neat.'

Sarah kept her head to one side as Jack placed a small bandage on her cut, using tape to keep it in place, 'Thank you,' she said, 'it wasn't as painful as I thought it would be.'

Jack nodded, then remembering his neighbours, he stood up saying, 'Mam can ye sort out the cut on Jake's head?'

Maggie nodded, 'Yes Jack,' as he stood reaching for his coat and hat that he had thrown on an armchair before seeing to Sarah.

Turning to Ian, Jack said, 'Ian, close the shutters so no one can see in here, I'll go and get the other gun and some ammunition before I leave, will you be okay with it.'

Nodding, Ian replied, 'Yes, and don't worry, I *will* shoot him if I have to.'

Walking into the vestibule with Ian, Jack buttoned up his Stockman's coat and pulled on his fur hat before loading two shells into his shotgun. 'Right lad, I've got half a dozen more shells and the rest of the box are on the telephone table, lock the door when I get out and only open it when you hear me knocking three times, pausing then knocking three times more and on until ye open up, okay?

Ian nodded nervously, replying, 'Yes, I'm ready.' Jack patted his arm then opened the door to the blizzard, pushing into it as Ian closed and locked the door behind him.

At Redesdale Camp, fifty-one-year-old, 'Young' Tom Fenwick was agitated, he should have been at the farm seeing to the sheep instead of sitting at a Formica topped table, drinking army tea in the large dining hall in the camp. The thirty or so occupants of the stranded vehicles were sitting exchanging stories of how they ended up there and where they were trying to get to, as well as enjoying the hospitality provided by Major Graham and his staff.

Tom did have misgivings, when he and his buxom wife, Claire left the farm yesterday afternoon and headed to Alnwick for her parents Golden Wedding Anniversary and it now looked, as he was right to have been worried.

Knowing how frustrated he was, Claire said, 'Maybe they'll manage te get the road open later teday Hinny.'

He shook his head, 'No, Aah cannit see that, not while this blizzard is raging, it'll tek all tha time just te get up te Byrness, if ownly we'd left an hour earlier.' Worried about his parents and their sheep, he rubbed his forehead and said, 'We'll be lucky if we survive this winter, we are struggling with the debt we have and Aah need to buy more forage and feed; this weather is killing us.'

Claire was about to speak but stopped when a side door opened and the lanky, PC John Carlisle was blown in by the blizzard. Stamping snow from his boots, he took off his snow-covered helmet and coat, placing them both on a table.

Looking at the gathering who were watching him with interest, he cleared his throat, then in a loud, clear voice, said, 'If I can just have a couple of minutes of your time,' pausing while chairs were scrapped on tiles by people turning to listen to him. 'It does look as if you'll all be spending the night here, the blizzard is making it very difficult for the snowploughs, but they will work as long as they can tonight and will start at again at four in the morning. They are hopeful that they can get through to Byrness in the morning for anyone who lives there but it is unlikely that the road over Carter Bar will be cleared in the next couple of days.' He paused for a moment, looking across to the RQMS who joined him from the behind the serving counter. 'Mick Reed here will answer any questions you have about food and sleeping arrangements.'

Young Tom shook his head, barely able to hide his frustration, 'Bliddy hell – that means me Mam and Dad will be on their own for another neet and nee forage for the sheep until the morn.'

'Your Mam and Dad will be fine Pet,' Claire said, 'They know how te look after themselves.'

CHAPTER 14

Friday 8th February – 11:30 am
Ashington

Shaking uncontrollably, Roger huddled under his duffle coat that he had pulled over his legs, wrapping his arms around them, trying to keep in what little warmth there was.

Billy tried once again to shout for help through the broken window but the blizzard whisked his unheard shout down the empty backstreet as few, if any at all were venturing out into the storm. His face frozen from the stinging, gale-driven snow, he gave up in despair, wiped the sleeve of his duffle coat across his face, and squatted down next to his brother. He wrapped his arms around him in a futile attempt to keep him warm as snow blowing in from the window began to coat everything in a white blanket.

Heat from the ovens in the rear of the bakery permeated through to the shop, clouding the large shop window with condensation that hid from view, the blizzard raging outside.

Jane Thompson, used a white cloth to wipe a window in the misted glass, studying the blizzard for a second or two before turning to speak to the bakery owner, Alice Kirkup, 'Alice, I'm worried about the boys at school is it alright if I pop home and phone Edward, I want to go with him to pick them up?

'Well we're hardly rushed off wor feet teday Pet, so, Aye go on, gan home for your lunch noo and see te them, I'll see you later.'

At home, a couple of minutes later, she rang Edward and arranged for him to collect her and drive round to Wansbeck School. The blizzard and road conditions made the drive from his office to their home difficult, taking Edward twice as long as normal and after collecting Jane, he turned the van around and drove carefully to the school

Parking his van outside the school, they hurried in through the snow, stopping on the long veranda that ran alongside the classrooms. Seeing through the floor to ceiling windows that the classrooms were empty, they walked briskly along to the hall where the Headmistress had gathered the children. They were sitting on the floor in classroom groups with their teachers, reading passages from books to each other.

Tommy waved when he saw his mother, his teacher smiled at her, then nodded to Tommy to go as Edward searched for Billy and Roger.

Not seeing either boy, he approached Tommy's teacher and asked, 'Where are the Grundy boys, we have come to take them home?'

Looking concerned, the middle-aged teacher replied, 'But Mrs North came and collected them this morning, just after half-past-nine.'

Edward thanked her and hurried back to Jane, repeating what the teacher had told him, adding, 'We'll drive around there now and see what's happening, hopefully, Ronnie will be there by now.'

After Tommy pulled on his coat in the large cloakroom, they hurried back along the veranda, Jane saying, 'I'll never forgive myself if something has happened to those two boys, we promised Jake we would look after them, I hope Ronnie *has* made it home?'

At that moment, Ronnie was struggling to drive up the bank from Stakeford Bridge, barely a mile from the Third Row.

The strength of the gale appeared to have increased as Edward, looked through the windscreen, trying to see through the snow that the blizzard was hurling at the van. Leaving the main road at the Plantation, he drove in between the end of terraces of the two blocks of colliery rows before turning into the Third Row and into the teeth of the storm; he could barely see five yards, the snow forcing him to drive at just a few miles an hour.

Inside the shed, Billy was becoming more worried about Roger, who was no longer shaking, sitting motionless as the wind continued to drive the snow in through the window, covering them both with an inch or more of snow that was no longer melting from their body heat.

Edward slid the van to a halt outside the Grundy's house and climbed out, the wind blowing the door out of his hand, slamming it shut with a bang. He then fought his way around the van and opened the passenger door, bracing his back against the inside to stop the wind slamming it shut, as Jane and Tommy climbed out and hurried across the small back yard and into the house through the unlocked door.

Billy was not sure but he thought he heard a bang and shook Roger asking, 'Did you hear that, there was a noise outside?' When Roger did not answer, he shook him again, harder, 'Roger, wake up man, Aah think tha's somebody outside.'

Roger still did not answer and Billy reluctantly let go of his brother, forcing his frozen limbs to work, he stood up, took a deep breath, and shoved his face to the broken window, squinting into the snow that stung his eyes. He could see little but snow blowing horizontally through the gap that kept forcing him to close them but he could make out the outline of a white van, just a few feet away, and shouted, 'Help,' but the blizzard stole his cries, whisking them off down the street.

Inside the house, Jane stood in the centre of the kitchen looking at the chaos that Edna had created when she ransacked the place, 'My Goodness, what has happened here?'

Closing the door against the blizzard, Edward walked slowly into the kitchen, stepping over a broken vase and crockery and looked through the connecting door to the sitting room.

Seeing the sofa lying on its back, cushions strewn across the floor and the contents of the sideboard scattered haphazardly around the room, he said, 'Someone has certainly done a canny job of wrecking the place, Aah wonder what they were looking for? The boys aren't in here, I'll nip upstairs and see if they are there,' and walking to the stairs, he took them two at a time, looking quickly in the three bedrooms before trotting down back down.

'No sign of the boys but it's the same up there, a right mess; they've even lifted the top of the stair carpet.'

Jane and Tommy were picking up crockery from the floor, standing it on the kitchen table but Jane stopped, worried about Billy and Roger, she said, 'I wonder if the neighbours might know where they are? This is very worrying and a little frightening.'

Looking around, Edward said, 'We best leave everything as it is until we know what's happened here and where the boys are, I am going to the houses either side to see if anyone knows what's been going on.'

'Hopefully, someone will know where they are,' said Jane, picking up a poker from the fireplace and stirring the embers of the coal fire before throwing on coal from the scuttle.

Head down, Edward pushed into the blizzard, struggling out of the yard and into the one next door. Knocking loudly on the wooden door, he waited a few seconds before the door opened a few inches, a woman's face appearing at the gap, squinting as the wind took advantage of the opening, blowing snow into her face.

Wanting to be heard over the sound of the wind, he almost shouted, 'Hello there, have you seen anything of Mrs North or the Grundy boys this morning?'

Blinking against the wind and snow she shouted back, 'I've seen nebody te day Hinny, I've not been oot me door and aah divin't intend to either until this bliddy storm stops,' and pushed the door shut.'

Still desperately trying to attract attention, Billy did not see Edward go to the next-door house, his vision obscured by the white van and the blizzard but every few seconds, he continued to shout, 'Help,' in a tired and scarcely audible voice,'

Backing out into the street and turning to walk to the house at the other side of the Grundy's, Edward stopped, unsure if he had heard a shout or if it was just the howling of the wind. Listening for a second or two and not hearing anything, he shrugged his shoulders and allowed the wind to push him along the snow-covered path, into the next yard.

Shivering violently in the shed, Billy blew into his frozen hands before he again wiped snow from his face, and saw Edward walk into the yard of the house to the left of the van.

Mustering his remaining strength, he tried to shout but just managed a feeble, 'Mista Tomsin – help,' not loud enough to be heard over the wind.

Big Jen's floral pinny struggled to retain her more than ample figure as she opened the door to Edward's knock, 'Eee, come on in oot of the snow,' she ordered, grabbing his arm, pulling him inside the hall before he could react.

Pushing the door closed behind him, She asked, 'And what can Aah dee ye for bonny lad?

Her chubby face, beamed with an infectious grin that made Edward smile involuntarily as he asked, 'Am looking for Mrs North and the two youngest Grundy boys?'

Jen took the question to be an invitation for a good gossip or, at the very least, a good natter; never one to mince her words, she let rip, 'That dorty brazen bugga, she's the last porson Aah want te see. She's nowt but a bliddy whooa; and the way she treats them bairns when Albert's not aboot is wicked, she wants locking up. Poor Albert doesn't have a clue, she has him wrapped roond hur little finga, she just flashes hor skinny arse at the lad and whey man he doesn't kna if he's coming or ganning if ye kna what a mean? Ye kna Aah used te cook Albert and the bairn's dinners for them just aboot iviry day until that witch got hur claws inte him and had the norve te tell me not to botha any more – botha, mind ye! Whey Aah telt hor it was nee bliddy botha, it was a pleasure but she says, she's cooking for Albert noo, so God kna's what tripe she's been sorving up te them, especially with them hands of hors which hev been deeing aall sorts of unmentionables!.'

As she paused for breath, Edward butt in, 'That's interesting, but have you seen her or the boys this morning?'

'Whey, Aah was coming te that man,' she replied, miffed at his interruption.

Pausing, she took a deep breath, crossed her arms under her mighty bosoms and restarted, 'Nur Aah hevn't seen hor or them this morning, my bairns went off te school this morning – mind Aah had te kick their backsides te get them oot the hoose. Aah telt them a bit of bliddy snow's not keeping them off school. Anyway, they alwas knock on next door and walk te school we Billy, Roger and that soft bugga Howard; so I suppose tha at school where tha supposed te be, but Ahh suppose ye've been roond there or ye wuldn't be asking wud ye ?'

'Thanks, but they were at my house first thing, I took them to school and Mrs North collected them not long afterwards and we don't know where she's taken them.'

Raising her eyebrows, Jen pursed her lips before adding, 'Noo that's a bliddy worry, that woman is not right in the heed, she's bliddy sackless, Aah wud get the polis in bonny lad cos she's boond te be up te ne gud, not that Aah want te worry ye like.'

Edward leapt in as she paused for breath again, 'Right, thanks, but I have to get on, we probably will have to go to the police,' and opening the door, he stepped into the blizzard as Jen shouted after him, 'Aah'll let ye kna if Aah think of oot else.'

Hanging onto the window frame, Billy saw Edward leave Jen's house and again tried to get his attention, shouting in feeble desperation, 'Mista Tomsin, Mista Tomsin.' He failed, and as Edward disappeared behind the van, Billy let go and collapsed onto the floor to sit sobbing next to his motionless brother, wrapping his arms around him again, trying to protect the weaker, Roger.

Jane listened intently while Edward gave her the gist of his conversation with Jen.

Her furrowed brow showed her worry when she asked, 'What shall we do Edward, do you think we should go to the police?'

'Absolutely but first I am going to the pit baths to fetch Albert, he needs to be here and he may know where the boys are.'

'Yes, that makes sense,' Jane said, 'I'll build the fire up in the sitting room, it's nearly out.'

Struggling around to the front of the van to reach the driver's door, Edward stopped and leaned forward and stared through the snow at Albert's shed, trying to focus on the window on the inside of the grill, it looked broken. He could see that the blizzard was driving snow into the shed and wondered what had happened.

Puzzled, he waded through the snow and peered through the grill and broken window, seeing that a layer of snow covered everything, including a large mound in the centre of the floor. Wondering how the window had been broken from the inside, he was just about to turn away when the mound moved.

Realising instantly what the mound was; he stepped around to the side of the shed, fumbling in his haste to lift the padlock from the hasp, he almost pulled the door off its hinges as he swung it back on itself, the wind holding it open as he rushed inside.

The mound stirred, snow falling away as Billy lifted his head to look up at Edward, saying weakly, 'Hello Mista Tomsin.'

Edward bent down on one knee and carefully took Billy's arms from around his brother, lifting him over his left shoulder before lifting Roger over his other and stepping out of the shed being careful not to catch the doorframe and struggled back to the house. Not wanting to drop either boy, he kicked the door several times, desperate to get the boys in and out of the storm.

Tommy rushed to the door, twisted the knob open, and fell back onto the stairs when the wind blew it wide open.

'Stepping in, Edward asked, 'Are ye alright Tommy?'

'Yes,' he replied and picked himself up to hurry after Edward who rushed through the kitchen and into the sitting room where Jane dropped the small shovel in her hand when she saw him.

'Lift the settee up Pet, they're both frozen,' Edward said still holding the boys close to him.

Jane and Tommy rushed to the back of the sofa and heaved it back onto its feet before lifting the cushions back into place, allowing Edward to lower, first Roger at one end and then Billy at the other.

Standing up, he looked at Jane and said, 'Here we go again Pet,' as he remembered the trauma of Ian and Tommy's rescue from an icy pond, three years earlier.

Jane did not answer, she did not want to think of that terrible time when she nearly lost two of her boys and, of the abuse, she suffered at the hands of her first husband. His execution later that year for murdering a police officer put an end to that dark time in her life.

Instead, she ordered, 'Tommy run upstairs and grab as many blankets as you can carry, Edward, see if you can find a bleezer and get the fire going, we need to warm them up.'

Billy sat up, pulling the hood of his coat back from his head, saying, 'Am aall reet Missus Tomsin, just a bit caad, how is wor, Roger?'

Unbuttoning the toggles on Roger's damp duffle coat, Jane eased him forward and slid the heavy coat off his shoulders as Tommy rushed in with an armful of blankets, dropping them next to Jane and rushed off to fetch more.

Touching Roger's face with the back of her fingers, Jane answered Billy, 'He's very cold but he still has colour...'

Behind his steamed up spectacles, Roger's eyes opened and after sniffing, he said matter of factly, 'Aah cannit see.'

Worried at what he heard, Billy sat forward, asking, 'Is he blind Missis Tomsin, me Dad'll kill me if he is?'

Taking off Roger's glasses to wipe them, she answered, 'No Billy, his spectacles were steamed up, that's all,' and then tucked two blankets around him before helping Billy off with his coat and then pulled off both boy's wet shoes and stockings.

Edward brought in a two-foot-square, metal bleezer he found in the pantry and placed it over the fire, opening the grate at the bottom, the updraft breathing life into the fire that began almost immediately, to roar.

'How are they Jane,' he asked as Tommy carried in the second armful of blankets.'

'Very cold but nothing too serious, I will check their feet to make sure they are alright but I hope they are just cold.'

'And hungry Mrs Triviln,' said Roger as he opened his eyes again.

As Jane tucked in blankets around both boys Billy said to his brother, 'Hoo come ye can speak to Mrs Tomsin but ye didn't speak te me in the shed?'

Beginning to shiver a little, Roger sniffed twice, wiped his nose on the blanket Jane had just tucked under his chin and replied, 'Cos Aah was ower caad man.'

Edward said, 'I'd best go and fetch Albert from the pit-head-baths, keep your eye on the fire Jane.'

She nodded yes and added, 'I'll see what there is to eat in the pantry.'

Edward walked to the door and pulling it open, stepped aside to allow Ronnie in out of the blizzard.

He looked at Edward and said, 'What an aaful drive up I've had – what are you doing here Edward?'

'Jane's in the sitting room with your brothers, she'll explain, I'm off to get Albert,' and hurried out to his van.

The short drive to the pit was difficult; Edward struggled to stop his wheels spinning but the van still slid when he drove around corners as the blizzard buffeted the slab-sided vehicle.

Just before the turnoff to the baths and canteen, he saw a police car parked by the colliery offices and wondered why it was there. He passed another outside the canteen and as he walked through the foyer between the baths and the canteen, he looked into the canteen and saw a uniformed policeman sitting at a table talking to a man wearing his pit clothes, who was still dirty from his shift underground. He also saw that there were quite a few more men inside sitting with, who he assumed were their wives.

Hurrying up the stairs into the warmth of pithead-baths, he found Albert sitting drinking a cup of tea, cigarette in one hand as he leafed through a copy of the Daily Mirror lying on the office table.

Surprised to see him, Albert asked, 'Aye Edward, what ye deeing here?'

Edward composed himself before replying, 'You need to come home Albert, it looks as if Edna has ransacked your house and locked Billy and Roger in yer shed, they are both a bit cold but alright, Jane's looking after them and your Ronnie has just got there but I think you should be there as well.'

Albert's eyes widen as he digested this information, thinking about what Jake had told him last night and again this morning, he asked 'Are ye sure the bairns are aall right? I'll niva forgive mesell if she's hurt, my lads.'

Placing his hand on Albert's shoulder, Edward replied, 'Yes, they'll both be fine but this needs sorting out and I think you need to do it.'

Minutes later, driving back to the Third Row, Edward filled Albert in on the events of the morning and Albert told Edward of the news circulating around the pit, the murders of Harry Weedon and Bill Robertson, and that Geordie Robertson was wanted in connection with both murders.

Cold and despairing, Yvonne, fought to hold back tears of fear and frustration as she allowed the blizzard to push her down First Avenue toward Weedon's betting shop. Her thick three-quarter length coat left her legs exposed to the blizzard and her shoes had done little to protect her feet on her exhausting walk from Station Road.

Desperate to get out of the cold, she was worried sick about her plight, as she wondered what Stuart Weedon would do when she told him that Edna had thrown her and Sandra out of the flat – 'Just so long as he doesn't take it out on me,' she thought.

Walking past Weedon's two-seater sports car and the betting shop whitewashed, painted window, she grabbed the door handle, pushed it open, and hurried inside where she stood shaking from cold, in the empty room.

Painted a drab, uneven battleship-grey by someone with no talent or training as a decorator, the room was depressing. A racing calendar on one wall and a blackboard with details of an old race meeting hanging on the opposite wall, failed to improve the ugliness. A short, plywood covered counter stood at the back with a door behind it leading to an office. Seeing that the shop was empty, she left a trail of melting snow as she walked behind the counter and opened the door to the office.

Sitting at a cheap, dilapidated wooden desk, flipping through pages in a thick tattered file, Stuart Weedon closed it when he saw Yvonne and asked her, 'What are ye deeing here, yer supposed to be cleaning that shite hole yer work in?'

She blurted, 'Edna's come back and hoyed me and Sandra oot, she said that she's living there noo and tha's nowt ye can de aboot it, noo that yer dad's deed.'

He leapt to his feet, knocking over the wooden folding chair he had been sitting on and screamed, '*WAAT?*'

Fearing he was going to attack her, she replied, 'She said, she's ganning te sort ye oot and Sandra's gone to her Mam's and said she's not ganning back and Aa divin't kna waat te de, I've got nee where te gan...'

'Shut frigging up,' the enraged Weedon snarled, 'this is aall Aah bloody-well need, I'll sort that ugly bitch oot once and for aall, ye stop here until I get back, lock the door behind me and divin't let any bugga in.'

Snatching up his overcoat, he stepped around the three-bar electric fire that was trying unsuccessfully to heat the small room, and charged out to his car, leaving Yvonne standing by the table, cold, alone and afraid.

A couple of miles away, having taken twice as long as normal, the Ashington to Morpeth single deck bus slid to a halt in Pegswood.   Grasping his holdall, eleven-year-old Howard North stepped off and leant into the storm, waiting for the bus to pull away before crossing the road. Despite the storm, he was happy as he slipped and slid his way to his aunt's house in the colliery rows.

A few minutes later, as he sat warming himself in front of a roaring fire, he did his best to answer the barrage of questions his aunty launched at him as she made a pot of tea, hoping that this time he would be here to stay.

CHAPTER 15

Friday 8th February – 11:40 am
Upper Redesdale

Before setting off for the Fenwick's farm, Jack checked the barns and outhouses around Treshinish House. Alert and cautious, shotgun at the ready, he searched them for any signs of the bruiser responsible for the havoc in his home, and the fear felt by everyone inside. The reduced visibility that blizzard created and the physical effort it extracted made the task tougher and more dangerous for Jack so that by the time he satisfied himself Robertson was not around, his nerves were a wee bit frayed.

Pushing through the snowdrift in between the courtyard and road, he turned left, leant into the storm, and ploughed through the snow toward the Fenwick's farm. After a few minutes, he came across the half-buried, red Ford that he guessed was Sarah's and stopped to look around before approaching it with shotgun raised in readiness for any trouble.

Seeing that drifting snow covered the driver's side up to the roof, he approached the car on the passenger side, keeping about two yards away, all the while, pointing the shotgun at the car as he moved closer. After ensuring that the car was empty, he pushed on toward the farm, alert for any signs of Robertson.

It took him almost fifteen minutes to struggle the half-a-mile before he reached the opening to the farm, stopping in the lee of one of the huge sandstone-block, gate-pillars on either side of the entrance. He carefully scanned the front of the house and farm buildings, paying particular attention to the windows in case Robertson was watching, he need not have worried; Robertson was busy in the kitchen at the rear of the house.

Ruby had helped Tom into a seating position with his back against the wall and having taken a small white handkerchief from the pocket of her dustcoat, tried without success, to stem the flow of blood from her husband's nose and split lip.

Unable to stand or crawl, their collie Nelson lay in a broken heap, whining between coughing up blood from his busted insides.

'If wor lads had been here they'd hev fettled this bliddy waster,' Tom whispered to his wife, as Robertson indulged in a feeding frenzy. Having devoured most of the scones, he looked inside Ruby's pride and joy, a Hoover refrigerator. Finding a plate of sliced ham and a tub of butter, he cut open a stottie, slapped butter inside before stuffing all of the ham in. Taking huge bites and hardly chewing, he swallowed the stottie in less than a minute, washing it down with a bottle of beer he had taken from the door of the fridge.

His hunger satisfied, he belched and walked menacingly over to Tom and Ruby, and spat, 'Me boots are soaking, hev ye got any size ten wellies or boots?'

Keen to get him out of the room, Tom replied through his split lip, 'Aye, there's a couple of pairs of size ten boots in the back passage.'

Pointing the revolver at them, he threatened, 'Reet, if either of ye move, ya deed,' and turning, walked to the kitchen door.

Expecting the front door to be unlocked, Jack approached it from the side and quietly turned the handle, pushing it slowly open before stepping into the vestibule, shotgun at the ready, carefully closing the door behind him. He waited for a few seconds, listening for any sounds - before he opened the inner door and took a step inside the brightly lit hall, placing his booted foot as quietly as he could on the wooden floor.

Lifting the shotgun up to the ready position, he was just about to shout, 'Anyone there,' when the kitchen door at the far end of the hall opened and Gerodie stepped through, heading for the door to the rear passage directly in front of him. Reaching for the door handle with his left hand, he glanced down the hall and saw Jack pointing his shotgun at him. Without stopping, he pointed the revolver down the hall, fired a single shot and bolted into and through the passageway bedecked with all manner of outdoor clothing hanging on a long row of hooks, a rack of assorted footwear below, and straight out the back door, out into the blizzard.

The speed of Robertson's reactions and the deafening bang of the wild shot that blew chunks of plaster from the ceiling took Jack by surprise but he was quick to respond. Running down the hall, he slowed and leaned around the door of the rear passage, checking that he was not walking into a pointed revolver. Glancing to his left, he saw Tom and Ruby sitting on the floor at the far end of the kitchen but intent on ensuring Robertson had left, he hurried outside into the blizzard and through the snow, saw the dark shape of the killer running toward the road. Not wanting to shoot him in the back, he lifted the shotgun to his shoulder and fired a single shot in the air, hoping it would send him on his way.

Stepping back inside, he bolted the door, walked quickly back to the front door, and bolted that, before walking to the kitchen.

Shocked and shaking, Ruby was struggling to help Tom to his feet, blood still flowing from his nose and lip as he steadied himself on the arm of his chair.

She tried to back him into his chair saying, 'Sit down now Tom,' but he was far too angry to sit.

'Sit doon! Nur am not ganning te sit doon, look at waat that bastard's done te poor Nelson, am ganning to get me gun and gan after that waster,' he fumed.

Leaning his shotgun against the kitchen dresser, Jack said, 'Come on Tom, Ruby's right, sit yersell doon, we need to stop that bleeding and anyway that bugga is long gone.'

Looking concerned, Ruby put her hand to her mouth for a second and said, 'Eee, what about Maggie, Jack, she'll be on hur own and that monster might be on his way doon there?'

Helping a reluctant Tom into his chair, Jack replied, 'She's not on her own, there's a couple of young soldiers with her and one of them has my other gun, I don't think – at least I hope - he won't try to get in there again.'

Tom looked up at Jack, and repeated, 'Again? Has that bugga been in yor hoose as weell?

While Ruby tended to Tom's cuts and bruises with the contents of the first-aid box she had taken from a cupboard in the dresser, Jack told them of the events at Treshinish and that Robertson bragged about having already killed two people that morning.

'I think he was trying to get away into Scotland,' Jack said, 'but this blizzard has left him stuck here. Our telephone lines are down so we can't let the police know that he's here, we just need to keep him out of our farms until the blizzard ends.'

Kneeling by a still whimpering Nelson, Ruby said, 'I think he's done for your poor Nelson, Tom, the poor dog is in pain.'

Jack knelt down beside her, examining the pitiful animal, trying not to hurt it anymore and then stood up, shaking his head, 'I think it would be best for him if I took out the back and helped him to sleep.'

Struggling to speak, through his split lip and swollen nose, Tom said, 'Thanks Jack but Aah will de that. Ruby, get a couple of guns and some cartridges from the gun cupboard and after Aah've said goodbye to Nelson we'll lock wor sells up in here and pray that swine comes back here and tries to get in.'

Tom stood up, steadied himself, and said to Jack, 'Will ye carry Nelson into the scullery for me?'

Jack nodded, knelt, and gently lifted Nelson up; the dog gave a pathetic yelp and then lay lifeless in Jack's arms as he followed Tom into the scullery.

Pointing to a stone bench and struggling to hold back tears, Tom said 'Lay him on there Jack, please.'

Jack left him alone with his pet.

A few minutes later, Tom shuffled back, sat down on his chair, and loaded a double-barrel shotgun. Leaving it open, he laid it across his knees as Ruby deftly loaded another, laying it on the kitchen table before saying, 'Well I divvin't kna aboot ye two but I could do with a cup of tea?'

Jack picked up his gun and said, 'No thanks Ruby, I want to check that he's not lurking about outside or, has gone down to my place looking to get in, so if you two are okay, I'll be off.'

Tom patted the gun on his knee, 'We'll be fine Jack, get yourself away but watch oot for that Bugga - Ruby lock the door behind him, Hinny.'

As Ian patrolled the inside of Treshinish house, looking out of windows, and checking doors, Davy, who looked upon Ian as a new 'big brother,' and having asked Ian if his swollen face hurt and if he could still see, followed on behind.

Standing at the kitchen table, Maggie and Sarah were making a couple of platefuls of sandwiches with cold meats and homemade chutney.

Slicing one of the loaves, she had baked yesterday, Maggie asked, 'Where were you going to?'

Sarah stopped buttering bread, and looked out of the kitchen window, as if searching for an answer, 'To my parents, near Dalkeith, they have a farm like this one but not in hills, my eldest brother runs it now, mainly beef.'

Maggie sensed sadness in her answer but also thought Sarah wanted to say more, 'Were you going just for the weekend?'

'I was just going up to drop Rosalind and Davy off then going back home myself tomorrow; I have to look for a new home for us.'

Maggie hesitated before continuing, 'A new home? Has something happened Pet, I have obviously noticed there is no man with you.'

Pulling a chair back from the table, Sarah sat down and put her hands in her lap, 'David - my husband, drowned three weeks ago. He was a pit deputy and although I have wanted to buy our own place for a few years, he preferred to stay in the colliery cottage, he used to say, "We have free housing and coal, why the hell would we want to waste good money on a hoose." Of course, now that he's gone, the NCB want the house back. I have a decent job but without his pay, I will have to look for somewhere to rent.'

Maggie rubbed Sarah's arm and said with sympathy, 'Am sorry to hear about yor man Pet, it is devastating; mine was taken by cancer during the war when Jack was away fighting.'

'That's the sad thing Maggie, we weren't close, we hadn't been for a long time, he resented me working in Newcastle and thought I was misbehaving but I wasn't. I like my job, I enjoy the responsibility, and I'm good at it. Anyway, he used to spend most of his weekends fishing as well as a lot of time at his allotment. We argued about it, especially on Saturday or Sunday mornings when Davy was playing football. David hated football and Davy hated fishing so there was friction there but he did love Davy and Rosalind. However, just like a lot of pitmen he wasn't good at showing his emotions and truth be told, our marriage was all but over, we were just going through the motions. Not that it makes his death any easier, I just which our last words to each other had been kinder.'

Maggie walked to a cupboard and opening it, reached up and pulled out two bottles, turning she held them up displaying the labels to Sarah and asked, 'Whisky or Sherry?'

Smiling at Maggie's forthright attitude, she replied, 'I don't think I could handle a whisky but a sherry will probably help – thanks.'

A few minutes later, Ian walked in with Davy close behind and looked through the window before checking the door was locked – again, then asked, 'Everything all right in here?'

'We are fine lad,' Maggie said, 'Tea and sandwiches in a few minutes, how are you feeling?'

Touching his face, Ian replied, 'It only hurts if I touch it.'

She smiled, 'Then don't touch it, how's your friend?'

'He's okay him and Rosalind are talking about some new group called "The Beatles," so he can't be in that much pain or, the painkillers you gave him are strong.'

Sarah asked, 'What are you up to Davy?'

'Stepping from behind Ian, he replied proudly, 'I'm helping Ian keeping us all safe.'

Ian rubbed his shoulder, saying, 'Come on soldier let's go and see what we can get on the radio in the sitting room.'

Looking up at a black and white plastic clock on the wall, Maggie said, 'Sam Costa will be on shortly playing his popular records on the light programme but I'll switch on my little transistor radio for the Home Service at one so we can listen to the news and weather. We are having a sherry, son, would you like one?'

Ian shook his head, 'No thanks, I've never tried that, besides, Aah want to be alert in case Geordie Robertson comes back,' and walked out, the open gun resting in the crook of his arm, Davy marching behind.

As Maggie and Sarah began placing the prepared sandwiches on two plates, Sarah asked, 'Was Jack injured in the war, Maggie?'

'Aye Pet, at Arnhem, he was blown up in a hoose and teken prisoner by the Gurmans, thcy didn't look after him very well, that's why his scars are so bad, he is very self-conscious about them, he says they make him look like a freak. Why do they upset ye?'

Leaning on the table, Sarah replied earnestly, 'Maggie, I didn't really notice them until you whispered to me, I was looking at his eyes, they are so blue and intense,' then realising what she was saying, she blushed. 'Sorry, Maggie but your son does have a certain presence, he is very striking.' Putting her hand to her mouth in embarrassment, she giggled, 'It must be the sherry, and I don't normally drink.'

Lifting the boiling kettle off the Aga, Maggie dropped the lid over the hotplate and poured the boiling water over tea-leaves in a large, brown teapot and said, 'I kna that Pet but he thinks wimin think he is ugly.'

Sarah suppressed another giggle, 'Not this one.'

Maggie handed the two plates of sandwiches to Sarah, 'Here take these in,' and grinning, added, 'I best carry the tea tray in case you drop it.'

Carrying the tray with the heavy teapot, and cups and saucers, Maggie was following Sarah into the front parlour when Jess started to bark.

CHAPTER 16

Friday 8ᵗʰ February – 12 am
Ashington

DS Dodson leant on the railing of the walkway, a few yards from the entrance of the cage that had just whisked them up six hundred feet from below. Sweating, despite the blizzard, he gulped in mouthfuls of snow-laden air and unfastened the navy-blue-overall he was wearing that the colliery had provided.

DI Norman smiled at him, 'Glad to be out Sergeant?'

Dodson lifted the pit-helmet off his sweating head and wiped his forehead with the back of his arm, 'Glad, sir – I am ower the bliddy moon, if I niva gan doon another pit again, it'll be ower bliddy soon. Hoo the hell they gan doon there iviry working day is beyond me, Aah've niva been so scared in aall me life, sir.'

Heading toward the lamp cabin with Dodson beside him, Norman said, 'We'll hand back this kit and head back to Ashington Nick. Hopefully, forensics will find Robertson's prints on that fishplate and the blood on it will be Weedon's, we just need a motive.'

Breathing heavily, as he tried to keep pace with the long-legged DI, as well as fighting the blizzard, Dodson said, 'We need to find out more aboot what Weedon and William Robertson were up to and where George Robertson fitted in.'

'Obviously, Sergeant,' the DI shouted over the wind, 'I don't think we will get much more out of Mrs Robertson today, that leaves us with Weedon's son – Stuart, we will have to ask him to come in for a few questions.'

'Aye, sir, Aah'll speak to Sergeant Malcolm and see if he can shed any light on what they were up to.'

The DI nodded, adding, 'You and Wilson can go round to Weedon's betting shop and see what you can find out, if Stuart Weedon is there, ask him to come down to Ashington Police Station, if he's not there, go around to his house. We may have to get search warrants for both places.'

Edward Thompson slowed his van to a sliding halt in the slush and snow in the Third Row, Albert opening his door before it stopped. He hurried inside, through the kitchen and into the sitting room, sighing with relief when he saw his two youngest sons. Wrapped in blankets, they were spooning bread, laced with condensed milk, sugar, and hot water from large mugs into their mouths.

Standing in front of the roaring fire, Ronnie greeted his father, 'Hi Fatha, this is a right carry-on, that bliddy woman all but killed these two and look at the state of this place, God knows what she was looking for.'

Ignoring the mess, Albert knelt down between his two boys asking, 'Are ye two alreet, what happened te ye?'

Roger sniffed and, using the handle of his spoon, pushed his glasses up his nose, a piece of hot, milky bread, slipping off the spoon and down his chin. He peered at his father and said, 'It was caad in the shed Dad and me feet are still caad.'

Billy added, 'It was missus North, Dad, she locked us in the shed, she said we could light the stove but loads of black smoke came oot and Aa had te put it oot and I smashed the winda cos we wor choking.'

Roger added, 'That's hoo we got caad, it was snowing through the winda.'

Standing behind the sofa, Jane said, 'They are both going to be fine Albert, I've given them some boily to warm them up and I have a pan of soup on the fire but I have to tell you, half an hour later and it could have been a lot worse.'

Sitting down in an armchair, Ronnie said, 'We did try to warn you about her Dad.'

Albert rubbed the heads of both boys affectionately and stood up, turning to look at Ronnie, he said, 'Ye did lad, ye and Jake - and Aah didn't listen and we nearly lost these two, Aah cud bliddy swing for that woman noo.'

Standing in the doorway, Edward said, 'I think this should be reported to the policc, Albert, it could easily have ended up being manslaughter or worse.'

Albert nodded and walked past him into the kitchen and through to the hall, climbing the stairs halfway before turning around and walking back into the sitting room saying in a low dejected voice, 'As I thowt, she's teken me bank book.'

'Bliddy hell, fatha' Ronnie said, 'was your compen money in there?'

Lowering his head Albert replied, 'Aye, so that's what she was after.'

'That and a cushy billet, look, Dad, by all accounts she was working as a prossy before she latched on to you, I'm sorry to have to tell you that.'

Having listened with interest, Roger asked, 'Is that a prosytitoot like Mista Hindmarsh said... whaat is a prosytitoot.'

Jane tried and failed to suppress a giggle and Edward turned away as Ronnie said, 'Not a nice person, Roger, that's all ye need to kna.'

'Aah kna,'Billy said, smiling.

'Aye whey keep it te yerself lad,' Ronnie, added.

Albert, moaned, 'Whey that's me money gone then.'

'Edward, asked, 'Was it just yor bankbook Albert?'

'Aye,' he replied.

'Well, in that case, I doubt if she was able to draw any cash out, not without your signature on a withdrawal slip or cheque but you need to confirm that with the bank.'

Ronnie stood up next to his father, saying, 'Mr Hindmarsh told me where the flat is that she used to live, so I'll go around and see if she is there and get your bankbook back before I go to the police.'

Edward, said, 'Drop me off at the police station and I'll report her Ronnie, it was me who found the boys.'

'Edward,' Jane butt in, 'I'm worried about Ian and Jake, I hope they reached Redesdale Camp this morning, I need to go home as Ian said he would ring at lunchtime.'

He replied, 'Okay, we'll use my van, it will be better in the snow than your Wolseley, Ronnie. I'll drop Jane off at home and then drive up to the police station, Albert says her flat is just a hundred yards along Station Road.'

Jane looked at Albert and asked, 'Will you be alright on your own with the boys, is there anything you need?'

'No,' replied Albert, we'll be fine, de what ye hev te de.'

His judgement clouded by anger, Stuart Weedon's day was not going well. Attempting to drive far too fast in the slush and snow, he slid across the road when he turned into North Seaton Road from First Avenue, bumping into the curb on the other side of the road. Climbing out to check the damage to his precious sports car, a passing double-decker bus sprayed him with slush, leaving his overcoat a sodden grey mess.

'Fucking bastard,' he yelled after the bus, his anger reaching the upper levels of the Richter scale.

Climbing back into the car, he slammed his door shut, leaving part of his coat sticking out and, tried to drive off but his aggressive driving resulted in the wheels spinning madly, while the rear of the car fish-tailed back and forth across the road. The inevitable happened; his rear end collided with a large oncoming, 1940's Rover P3. The collision spun his car round leaving him facing the wrong way, on his side of the road, a large dent in his rear wing.

Screaming with rage, his weasel-like features distorted almost beyond recognition, he beat his fists on the steering wheel, yelling obscenities until the driver of the Rover, a huge, burly man, opened his door and asked, 'Are ye alreet?'

'*Alreet – aall-frigging-reet*! Nur am not aall-frigging-reet, ye sackless bastard!'

A big mistake - the other driver, grasped the front of Weedon's overcoat and pulled him bodily out of the sports car, holding him so that he had to stand on his tiptoes as the blizzard tore into them both, the big man ignoring it.

'Listen, ye little, short-arsed waster, calm yersell doon or Aa'll fettle ye, that was your fault, driving like a bliddy idiot, ye've scratched me bumper, whaat are ye ganning te de aboot that?'

Weedon looked back at his battered rear wing and yelled, 'Scratched yer bumper, look at my frigging car, ye've knackered it.'

'Not as much as Aah'll knacker ye if ye divin't pay up.'

Wriggling like a fish on a hook, Weedon, snarled, 'Put me doon, put me doon,' and when the man lowered him but did not let go, he pulled back his sodden overcoat and reached into his pocket pulling out three wrinkled pound notes. Shoving them at the man, he said, 'Here, noo let me go,' and climbed back into his car when he was released.

The burly man leant on the soft top of Weedon's car, and holding his door open, said with some sarcasm, 'Drive carefully bonny lad,' slamming the door shut before walking back to his Rover.

Weedon waited until the Rover drove off, before driving away with much more care, turning his car around, and heading toward the Grand Corner. There he turned left and drove along Station Road, until he crossed Station Bridge, turning left and then right so that he was at the rear of Station Road where deep snow halted his drive.

Climbing out, he hurried through the storm to the backyard of the flat that he quickly crossed and charged through the door to the stairs, taking them three at a time, his anger driving him on.

Scrubbing pans at the small kitchen sink, Edna, heard his heavy footsteps followed by the door handle rattling and then heavy thumping on the door.

Gritting her teeth, she said to herself, 'Stuart,' and dropped the Brillo pad she was using into the sink, reaching over the drainer to pick up a heavy metal frying pan.

As the thumping continued she walked to the door and knowing the answer, shouted, 'Who is it?'

Barely able to speak because of his rage, he snarled, 'Open this frigging door, ye bitch.'

Edna took a deep breath and replied just loud enough, for him to hear, 'No, go away.'

Totally out of control, he hurled himself at the door but the mortice lock and bolt held and he bounced off, rubbing a bruised shoulder. About to kick to the door he stopped when he heard the key turning and, the bolt sliding back.

She stepped back from the door as he charged in, almost skidding to a halt, then slipping as he took a wild swing at Edna who dodged sideways swinging the frying pan with all her might, smacking Weedon on the side of the face, dropping him like a felled tree.

Semi-conscious, he rolled onto his belly and pushed himself up on all fours, glaring like a vicious hyena as he tried to clear his head.

Leaning back onto his knees he shouted, 'You frigging bitch, Aah'll bliddy kill you,' as Edna swung the pan at him again.

Seeing it coming, he raised his left arm just in time, deflecting the blow over his head, before springing to his feet and rushing Edna, knocking her backwards, crashing into the kitchen table and chairs, skinning an elbow, and bruising her back. Before she could recover, Weedon, was above her, kicking with his full force, once full in the face that snapped her head back against the corner of the table, splitting her scalp, and one in her ribs, the toe of his shoe snapping two ribs just below her right breast.

She screamed in agony from the pain of the second kick. The scream splattering blood from her split lip and broken teeth as she instinctively swung the pan that she still grasped, making solid contact with Weedon's shin.

It was his turn to scream out in pain as he hopped back clutching his leg as Edna tried to stand up. The sharp pain from her cracked ribs was too much, she curled up as Weedon stopped hopping and limped toward her. Grabbing a chair, he forced it over her, the chrome plated legs trapping her.

Stamping on her hand that held the pan, she released her grip and he kicked the pan away before kicking her again in her unprotected face. Moaning in agony, she tried to curl up even more as Weedon threw the chair to one side and grabbed her hair, dragging her from the table, determined to beat her to a pulp.

Turning her onto her back, he forced her arms up, straddled her just below her throat, and pinned her arms down with his knees.

Salvia dripping from his mouth like a rabid dog, he snarled, 'Right ye bitch am ganning te teach you a lesson ye'll niva forget,' punching her unprotected face a couple of times with his bony fists, splitting skin on both cheekbones. Then leaning back, he began to strike her with long swinging slaps that rocked her head from side to side, as she slipped into unconsciousness.

Having parked at the side of Ashington police station, DI Norman and DS Dodson hurried inside and into the main hall after the Duty Sergeant unlocked the door, saying, 'The top brass are here sir, in the Superintendent's Office.'

Grimacing, Jamie said, 'That's all we need,' then turned to his DS, 'Take Cotton and go to the betting shop and speak to Stuart Weedon while I'm briefing the bosses.'

Dodson nodded and hurried off as Inspector Brian Smith stepped out of his office, 'Aah Jamie, Chief Superintendent Garrity and DCI Fairbanks are in with our Super', they want a briefing on events so far.'

Norman grimaced, saying, 'Come on then Brian, let's face the inquisition.'

During the drive through the ever-deepening snow and slush to their home, Edward told Jane and Ronnie what Albert had told him about the murders, that Harry Weedon had apparently been murdered down the pit and a rumour was circulating that Bill Robertson had been murdered in his home and, that his son, Geordie, was the chief suspect. Ronnie remarked that Ian and Geordie Robertson had fought a vicious fistfight four years earlier and that during the intervening years, Robertson earned himself a reputation as a hard case.

Edward helped Jane into their house before driving the half-mile to Ashington police station, parking directly outside the main entrance.

Sitting on the long bench seat next to Edward, Ronnie said, 'The flat is just a hundred yards up the street, Aah'll nip along and see if Edna is in and get me Dad's bank book off her.'

Edward replied, 'Okay, I'll go in and report her treatment of the lads and her theft of the bank book, see you in a minute or two,' both men climbing out into the storm, Ronnie pausing for a second to pull up the collar of his heavy, navy-blue reefer coat.

It only took him a couple of minutes to find the number he was looking for, screwed on the wooden-gate to the backyard of the shop and flat. It was open as was the door to the stairs that led up to the flat. Kicking away some of the snow that had blown into the small hall, he closed the door behind him before climbing the steep stairs.

Approaching the top, he saw that the door to the flat was slightly ajar and hearing a smacking sound, he rushed in, pausing for a second to digest what he was seeing. Two kitchen chairs lay on their sides, a frying pan next to them but it was what he saw between the table and sofa, which shocked him. A scrawny figure in a dishevelled overcoat was kneeling over Edna, raining viscous slaps on her bloody face. So focused on attacking the now defenceless woman, Weedon did not see Ronnie until the last moment.

Ronnie grabbed him by the shoulders and threw him across the room, asking, 'What the hell are ye doing?'

Weedon did not answer; crouching on all fours like a cornered rat, his eyes not focusing, he looked insane.

Looking down at Edna, Ronnie could not believe the damage inflicted upon her by Weedon. Her mouth was a bloody crimson mess, blood from her nose, lips and teeth, smeared across her face and down her neck; both her cheeks were cut and bleeding and her eyes were puffed and closed. Bubbles of blood spurted from her mouth as she struggled to breathe as her own blood ran down her throat, choking her.

Bending down, Ronnie carefully rolled her onto her side into the recovery position, pushing a finger into her mouth, ensuring her tongue had not fallen back and she could breathe. Weedon seized his chance, springing to his feet he rushed toward the door but Ronnie was quicker, grabbing him by the arm, he jerked him to a halt, spinning him around before kicking his legs from under him, hurling him to the floor where he slid across the worn linoleum, crashing into the kitchen cabinet.

Standing over him, he warned, 'Stay down and don't move, you are going nowhere until this is sorted out.'

A long, low moan came from Edna as she began to regain consciousness, curling into a protective ball, in too much in pain to be aware of what was happening.

As Ronnie turned to help Edna, Weedon sprung to his feet and snatching a paring knife from the draining board, pointed it at Ronnie, snarling, 'Right ye bastard, get oot me way, am leaving and yor not stopping me.'

Ronnie did not reply, he moved quickly, positioning himself between Weedon and the door, standing with a wide stance, knees slightly bent his arms open at shoulder height, waiting. Weedon hesitated before making a wild stabbing lunge at him with the knife but Ronnie moved quickly to his right, bringing his left hand crashing down on Weedon's forearm, knocking it down as he followed up with a swinging right into his nose, sending him crashing to the floor. Weedon curled up, his left hand to his nose, blood running between his fingers, the knife still clenched in his right hand.

Ronnie stepped onto his right forearm, pinning it to the floor and bending down, twisted his hand back, forcing him to release the knife. Ronnie picked it up and placed it on the table. Then taking a cushion from the sofa, he knelt down placing it under Edna's head table as the door swung open.

Sergeant Malcolm stepped into the room, while behind him Edward blocked the door.

Surveying the scene, Malcolm asked Ronnie, 'What's happened here, lad?'

Still kneeling by Edna, he composed himself, before replying, 'I came up here to see if she had my Dad's bank book and Aah found him kneeling on her battering so I hoyed him off.' Pointing to the knife on the table, he continued, 'He had a go at me with that when I was trying to help her so I smacked him one but she needs an ambulance.'

Weedon pulled himself into a sitting position, his left hand still trying to stem the flow of blood from his nose as Malcolm bent down to look at Edna.

Shaking his head he stood up and glared down at Weedon, recognising him, he said, 'Stuart Weedon, now why are you here? You've made a right mess of this lass, this is all very interesting because we wanted a chat with you anyway.'

Opening his overcoat, he reached in and pulled out the antenna on his Pye pocket phone, pressed the transmitter button and asked for an ambulance and assistance.

Taking his handcuffs from under his tunic, he reached down and hauled Weedon to his feet, turning him around and deftly snapping the handcuffs on him.

It took Jane a few minutes of searching through telephone books to find a number for Redesdale Camp, the operator connecting her with the Camp Commandant's Office who transferred her call to Major Graham.

'QM,' he snapped down the receiver.

Jane, took a deep breath, and asked, Major Graham?'

'Yes,' he answered curtly.

'Good afternoon, my Name is Jane Thompson; I am trying to find out if my son, Gunner Ian Trevelyan and his friend

Lance Bombardier Jacob Grundy arrived back there this morning as I was expecting a call from him, I am worried they may have been caught in the blizzard?'

Major Graham, paused, dropped his curt speech, and replied, 'Mrs Thompson, Ian and Jacob arrived back here early this morning – but - in response to a police request, I sent them along the road to Catcleugh Reservoir looking for stranded cars. 'That was at eight-thirty this morning, as of yet they have not returned.'

Jane felt her stomach do a cartwheel, 'So are you saying, they are now stranded?'

'No, we don' think so, a large recovery vehicle followed along behind them a little while later. The driver lives on a farm at the far end of the reservoir and we believe they may have taken shelter with him.'

Trying to conceal her fears, she asked, 'Can't you phone the farm and find out?'

'I'm afraid not Mrs Thompson, the storm appears to have brought the telephone lines down beyond Byrness but you know your son, he is a good soldier as is Bombardier Grundy, they both know how to look after themselves. We are doing everything we can to clear the road. We have a snowplough and digger working trying to clear the road and the few men I have to spare are out there helping.'

'I see; can you keep me informed on progress?'

'Yes of course Mrs Thompson,' he paused, 'I do not want to worry you unduly, but there is a very remote possibility that a man wanted by the police could be in a stranded car somewhere along the road. There are police here and more are trying to get through but the blizzard is hampering progress, and, as I said it is far from certain that he is actually here.'

Jane asked quietly, 'What is he wanted for?'

'Murder I believe Mrs Thompson.'

'Oh my God,' Jane muttered before saying clearly, 'if this is the murders in Ashington this morning, I need to tell you that there is history between the wanted man and my son and Jacob. They were all at school together, Ian fought with this Robertson, I hate to think what will happen if they meet, I must come up there.'

Of course Mrs Thompson I can see that but the roads; that's the A68 and A696 are still blocked at the moment.'

Trying to remain calm despite her rising panic, she asked, 'Can you telephone me when the roads are open?'

'Yes, of course, I will, I think you should also tell the police about the connection between the wanted man, and your son and Grundy.'

'I will,' replied Jane and gave Major Smith her telephone number before ringing Ashington Police Station.

She asked if Edward was there, the Duty Sergeant telling her that he left earlier for Station Road with Sergeant Malcolm. When Jane told him of the connection between Robertson, and Ian and Jake, he told her that he would brief either DI Norman or DS Dodson when they were available. Remembering Jamie Norman, Jane asked the Sergeant to have DI Norman ring her when he was available.

Unaware that Stuart Weedon was under arrest for assault, DS Dodson and DI Cotton pulled up outside the betting shop in First Avenue.

Looking out through the cleared part of the windscreen, Will Cotton said, 'Lights are on in there so hopefully he will be in.'

Dodson took the last drag from his cigarette before stubbing it out in the ashtray, 'Great, here we gan again, back oot inte the bliddy blizzard, it's a helluva a day and we not haf way through it yet.'

Climbing out of the protection of the car, the gale helped them across the pavement, pushing them into the doorway of the shop, which Cotton tried to open.

Unable to see through the whitewashed glass he shouted, 'It's locked but there must be someone in there,' and banged loudly on the door.

After a few seconds, they heard someone inside shout, 'Who is it?'

'The Police, open this door now,' shouted Dodson, wanting to get out of the storm.'

Yvonne unlocked the door and stepped back, she looked cold, tired, and terrified.

Cotton held up his warrant card, I am Detective Constable Cotton and this is Detective Sergeant Dodson, is Stuart Weedon here?'

Backing up to the counter, Yvonne began shivering as she replied, 'No he's gone to his Dad's flat in Station Road.'

Brushing snow from his car coat, Dodson asked, 'Who are you then Pet?'

'Yvonne Carter, am a friend of Stuart's he's asked me to look after the shop until he gets back.'

Smoothing back his snow-dampened hair, Cotton asked, 'Mind if we have a look round, Miss?'

Worried that the two detectives were going to ask her questions about her relationship with the Weedons, she nodded, 'Okay.'

With nothing to see in the shop, both detectives walked through into the office and straight to the six-drawer desk, the only piece of furniture in the room, of any note.

Cotton looked at the open file on the desk and began reading lists of names and addresses with scribbled amounts and dates next to them as Yvonne's fear were realised, Dodson asking, 'What's your relationship to the Weedons?'

'Am just a friend,' she lied.

'Friend of who, father, or son?'

Not sure how to reply, she blurted, 'Both.'

His suspicions aroused, he continued, 'Where do you live Yvonne.'

'With me mam and dad,'

'Where's, that?'

'Poplar Street.'

Dodson smiled, ''That's just around the corner, what number, we'll go and have a word with them when we are finished here.'

She panicked, 'No ye cannit, sorry, - Aah mean they might not be in - Aah divin't live there anymore.'

'What is it Yvonne, they might not be in or you don't live there anymore, what ye hiding Pet?'

Shivering even more and terrified, she replied, 'Aah divin't live at home anymore.'

Cotton took a loose piece of paper from the file, 'You live in the flat in Station Road, don't you, it says so on here.'

'I might.'

Dodson walked over to her holdall, lying by the door, tapping it with the toe of his shoe, 'Is this your's Yvonne? Just why are you here Pet?'

It was all too much for her; she collapsed into one of the wooden chairs by the desk and burst into tears.

Cotton interrupted, 'Sarge, you need to read this file, it looks as if the Weedons and Robertsons were running a loan shark business as well as something else at the flat in Ashington as well as two more flats in Blyth.'

Dodson walked across and began reading the file while Cotton stood by the still crying Yvonne, 'Did you work for Harry Weedon?'

Sobbing, she nodded, 'Yes.'

'How long for?'

Looking up at him, she took a deep breath and replied, 'A few months.'

'How did you end up working for him?'

A deep sob wracked her slim frame, 'Me Mam owed him money.'

'Your Mam? So why are you working for him, could your father not pay off the money?'

'He doesn't know about the money, he just thinks I'm a slut and winnit have anything te de with me.'

Leaning on the desk, Dodson said, 'Bliddy hell lass, Aah divvin't kna who's warse, ye mam or ye dad, probably yer mam for letting this happen te ye.'

Yvonne was crying again, uncontrolled, body shaking crying.

Rummaging through the drawers of the desk, Dodson found four more full files in a lockable drawer that in his haste to get to the flat, Weedon had left unlocked, the key still in the hole. Stacking them on top of the file on the desktop, he looked at Yvonne.

Trying to connect names, he realised where he had heard 'Carter' before, 'Is your father William Carter and does he work at Ashington Colliery?'

'Yes,' she replied, sniffing loudly, 'how did you know that?'

'Because he found Harry Weedon's body.'

Cotton exclaimed, 'Bliddy hell, Sarge, is that right?'

Dodson gave him a withering look, 'Aah wouldn't hev said it if it wasn't, would Aah.' Picking up the files he said, 'Right, we are going to have to ask you down to come down to the Station with us, I am not arresting you – yet, we need your help with our investigation into the Weedons. I wouldn't worry too much about them, Harry is dead and I think Stuart Weedon is in big trouble, are you happy to come with us and are you happy to give these files to us?'

Sniffing and wiping her eyes with the back of her hand, smearing her mascara, she said firmly, 'Yes.'

CHAPTER 17

Friday 8th February – 12:15 am
Treshinish House

Despite the freezing temperature made doubly worse by the biting wind-chill, Geordie Robertson was sweating.

His sodden T-shirt clung to him as sweat, seeped through his heavy woollen pullover into his greatcoat. Fear of feeling shotgun pellets blasting into his back and the force of the blizzard propelled him through the snow, forcing him to gasp for breath as he tried to keep on running. Not pausing or turning around to look to see if Jack was chasing him, panic drove him on until his bursting lungs brought him to a halt by the snow-covered, abandoned Ford.

Bending over, hands on knees, he gasped and spluttered as he tried to gulp in air and control his breathing. After a minute or so, he stood, leaning his back into the gale, to take another deep breath before turning to squint into the wind-driven snow, looking for Jack, the blizzard making it impossible to see more than a few yards.

Desperate to get away from Jack and the shotgun, he plodded on, the realisation that he was not going to reach Scotland, forcing him to rack his fear-filled mind for a way out. 'The big truck, that's it, he drove it through the blizzard, I'll take that. Jake's shot and if Ian tries to stop me, I can fettle him, nee bother.'

Unafraid of the people inside, he allowed the wind to push him across the courtyard toward the Scammell, climbing into the cab from the passenger side to see if the keys were in the ignition. Seeing they were not there, he opened the driver's door and stepping down into the sheltered spot between the two vehicles; he climbed up into the cab of the Austin army truck to check for keys. That was when Jess began to bark.

Not finding the keys, he decided to use his revolver to threaten those inside the house and, to have them give them the keys to one of the vehicles. Climbing out the cab, he stood in the shelter of the truck, fumbling in his greatcoat pocket to pull the revolver out when to his right; he saw the nearest dining room window slide up.

When the bottom of the sash window was up to its stops, Ian's battered face appeared as he lent out, the butt of the shotgun pulled into his shoulder, the muzzles pointing at Robertson.

Tipping his head toward the wind, Ian shouted, 'Give up Geordie, bring your revolver slowly out your pocket and throw it on the ground, we'll let you in out of the storm if you do.'

Robertson stood motionless for a few seconds before trying to whip to revolver from his pocket but it snagged, as Ian lifted the shotgun and fired above his head.'

Ducking to his left, he shouted, 'Bastard,' and ran off into the snow, throwing himself over the stone wall between the house and cattle barns and staggering off into the woods next to the reservoir, screaming obscenities, angry and frustrated and having failed to take a truck and being chased off by Ian.

Ignoring the blizzard as best he could, Jack Gray, alert and on edge checked the outhouses and barns around the Fenwick's Farm for any signs of Robertson. Satisfied that he was not about, he set off for home worried that the murderer may be on his way there and hoped that young Ian would be able to protect the folk there.

Holding the shotgun ready to fire, he trudged through the snow, the wind pushing him along, his eyes sweeping left to right, searching for any sign of Robertson. It was both physically and mentally tiring but he did not relax, cautiously wiping snow from the rear window of the Ford to check that Robertson had not sought shelter inside.

Reaching Treshinish house, he looked inside the two trucks in the courtyard before banging three times on the front door, pausing, and then banging three times more.

Ian shouted from inside, 'Who is it?'

'Jack Gray,' he shouted back.

Unlocking the door, Ian turned the handle and standing back with the shotgun ready, he let the wind blow the door open, revealing a snow-plastered Jack leaning into the blizzard.

Jack stepped into the hall and helped Ian and Davy force it closed against the wind, shouting, 'Everything alright lad?'

Shaking his head, Ian replied, 'Robertson was looking around the trucks ten minutes ago, I opened the dining room window and chased him off with a blast from this, he ran off toward the reservoir.'

Unable to hide his excitement and admiration for Ian, Davy said, 'Ian said he could come in if he surrendered but he wouldn't so Ian fired a shot in the air and chased him off, it was a really big bang.'

Jack smiled at Davy, then lifting his fur cap, he rubbed his forehead and thought for a few seconds before saying, 'We cannot just sit here and wait for him to try something else; I'm going after him.'

Shall I come with you or stay here?'

'Jack patted Ian on the shoulder, 'Stay here and protect the women, you and young Davy here are doing a grand job, I'm going to hunt the bugga doon and I'm going now before the blizzard covers his tracks, tell me, Mam...'

Maggie opened the inner hall door and asking, 'Tell me what Jack?'

'I'm going after Robertson, I'd prefer to have him here where we can control him than out there not knowing what he is up or even freezing to death.'

Maggie furrowed her brow, 'Whey tek care lad and keep yor distance until ye get that revolver off him, ye wor always ower kind for yor own good, mebe's he would be better of freezing to death oot there because he is going to hang if he has murdered anyone.'

He smiled at his mother's blunt statement and said, 'Mam, dig out some rope or straps so that we can tie the big bugga up if I catch him, and lock up after me. Ian, keep a look out the window for me coming back.'

Opening the door with Ian, he stepped out into the lee of the Austin, unfastening the lower buttons on his long, heavy coat so that he could move faster.

Despite the blizzards best efforts to hide it, Robertson's trail was easy to follow through the deep snow, Jack hurried across the yard and clambered over the four-foot-high wall, pausing to study the trail ahead, searching for any signs of his prey.

Leaning into the ferocious wind, he moved forward at a good pace, concentrating on looking ahead as far as the blizzard allowed him, the deep furrow in the snow showing the way. He stopped when the trail reached the side of the reservoir indicated by a drop of a few feet onto an expanse of snow that resembled a snow-blown, level field. Checking that the trail thankfully did not go onto the thin ice, he moved on, the trail following the reservoir bank.

Two hundred difficult yards further on, he slowed, lifted the butt of his shotgun to his shoulder, and stopped, staring at a large, snow-covered mound, ten yards ahead. Keeping his shotgun pointed at the mound, he moved to the left, one careful step at a time, until he was level and could see that it was the snow-covered, hunched-figure of Robertson. The lad looked to be on his knees with his head in his hands and judging from the weird sounds coming from him he was crying like an injured dog.

Jack moved a few more steps; stopping five yards in front of the wretched figure and pointing the gun at him, shouted, 'Robertson!'

His head shot up, looking like a frightened schoolboy, he held his empty hands up in front of him, tears rolling down his cheeks and began pleading in short, breathless sentences, 'No, please - no, I give up. I'm lost. Aah divin't kna where Aah am. I'm tired. Aah hev't slept since yesterday. Aah cannit tek it any more. Am caad and knackered. Please.'

Jack kept the gun steady, shouting, 'Where's your revolver?'

'In my pocket,' he replied, reaching for it.

Jack Yelled, 'Don't move until I tell you too, Now keep your left hand in the air and very slowly bring the revolver out of your pocket with two fingers and drop it in front of you.'

He nodded, lifting the revolver out of his greatcoat pocket; he dropped it on the ground in front of him, sniffing up accumulated snot and tears.

Jack took a step closer and ordered, 'Stand up and move to your right – slowly,' Robertson complied, halting when Jack ordered, 'Stop.'

'Keep your hands up, turn around, and take a step forward.'

Robertson did as he was told, ignoring the snow blasting into his face, he was spent, finished, he just wanted this nightmare to end.

Moving forward, Jack picked up the revolver and shoving it into his pocket, shouted over the storm, 'Right, we are going back to my house, follow our tracks and don't try anything stupid because I will shoot you.'

Struggling into the blizzard lashing their faces, they slowly retraced their trail back to Treshinish, Jack ordering

Robertson to walk around to the main entrance rather than climbing the wall again.

The big lad was staggering from fatigue as they approached the front of the two trucks, turning behind the Austin. Ian watched them approach and opened both the front door and the door to the inner hall allowing them to walk straight through, closing the doors behind them.

Standing in front of the stove in the sitting room, Sarah Rosalind and Davy watched him shuffle past the door, Sarah wrapping her arm around her daughter's and son's shoulders as Jake raised his head and peered over the back of the sofa.

'He doesn't look so hard noo.'

Jess was barking and growling from behind the kitchen door where Maggie had taken him just before Ian opened the front door. Maggie stood at the end of the hall, three long leather luggage straps hanging over her shoulder, a length of rope in her hand.

'Bring him in here son,' she said, opening the door to the rear passage and then the scullery door, I have a chair in there and I've switched on a bar of the electric heater to keep the chill off.'

Head down; defeated; Robertson shuffled past a glaring Maggie, into the eight-foot by eight, scullery and sat on the stout wooden kitchen chair without looking around when Jack ordered him to do so.

Keeping his gun pointed at Robertson, Jack said to Ian who had come up behind him, 'Leave your shotgun in the hall and use one of the straps me Mam has to fasten his hands behind his back and the other two to strap him to the chair.'

Ian set to, pulling the straps as tight as he could. Robertson said nothing, his head lolling forward; he appeared to be past caring.

When Ian finished, Jack said, 'Cut two lengths of rope, and tie his ankles to chair legs; that should keep him secure.'

Once Ian had finished, Jack backed off into the hall, pointing with his head for Ian to follow him.

In the hall, he asked Maggie, 'How is everyone?'

She replied, 'Davy and Rosalind are both fine and the cut on Sarah's face doesn't seem to be bothering her but she has a nasty bruise on her head where that big brute punched her. Jake's another matter, he's not complaining but I can tell he is in a lot of pain, I am worried the bullet might have damaged something inside him.'

'I don't think so Mam, it was a glancing blow so most of the power would not have gone inside him, hopefully, all his insides will be okay,' and looking at Ian's swollen and bruised face, he asked, 'What about you lad, how is your head?'

'Sore but, that's all, nothing broken as far as I can tell, I'm okay.'

'Good,' Jack said, 'I don't want to leave this evil bugga on his own for a minute, have you had anything to eat?'

'Yes, a couple of sandwiches.'

'Then you can have the first watch while I get a bite to eat, get another chair from the kitchen and take it in there but keep well away from him,' and pointing at Robertson, said, 'mind he looks knackered now.'

Robertson's chin was resting on his chest, his body appearing to have collapsed in on itself, as he snored loudly.

Ian walked back in carrying a chair as Jess darted past him, lying on the floor a few feet from Robertson, her eyes fixed on him, silently waiting for him to move.

'We'll give him a bite of food and a drink when he wakes up,' said Jack, and taking his coat off, he placed Robertson's revolver on the hall table before heading into the warmth of the kitchen.

CHAPTER 18

Friday 8th February – 12:30 am
Ashington Police Station

A relieved DI Jamie Norman winked at Inspector Brian Smith as they walked out of the Superintendent's office, 'Och, that seemed to go well enough,' he whispered, hoping that he had answered the many questions thrown at him by his senior officers, to their satisfaction.

Brian said, 'Yes now let's get some work done, are you going back to Morpeth?'

Norman did not answer, his attention drawn to the Duty Sergeant opening the front door to allow in DS Dodson and DC Cotton with a nervous looking Yvonne Carter between them.

Stamping snow off his shoes and brushing snow from his coat with his left hand, his right clutching files, Dodson said to Cotton, 'Take her into one of the interview rooms, and I'll brief the boss.'

As the three of them walked down the narrow hall toward the DI, the Duty Sergeant appeared out of the main office and squeezed past them saying; 'It's getting like Piccadilly Circus in here,' opening the front door again.

Sergeant Malcolm strode in, his right hand gripping a handcuffed Weedon whose nose still dribbled blood, followed by Ronnie Grundy and finally by Edward Thompson who stood at the back of the group.

The narrow hall was now full of damp-clothed, wet-shoed people; jostling for position like a greedy crowd waiting to enter a department store for the January sales.

Jamie raised his voice, 'Everybody just standstill for a moment until we find out what is going on.'

The Duty Sergeant spoke first, 'Sorry sir, there's someone else at the window, I'll have to see who it is,' and disappeared into the front office.

The noise level increased as shoes and boots were stamped, coats shook free of snow and throats cleared.

Seeing Yvonne, Weedon spat, 'What's she deeing here she's supposed te be looking after the betting shop,' then recognizing the bunch of files under Dodson's arms, asked, 'What ye deeing with them?'

DS Dodson replied, 'Miss Carter gave them to us and now shut up, yer in enough trouble as it is.'

Squeezing through the noisy throng in the long narrow hall, the Duty Sergeant opened the door again, allowing Bill Carter to step in and join the melee.

Showered, shaved and fed, he took off his flat cap, shaking snow off and added to the noise when he saw his daughter, saying in a loud voice, 'So ye've been caught hev ye, whey it serves ye right.'

DS Dodson rounded on him, 'Listen ye bliddy idiot, ye need to speak to your wife, this lass is paying off hur debt not hur own.'

Weedon snarled, 'She's just a frigging whore.'

Carter shouted, 'Who the fuck is that little shit?' Any answer was lost in the rising crescendo of voices as they all tried to talk at once.

Brian Smith yelled, 'QUIET!' An instant embarrassing silence, broken by shuffling of feet, and nervous coughing indicated that they had heard his order, 'Thank you, 'he said, 'Now carry on quietly.'

Brian felt a tap on his shoulder and turned to look into the red face of the Superintendent, 'The Chief thinks he has walked into Bedlam Brian, sort these buggas out now.'

'As you can see, sir, - I am,' he replied and turning back to the throng said, 'Right line up and wait while the Duty Sergeant books you in.'

Jamie grabbed DS Dodson by the arm, 'Put her in the interview room and come and brief me on why you have brought her in.'

As Dodson took Yvonne down the corridor, Brian Smith asked Sergeant Malcolm, 'Who is this?'

'Mr Stuart Weedon sir, I arrested him for GBH; his victim, Mrs Edna North is in Ashington Hospital. PC Ryan is with her as she is suspected of theft and, physically abusing two boys. I believe Sergeant Dodson is investigating Mr Weedon on other matters.'

Leaving DC Cotton with Yvonne, DS Dodson briefed Jamie Norman on events at the betting shop; Jamie listened, nodding occasionally before saying, 'Have Cotton take a statement from the girl and then release her. Once Sergeant Malcolm has booked in Mr Weedon, get him to brief me on what happened. We need to interview Weedon to see if we can establish any reason that Robertson may have had to kill his father.'

DI Dodson replied, 'Right ye are, sir, what aboot, William Carter, what de ye want deeing with him.'

'Tell him to take a seat; Cotton can take a statement from him when he is finished with the girl.'

Ten minutes later, Sergeant Malcolm explained to DI Norman that he had gone to the flat to arrest Edna North on suspicion of theft of a bankbook and, locking two boys in a shed but on arrival at her flat, discovered that Stuart Weedon had assaulted her.

'Mr Grundy had gone to the flat to tackle Mrs North; he wanted to get his father's bank book back but he found Weedon beating the girl. Weedon attacked Grundy with a knife so he clobbered him. It was me that told Weedon of his father's death earlier this morning, sir. He was also unable to tell me where Mrs Weedon was, all he could say is that she left a couple of years ago and claimed he has no idea where she went, I did warn him that we would be questioning him again about his mother's disappearance.'

'Thanks,' said DI Norman, 'very disturbing – it appears the Weedons were up to a lot more than running a betting shop, see what you can find out about Mrs Weedon please.'

Turning to DS Dodson, he said, 'Let's get Weedon into the interview room and I'll draft up a list of questions we want to ask him.'

While DS Dodson waited in the hall for Weedon to be processed, the DI walked into Inspector Smith's office and asked, 'Mind if I sit here for a couple of minutes to draft a few notes, Brian?'

'Not at all Jamie,' and handing a piece of paper to him, said, 'Oh, by the way, the Duty Sergeant gave me this telephone number, it is a Mrs Jane Thompson, she would like to speak to you as a matter of urgency?'

The mention of Jane's name made Jamie sit up, memories flooded back, how her stunning looks and dignified, inner-strength had left him like a smitten schoolboy, stumbling physically and verbally in her presence. Distraught when she became engaged to Edward Thompson, to his shame, he sought to discredit him. Although he was married and worshipped his wife, hearing Jane's name, still excited him.

'Mind if I use your phone, Brian?'

'Go ahead, I'm going next door.'

The DI dialled the number and waited, holding his breath.'

'Hello, Jane Thompson here,' her voice as sweet as ever.

The DI cleared his throat nervously, 'Hello Jane, Jamie Norman here, you, er want to speak to me?'

'Oh, yes Jamie, the sergeant there told me that you were investigating the murders that happened this morning?'

'Yes, I am Jane, why?'

She told him about Ian and Jake being lost somewhere in Redesdale and that an army officer there had told her that the murder suspect may also be in Redesdale, possibly stranded in the blizzard and that she was worried that the two boys had not been heard from for several hours.

The DI forced himself to listen to what she was saying and stop enjoying the sound of her voice, 'Sorry Jane, it is possible that the suspect may be there but we have no concrete information at the moment, he could be anywhere.'

Pausing, Jane took a deep breath before continuing, 'If your suspect is George Robertson, I need to tell you that there is bad blood between him and my son so I intend to go up to Redesdale as soon as the road opens regardless of any concrete information, it is very worrying.'

'I can understand that Jane but until we have something definite we will be concentrating our investigations here. Hexham Police are dealing with the situation; they already have a couple of officers there and more are on their way but they are struggling to get through. If I get any more information on the suspect's whereabouts I will call you if you like?'

'Yes please, Jamie that is very kind of you.'

'I have to go now Jane, things are very hectic here at the moment.'

After Jane thanked him and rang off, he stood up and headed for the interview room bumping into Edward, Jane's husband in the Hall.

Edward spoke first, 'Hello Jamie, it looks as if you are a wee bit busy?'

Surprised at the coincidence of Edward being there, the DI replied, 'Och, yes very busy, I have just been speaking to

Jane, she is very worried about young Ian, but what are you doing here?'

In a couple of sentences, Edward explained how he had found the two Grundy boys and coming into the station to report it before asking, 'Did Jane say why she is worried about Ian?'

'Apparently, he is missing in Redesdale and an army officer has told her that our murder suspect may be there.'

'Is that true, I mean your suspect being there?'

DI Norman replied, 'Just a possibility, a remote possibility.'

'Edward looked worried, 'Thanks for that Jamie, I best be off home,' and hurried out into the storm.

DI Norman walked along the hall to the interview rooms where DS Dodson, who was still wearing his car coat, was lounging in the hall, smoking a Capstan while he waited for the DI.

Standing, he asked, 'Ready sir?'

The DI stopped outside the closed door, replying, 'Aye Sergeant, I am that, first we'll see what we can find out about the connections between the Weedons and Robertsons and what criminal activities they were involved in...'

DS Dodson interrupted, 'Prostitution, loan sharking, gambling and protection, according to the files we picked up.'

'Yes Sergeant, plus why he attacked Mrs North and what he knows about his mother's disappearance, it is going to be a long afternoon.'

CHAPTER 19

Friday 8th February – 2 pm
Treshinish House

Head bent because of the restricted headroom, Geordie Robertson knew from the smell of the warm air wafting over him that he was standing in the cage at the top of the updraft-shaft at the colliery. The soft breeze blowing up and through the cage smothered him with the dank aromas it had collected from far below since it entered the coal mine through the downdraft shaft. The breeze carried the smell of warm electric machinery, rusting girders, decaying timbers, stinking pools, dripping water, dust, and, the stench of the sweat of the men toiling far below; all rolled into one fetid slap of his senses.

The clanging of the signalling bell shook him, shattering his thoughts as he tried to understand how and why he was there. A second later, the winchman eased off the brake of the massive winch-drum in the winder-house and the cage plummeted downwards into pitch-blackness. For the first time in ages, Geordie experienced once again the feeling of his stomach hitting the roof of his mouth, a feeling he had become used to during the past three years as the cage hurtled downward, ever faster.

His slightly bent knees began to tremble as the speed of the descent continued to increase, the cage began to rattle and groan, sparks flying off the steel guides. Terrified; sweat ran down his face and body as he gripped the sides of the cage with one hand to steady himself and tried to unfasten his tight greatcoat but the buttons would not budge.

He became aware that he was not alone in the plummeting cage and struggled to lift his head to shine the light from his headlamp forward to where he felt the presence of others in the ten-foot by six cage but the lamp began to flicker and he could not see them clearly.

Reaching up, he twisted the knob on the side of the lamp but he was unable to steady the light.

'Shite,' he shouted and followed the cable from the lamp, around to the back of his helmet and then down his back to where the large battery should be strapped to his belt but it wasn't there, the cable ended in frayed loose ends.

His whole body now trembled with fear as the cage hurtled on and on as he tried to brace himself for the inevitable crash when it hit the bottom. To his horror, the two figures in front of him began to move forward, slowly coming out of the dark into focus. Opening his mouth wide, he tried to scream but although he could hear the scream in his head, no sound came out of his wide-open mouth as he tried to back away but found he was unable to move his booted-feet.

Tears ran down his cheeks, joining the sweat and spittle dribbling from his mouth as the figure of Harry Weedon, half his head replaced by a gory bloody pulp, dead eyes wide open, reached out for him with a hand like a raven's claw.

Geordie began another silent scream as the other figure came into focus, his father. He appeared to be bulging out of white skin, laced with pulsating, blue veins, a huge, bloody hole in the centre of his forehead. The figure of his father moved toward him, raising its hand, ready to strike Geordie.

He yelled in his familiar threatening voice reminding Geordie of the beatings he had inflicted upon him when he was a child, 'Ye bliddy little waster, Aah telt ye te hoy them coals inte the coal hoose, I'm ganning te give ye a hiding ye'll niva forget,' and reaching forward, grabbed Geordie's shoulder shouting, 'Robertson, Robertson!'

Geordie snapped his head back, the gruesome, bloated figure of his father replaced by the backlit silhouette of a slimmer man who was shaking his shoulder, 'Come on wake up, ye were having a bad dream, I've brought ye a sandwich and mug of tea.'

Breathing heavily, trembling, his face glistening with sweat, spittle running down his chin, his eyes glazed and unfocused, he looked pathetic as he shook his head as though he could shake out the nightmare that had just attacked him.

Jess raised herself an inch or two, remaining crouched, ready to spring, she growled, low and deep, eyes fixed firmly on Geordie.

Jack waited until Geordie regained his senses and said, 'I'm going to feed you; I'm not going to risk untying you, do you want this.'

Geordie swallowed the spittle that filled his mouth, coughed, and grunted, 'Aye, can you loosen these straps and my coat; I'm sweating like a pig.'

Jack looked at him without pity, 'No – we listened to the one-o'clock news; I'm not letting you lose, now do you want this?'

'Aye man but listen, I winnit try owt, am too knackered man, just loosen them a bit.'

Ignoring his pleas, Jack said, 'Shut up and open your gob,' and pushed the sandwich into his open mouth. Ravenous, Geordie took a large bite and in his haste and greed to eat, tried to swallow without chewing it fully, before he took another bite of the sandwich. He began choking and coughed out half the food in his mouth, waving his head from side to side, as he tried to swallow the remainder.

'Gis a drink man,' he begged, wanting to wash the half-chewed remains down his throat.

A look of disgust on his face, Jack held the mug up to Geordie's lip and watched him take a large gulp of the hot liquid, immediately snorting it out through his nose and mouth, yelling, 'Yer frigging freak ye, that's boiling, ye've scaaded me, ye scar-faced git ye.'

Controlling his anger, Jack turned and walked past Ian who was sitting with a shotgun on his knee, and into the kitchen where he emptied the tea into the Belfast sink and threw the remains of the sandwich into a large, metal kitchen bin.

Sitting at the table in the centre of the room, Maggie, and Sarah with Davy leaning on her, watched him, Maggie asking,' Was he not hungry?'

Ensuring the disfigured side of his face was away from them, he muttered, 'Yes he is but he's getting nowt until he learns some manners,' and walked back to the scullery.

Geordie looked at Ian, seeing for the first time the damage his beating had done to him, the flicker of a smile that showed his pleasure, disappeared when Jack walked back in

He tapped Ian on the shoulder, 'I'll take over now Ian lad, Mam's got some soup for you in the kitchen.'

Eager for the break, Ian stood up and handed the gun to Jack and after stretching, said, 'He has been asleep all the time until you woke him,' and walked off into the kitchen.

Jack sat on the chair, laying the gun across his lap and Jess, without taking her eyes from Geordie backed up and hunkered down next to Jack to continue her guard duty.

Jack patted his dog and stared at Geordie who spat, 'Aah need a drink, man.'

'I might let you have a drink of water – when I'm ready.'

Geordie wriggled in his chair, flexing the leather straps that Ian had fastened tightly and muttered, 'Bastard.'

Jack leant back, unable to hide his contempt for the monster in front of him, and said with deliberate scorn, 'Maybe but I'm not the one that murdered his father and workmate, nor do I have half of Northumberland Police Force out looking for me.'

'Aye, but they hevn't caught me yit.'

Jack gave a crooked smile and said, 'You look pretty well caught to me, and it's only a matter of time before the storm ends and the road is opened.'

Wriggling in the chair, Geordie spat, 'Ye cannit keep me trussed up like this, hoo lang is that bliddy blizzard ganna last.'

'Make yourself as comfortable as you can lad, you'll be sat there all night - at least. Don't expect any sympathy from me, you nearly shot my mother, and you did shoot young Jake and, battered Ian, you deserve everything that's coming your way.'

Geordie lowered his head in despair.

'You made the second spot after the blizzard, on the news on the radio; the police have a country-wide alert out for you but they did say you could be trapped in the blizzard on the A68.'

Looking up, Geordie said, 'So you've telt them I'm here?'

'Yes, on the telephone,' Jack lied, 'they are going to let me know when they expect to get through to us.'

Geordie sunk down again; the hostility disappeared from his face, replaced by a look of frightened resignation.

After a few minutes, he raised his head, asking, 'Do ye think Aah will hang for this, Aah niva meant to kill them, it was self-defence; they attacked me.'

Jack was curious, 'What happened; according to the report, you are wanted in connection with a man killed doon Ashington pit?'

'We had an argument and the bastard attacked me with a fishplate...'

Jack interrupted, 'What sort of fishplate?'

'One of the ones we use underground for bolting the tub rail-lines together, it's a piece of metal with holes in it.'

'So he attacked you with that, what did you do?'

Geordie lifted his head and starring with wide eyes at Jack, said, 'Aah took it off him and smashed his heed in with it!'

'Hardly self-defence, how big was this fella?'

Geordie looked away as if he did not want to be reminded of his brutal attack, 'He's aboot five-foot-five, but the bugga was kicking me with his pit boots.'

'So you took this fishplate from a small fella and bashed his head in with it, hardly self-defence is it. Why did you murder your father?'

'Noo that was an accident and self-defence - whey at forst it was anyway. He tried to stop me teking his money and I'd picked up his gun te tek with me, anyway, tha was some pushing and shoving and the gun went off and he was shot in the belly.'

Jack looked puzzled, 'If that's true, you could plead it was an accident?'

'Aah could hev but Aah was that mad, I shot him again – in the heed.'

Shaking his head, Jack said, 'It looks like you are going to hang lad. They'll come for you early in the morning and put a black bag over yor big, ugly head, take you into a bare room, onto a platform with a drop-hatch. Then they'll put a noose of rough, hemp rope around your neck and let you drop through the hatch, choking the life slowly out of you as you wriggle and dance like a fish on a hook.'

Leaning into the leather straps, Geordie began to slowly rock, his head nodding in rhythm as he lost himself in self-pity and silence.

Earlier, Rosalind helped Jake off with his boots and helped him lie down on the sofa, covering him with a blanket that Maggie fetched from upstairs. The two of them sat talking for a while as Rosalind attempted to take Jake's mind off his wound. Not wanting to appear 'soft', he put on a brave face but she could tell he was in a lot of pain and sat quietly in an armchair wondering what she could do to help as Jake fell into a fitful sleep.

He was still asleep when Rosalind joined her mother, Maggie, Davy, and Jack in the kitchen to listen to the one-o'clock news on Maggie's, Bush transistor radio. After the news, the four of them ate the soup that Maggie made from lentils and bacon bits discussing the news before Rosalind went back to sit with Jake, fetching him soup when he woke up at one-thirty.

After he ate most of the soup, Maggie gave him another codeine tablet, saying have this Jake and try to go back to sleep, I can't give you any more for five or six hours. He was asleep again in minutes.

Ian finished his soup and said to Maggie, 'I'll take my ammunition boots off so I'm not clumping around your house, I'm sorry for the noise they make.'

Maggie smiled at him, saying, 'Make yourself comfortable lad, we got a canny few hours to go before anybody gets through to us and ye look as if ye could de with a rest.'

In the scullery, the events of the past nine-hours, the lack of sleep and panic-stricken fear had taken their toll on

Geordie's mind.   Almost imperceptibly, he lifted his head, just enough to allow him to stare up through his eyebrows at Jack, a twisted grin on his face.

Evil intent shining from his eyes, he directed his demonic look at Jack, unnerving him.   He had felt no fear of the murderer until now but looking into his eyes, he thought, 'He looks insane, God knows what he would do if he broke loose.'

Geordie was on the edge of madness; only the occasional blink, the rise and fall of his chest and the fire of hate burning in his eyes showed that there was life in the motionless murderer as he plotted in malevolent silence.

CHAPTER 20

Friday 8th February – 4 pm
Ashington

The organized chaos in Ashington Police Station had subsided, After giving a statement to Sergeant Malcolm; Ronnie left the station and found Edward sitting in his van waiting to give him a lift home.

Edward waited until Ronnie made himself comfortable before asking, 'How did it go?'

Wiping melting snow from his face, he replied, 'Okay, Sergeant Malcolm is coming round to take a statement from my Dad tomorrow and speak to Billy and Roger. He reckons Edna will be facing a few charges - depending on what my Dad wants to push but knowing him, he'll probably not complain, especially when I tell him she's in hospital after having the shit kicked out of her.'

As the inside of the cab began to steam up from the dampness carried in by Ronnie, Edward wiped the inside of the windscreen with a chamois-leather saying, 'I divvint want to add to your worries but Inspector Norman told me that Jake and Ian are missing on the A68 past Redesdale Camp. They think they may have taken shelter in a farm but the telephone lines are down and the road is blocked so they can't confirm that.'

'Bugga, I hope they are alright,' said Ronnie.'

'That's not the worst of it; they think Geordie Robertson might be along there somewhere. You might remember that Ian and him had a helluva fight at school and your Jake had a couple of bits of bother with him as well.'

Ronnie straightened up; this isn't good is it, I'm ganning up there to see what's happening.'

'Jane and I will be going there as soon as we hear the road is open; you can come with us if you want?'

'Yes thanks that will be great, I'm going to have to think of a way of telling Dad without worrying him.'

Edward smiled, 'Good luck with that,' and drove carefully off.

DC Cotton had spent an hour taken a statement from a tearful Yvonne, stopping twice to make coffee for her. She opened up, not holding anything back, telling Cotton of how her mother had become indebted to Harry Weedon through under the table betting at the new Bingo hall in the converted Pavilion Cinema. Afraid to tell her husband Bill, she continued to try to gamble her way out of debt, ending up owing over a hundred pounds that increased weekly when she was unable to pay.

Knowing she had an attractive daughter, Harry Weedon, as in other loans, handed it over to Stuart to deal with.

Terrified at how Bill would react if he found out, Mrs Carter asked Yvonne for help, initially using her pocket money from her job at the Welwyn electric components factory. However, as the debt continued to increase, Yvonne agreed to Stuart Weedon's demands to meet him socially.

After plying her with drinks in the Grand Hotel, he raped her in the old stable block at the rear of the hotel and warned her if she told anyone, he would tell her father of her mother's debt; and, that she did not just give herself willingly to Weedon but that she was also taking money from him. He also warned her that he expected regular sex with her, or Bill Robertson would pay her mother a visit.

Within six weeks, all self-esteem lost and close to suicide after a back-street abortion, and thrown out of her home by her father, she went to work for Stuart Weedon.

Emotionally drained and physically exhausted, at the end of the interview, she sat, head bowed with tears running down her face. The dapper DC Cotton had found it increasingly difficult to hide his sympathy for her and his growing loathing of the Weedons. After making her another coffee, he left her in the small, dingy room for a few minutes to compose herself and stepped into the hall where her father, Bill Carter, was sitting in a chair, waiting to give a statement on his discovery of Weedon's body.

Cotton stopped next to him, staring at him, struggling to hide his contempt.

Carter looked up at him, asking, 'Anything the matter?'

'Anything the matter – yes there is something the matter, you are not much of a man are you?'

Carter stood up, gritting his teeth and clenching his fists, demanding, 'Waat de ye mean by that.'

Struggling to control his anger, Cotton hissed, 'I cannit tell you what your daughter has said but I suggest you tek her home and talk this all through with her and yer wife,' and turning, walked back into the interview room.

Yvonne looked up when he entered and asked, 'Is that it?'

Cotton, sighed, releasing his anger, trying to be formal, 'Yes that's it, thank you for your statement Miss Carter and thanks for coming in, can I arrange a lift for you?'

She shook her head, I'm not sure where to, I can try my aunty at Newbiggin.'

'If you want to wait outside, I'll arrange that, then I have to take a statement from your Father who is waiting outside the door.'

Yvonne followed DC Cotton outside, trying to avoid her father but he stepped forward and grabbed her arm, 'Listen, Pet, wait for me and I'll take you home and we can sort things out with your mother.'

She gripped his hand and pulling it from her arm, said, 'It's too late for that, 'I'm ganning te my Aunty Wendy's at Newbiggin,' and stepping around him, sat on one of the chairs as DC Cotton ushered him into the interview room.

Cotton came back out and strode off down the hall to the main office, returning a few minutes later to say to Yvonne, 'A uniformed officer will come and collect you shortly and take you across to Newbiggin. If there's anything I can do to help just give me a call,' handing her a piece of paper with the telephone number of his Morpeth desk.

Taking the slip of paper, she thanked him and he walked back into the interview room, closing the door behind him.

Cigarette smoke hung heavily in the air of the main interview room where DI Norman was enjoying playing 'Good Cop' to DS Dodson's 'Bad Cop,' the two of them wearing Stuart Weedon down with nonstop questions, some sounding like innocent comments while others were direct accusations. The relentlessness of the questioning and, the tearing apart of his answers slowly backed him into a corner that he was unable to get out.

By four o'clock, the day's events and the expert questioning resulted in him admitting to the savage attack on Edna and threatening Ronnie Grundy with a knife. Faced with the evidence contained in the file from the betting office, he also admitted to running three flats for prostitution, aiding his father in his loan shark business and his involvement in a protection fraud operating in Ashington and Blyth.

It took another hour before DS Dodson finished writing out Weedon's statement. After he signed it, Dodson handed him a cigarette and said, 'There'll be a canny few folk in Ashington and Blyth a lot happier in the next few days when they larn that they no langer owe ye and yer fatha any money, your canny little life is ower lad.'

'That's enough Sergeant,' said DI Norman, who had been sitting quietly watching and listening and now found it difficult not to smile at his DS's comment. Standing he said, 'Leave him there for a minute,' and he walked out into the hall followed by Dodson who closed the door behind them.

The DI smiled at Dodson, 'Well done, you can read out the charges against him and have him locked up for the night. We need to get back to the hunt for Robertson, that interview has not provided us with any idea of a motive that he might have had for killing Harold Weedon, I am beginning to think it was just a result of some sort of argument.'

Dodson took a long drag from his cigarette, sucking it into his lungs before saying, 'Aye, whey there are aall nasty bastards, so it wouldn't surprise me,' and tipping his head back, he blew smoke up to the ceiling.

DC Cotton walked down the corridor and asked, 'How did it go, sir?'

Wafting away cigarette smoke, the DI replied, 'Och, it couldn'a have gone better, he's confessed to everything but stealing the crown jewels.'

Cotton straightened his already straight tie and said, 'Well we need to question him about the rape of Yvonne Carter, sir.'

Norman frowned, 'I see, we'll wait until we visit his other two flats and bring the girls in for questioning, there may be more than one rape charge, I'm thinking. Right now though we need to find out how the search for Robertson is progressing.'

Cotton cleared his throat and said, 'I've just checked, with Morpeth and Hexham, sir, no news at the moment, the blizzard is the problem. Hexham have said that they are hoping that the A68 to Otterburn will be open in a few hours and Morpeth reckon the A696 should be clear by morning.'

Dodson shook his head, 'Who are they kidding, the bliddy blizzard doesn't look like it's iva ganning te end.'

In the Third Row, Ronnie Grundy found his father tidying away the last of the mess Edna had created earlier in the day. He took him into the kitchen leaving Billy and Roger lying under blankets on the sofa in the sitting room reading old comics.

He told him what happened at the flat; of him finding Stuart Weedon beating Edna and threatening him with a knife, Albert smiling when Ronnie told him of the punch he threw that knocked Weedon down.

Taking a deep breath, Ronnie said, 'Anyway, Edna Bliddy North is in hospital, Weedon is locked up, the police have your bankbook, and – Jake and Ian are stuck in the blizzard somewhere past Redesdale camp but they are most likely holed up in some nice farm with the farmer's daughter.'

Albert listened unemotionally until Ronnie mentioned the problem with Ian and Jake, and standing up said, 'Waat?'

On the drive back from the police station, Ronnie had decided not to tell his father that Robertson may be in the area where Jake and Ian were missing and now, he was glad he hadn't.

'I'm driving up to Redesdale with Edward and Jane as soon as the road is open; you are going to have to stay here with the two lads if that is okay.'

Albert nodded, 'Aye, that's probably best.'

Before Ronnie could say anymore, the front door swung open, the blizzard blowing Big Jen into the hall where she swung the door behind her, leaning her back into it and slamming it shut. Puffing and panting, she stepped into the kitchen and leant forward to recover her breath, looking like a Sumo Wrestler about to charge.

Standing up, she eased her back and dusted the snow off the cardigan she had pulled on, her only concession to the blizzard as she shook slush of her tartan slippers.

Albert and Ronnie watched in awe as she brought her forearms up in front of her, moving them from side to side, adjusting the huge bra that struggled to contain her more than voluptuous breasts.

Smoothing back her lacquered hair that the blizzard had transformed into a sodden, sticky mess, her chubby cheeks glowing a fetching red, she said in her high-pitched, excited voice, 'Ye buggas aah hell, it's wild oot there - noo then waat on earth is happening? Edward Thompson called in this morning and telt me that frosty fyeced harlot has buggared off we your bairns?'

Albert smiled and opened the door to the sitting room, said, 'Tha in there, look, snug as two bugs in a rug.'

Jen looked in and turning pulled out a chair from the kitchen table, plonking her large backside down, the chair groaning in protest.

Leaning her mighty forearms on the table, she ordered, 'Right Albert lad, tell me what the buggary has been ganning on. Ronnie son, Aah'll hev a cup of tea and a biscuit – or two, and before ye start Albert, divin't worry aboot dinna tonight, Aah've got a couple of pans of mince and dumplings on for my tribe, tha's plenty for ye lot as weell, noo come on tell me whaat's happening.'

CHAPTER 21

Friday 8th February – 6:pm
Treshinish House

Rosalind took Jakes hands in hers, taking the strain as he eased himself up from the sofa, being careful not to stretch his side.

Once he was upright and balanced, she took his right arm and placed it around her shoulder saying, 'Put your weight on me and take it nice and easy,' as she moved past the sofa, helping him to the kitchen where Maggie and Sarah, had set the table for dinner.

Feeling the wound move, Jake gave a low grunt, his arm tightening around Rosalind's shoulder. Although the pain he felt was sharp, it was not debilitating but he was not going to let her know that, he was enjoying her ministrations far too much. Walking with his arm around her felt good and he was not going to hurry.

The smell of cheese baking on top of a large shepherd's pie in the Aga masked the not so pleasant aroma of freshly boiled Brussel sprouts and carrots but combined, they provided a welcoming, nasal-delight that brought an air of normality to the house.

Ian, who had been sitting at the table with his new shadow, Davy, pulled out a chair for Jake, asking, 'How ye feeling?'

His arm still tightly around Rosalind, he feigned a pathetic smile and replied, 'Not too bad, just a wee bit sore but hev ye seen your face, it looks as if you've just done ten rounds with Henry Cooper.'

Ian nodded, 'And that's just how I feel.'

Waiting to take the pie out of the oven, Maggie, with a knowing smile on her face looked at Sarah and, raising her eyes, dipped her head, pointing toward Jake and Rosalind; Sarah smiled back before emptying the water from the cooked sprouts.

Maggie, waited until Jake and Sarah sat down before lifting the pie onto the table, then slowly looked around before saying, 'Welcome to my dinner table, am sorry that it has to be at such an awful time, thanks to that wicked lad next door and the storm. Anyway, I do always try to look on the bright side of things, ye de when ye live out here, so the two have brought us all together and I do hope it's not the last we will see of each other when this nastiness is over.'

Sitting in the scullery with Jess at his feet, Jack sniffed in the aromas from the kitchen, looking forward to Ian relieving him so he could enjoy his share of his Mam's home cooking.

Earlier, Jack watched as Geordie Robertson, with evil in his eyes, glared at him until fatigue once again conquered him, his chin dropping onto his chest as he fell into a deep, troubled sleep.

Fifteen minutes later, Ian and Davy took over guard duty from Jack who stood up, handed the shotgun to Ian, and stretched saying, 'He's been asleep for well over an hour, I'll bring him some food after I've eaten.'

With Jess following, he walked out into the rear passage, into the hall, stopping at the kitchen door for a second to clear his mind as Maggie pointed to a chair opposite Sarah, and said, 'Come and sit doon Bonny Lad, yer dinner's ready for ye.'

Sitting down, he gave Sarah a self-conscious smile and turned to Jake, saying, 'You're looking better, Jake.'

Jake did feel a lot better, he was over the shock he felt earlier after Robertson shot him, the pain was manageable and Maggie's homely but delicious shepherd's pie, lifted his spirit, 'I feel a lot better thanks, Mr Gray,' he replied.

Realising she was staring at Jack, Sarah dropped her head for a moment to collect her thoughts before raising it, asking, 'How is that monster in the scullery?'

Jack raised his head; looking into her deep, hazel eyes, the compassion, and tenderness he saw took him by surprise. During the fast-moving events of the day, he had subconsciously noted that she was an attractive woman but now he could see she was more than just attractive. She had an aura of self-confidence without brashness, a classic red-haired beauty, she reminded him of the proud but demure Maureen O'Hara in 'The Quiet Man.'

Feeling awkward, he automatically lowered his head slightly to the left, turning his scars away from her, and replied, 'He's asleep; he looked as though he was completely mad before he nodded off.'

Maggie leant back in her chair and said, 'He has to be mad, the things he has done today, no sane person would do. I'll be glad when this blizzard is over and we can get rid of him, I felt normal for a wee while there, now the thought of him sitting in my scullery makes my flesh crawl.'

Enjoying his dinner, Jack, asked Sarah why she was travelling to Scotland and Jack listened in respectful silence as she told him of the loss of her husband and her still uncertain, vague plans for the future.

Finished eating, he placed his knife and fork on his plate and looking into Sarah's eyes said, 'You're going through a hard time and being caught in this blizzard with a madman in the house can't be helping – if there's anything...'

Sarah replied, 'Thanks Jack, you, and Maggie have both been fantastic, we would not have survived without you.'

Embarrassed, he replied, 'It was young Jake and Ian that rescued you from the storm,' and turning to his mother said, 'I'll take that bowl of shepherd's pie in to feed that bast... er bugga and a glass of water.'

When Jack carried the food into the scullery, he found Ian and Davy in deep, whispered conversation. Davy had told Ian of his passion for football and listened spellbound as Ian enthralled him with tales of his older brother Mike who also lived for football, currently playing for the Colliers.

Geordie Robertson knew he was standing outside the cage at the top of the shaft, what he did not know was why his hands were tied behind his back and why his arms were fastened to his side by a huge leather strap or why he had shackles on his feet.

He saw and heard the cage door open just before someone standing behind him pulled a black hood over his head, stealing his visual awareness. Hands gripped his arms from behind, nudging him forward into the dangling cage, feeling it move under his weight as the smells of the pit seeped through the hood.

He tried to ask - to scream, 'What are you doing to me,' but he found himself unable to speak. Trembling with fear again, his knees buckled as unseen figures gripped his arms stopping him from falling when he felt someone place a heavy rope noose around his neck.

Hearing a monotonous voice chanting prayers in the background, he screamed in silence, knowing what was to come. The cage floor swung open and he plunged downwards, waiting for the inevitable jolt when the rope jerked tight, snapping his neck and choking the life out of him but he just kept falling and falling plummeting down the never-ending shaft...

The rope tightened and he awoke screaming at a startled Jack, who, having just shaken him, stepped back and waited until he came to his senses.

'Another bad dream Robertson, hopefully, you'll have one every time ye close your eyes. I have food and a glass of water here for you and this time divin't mek a pig of yourself and I'll try and get as much of it as I can down your gob.'

Robertson shook his head, coughed, and opened his mouth like a fledgeling starling waiting for a worm.

Ian and Davy watched open-mouthed as Jack spooned food into him as though he was a monstrous baby. Davy, unable to hide his surprise and amusement, sniggered loudly, the snigger changing into a nervous, belly chuckle when Jack held the glass of water to Geordie's mouth and he guzzled the water from the glass, splashing more of it than a thirsty dog.

Past caring, Geordie forgot his plight for a minute or two while he quenched both his hunger and his thirst.

Jack stepped back; looking down at him with disgust, mince, and mash smeared across his chin and under his nostrils, 'Wipe my face,' demanded Geordie.

Shaking his head, Jack turned away, saying to Ian, 'I'll take over again until nine-o'clock, then you can do nine to eleven and I'll do the rest of the night until early morning, okay?'

'Yes, okay but I'll relieve you at three, so you can get some kip as well.'

Jack nodded and taking the gun off Ian, after he got up and walked out with Davy, sat down on the chair as Jess slunk in and settled at his feet.

Robertson listened to the exchange of timings and having earlier looked down the passage into the hall and seen his revolver lying on the hall table, lowered his head, and began, once again to plot.

While Maggie and Sarah chatted as they washed the dinner plates and pans, Ian and Davy walked into the parlour where Jake had taken up his previous position on the sofa, and

Rosalind was trying to tune in Radio Luxemburg on the radiogram.

Unable to capture the pop channel, Rosalind gave up and the four of them sat chatting until they were joined a few minutes later by the two women, Maggie opening the stove and throwing a couple of logs into the already roaring fire.

At five to nine, Ian, accompanied by Davy, relieved Jack who handed over the gun once again, saying, 'He's asleep, see you at eleven,' and walked off to the parlour.' Robertson was far from asleep.

Maggie was busy allocating beds to bodies, 'Sarah and Rosalind will have the front, spare-bedroom with the double bed, Ian and Davy can have the two-single beds in the back bedroom, and Jake can bide where he is, I'll just gan up and mek sure they're all ready.'

Sarah went with her as Jack sat down in an armchair by the stove.

Just after ten, Sarah and Rosalind went off to bed leaving both Jack and Maggie, asleep in the chairs by the stove.

In the scullery, Ian was teaching Davy how to play patience when Robertson sat upright, startling both lads, 'A piss, I need a piss, noo,' he demanded.

Ian collected the playing cards and pushed them in his pocket, saying to Davy, 'Go and ask Jack to come in.'

Robertson spat, 'Waat de ye need him for. Aah just need a piss, am not ganna try owt, I'm too knackered, and anyway, ye have that frigging shotgun.'

Ian did not answer, waiting for Jack but Davy returned and said, 'He's fast asleep in there, they all are.'

Geordie looked desperate, rocking back and forth, he said, 'Howway man Ian, am not ganna de owt, Aah just need a piss, Aah hevn't had one since Aah came in here.'

After a minutes thought, while Geordie kept on pleading, Ian said, 'Alright, but I will blow your bliddy head off if you try anything.' He stood up a few feet from Robertson and pointing the gun at his head, said, 'Davy untie the rope from around his feet,'

Nervous and just a little afraid, Davy knelt at the side of Geordie's chair and untied the rope around his left ankle before moving around to the other side and untying his right ankle.

'Good lad, now go around the back and unfasten the two buckles holding the straps around his arms.'

Davy struggled to release the tension on the straps but eventually managed when Robertson pulled his arms in. Unwinding the straps, he hung them on the back of the chair as Geordie stood up to stretch, towering above the eleven-year-old.

Easing his shoulders, he stepped forward until Ian stopped him, 'Wait, and listen carefully, when I tell you, follow me out of the scullery and into the passage, then you back-up along the passage, the toilet is the next door along on your left as ye back-up, Davy come behind me lad.'

Robertson nodded, slowly following the muzzles of the shotgun pointed at his face as Ian inched back through the door. Once into the passage, Ian said, 'Move backwards, slowly.'

Obeying, Robertson inched backwards, down the dimly lit passage until he was level with the open toilet door and turned around pushing his still strapped hands toward Ian.

'What?' asked Ian.

'Whey man Aah cannit hev a slash we me hands tied behind me back, unless the kid is ganning te tek it oot and howld it for me?'

Davy shuddered and said, 'Am not deeing that.'

Ian hesitated as Geordie said, 'Howway man, am ganna piss mesell in a minute.'

Ian warned, 'Don't try owt or yer dead,' and without taking his eyes off Geordie, said, Davy, unfasten the strap around his wrists, and step behind me again.'

A little hesitant, the reluctant Davy did as ordered, hurrying back behind Ian with the strap in his hand as Geordie rubbed his wrists before stepping into the toilet, fumbling with the zip of his jeans.

Ian stepped forward, standing in the narrow passage with the shotgun still pointed at Geordie's head as the big lad emptied his bladder noisily into the toilet bowl.

Finished, he tucked himself away, and said, 'That's better,' and began to turn.

Ian stopped him, 'Don't turn around; put your hands behind your back and move slowly back out.'

Geordie made a show of moving his hands behind his back and slowly shuffled backwards as Ian backed down the passageway, the barrels of the shotgun still pointing at Geordie's head.

As he took the last step out of the toilet, Geordie, ducked to his left, toward Ian and at the same time swung his left arm up knocking the barrels in the air as Ian pressed both triggers. The noise from the blast of both barrels was deafening as Geordie swung his right fist, with all of his force into the side of Ian's head knocking him onto his back, unconscious.

Davy who was still stunned by the blast, stood motionless as Geordie strode forward wrapping his left arm around the lad, lifting him off his feet as he hurried into the hall; snatching his revolver from the table just as Jack stepped through the parlour door.

Geordie pushed the revolver into the cheek of the petrified lad, growling at Jack, 'Fucking move and Aah'll blow this little bastard's heed off.'

Jack leant forward as if to spring but a scream of 'No Jack,' from Sarah who was standing on the half-landing of the stairs, stopped him.

With Davy pulled tightly to his chest, the revolver pushed hard into the lad's face, Geordie moved toward the inner hall door keeping his back against the wall opposite Jack.

'Open the door,' he said to Davy, who despite his fear and trembling, grasped the handle and opened the door, swinging it inwards.

Robertson backed into the vestibule as Jack inched forward and standing to the side of the door, ordered, 'Right ye little prick open the front door.'

Davy reached over and twisted the large cast iron handle, releasing the door, the blizzard smashing it open and blasting snow into the hall as Jack lunged forward.

Geordie hurled Davy at Jack who caught him, falling backwards from the momentum of the throw and the wind as Geordie disappeared into the blizzard – again.

Sarah screamed when the front door swung violently open and rushing downstairs grabbed her boy from Jack as he struggled to stand up. On his feet, he forced the door shut against the storm and slid home the top and bottom bolts.

'That's it, that bugga can freeze to death oot there,' he said as he turned around and stepped into the hall to close and lock the vestibule door.

Jake was standing in the parlour doorway with a bewildered look on his face as Maggie wrapped her arm around Sarah who was holding Davy close to her and led them into the parlour with Rosalind following.

Davy wriggled in his mother's arms, saying, 'Let me go, Mam, I've got te help, Ian, that man knocked him oot.'

Ian staggered into the hall from the rear passage and leant against the wall, still dazed, all he could say was, 'Sorry, I buggared it up,' and dropped to his knees as Davy hurried into the hall.

Jack rushed over, helping Ian to his feet, steadying him before asking, 'What did he do to you; you haven't been shot have you?'

Ian took a deep breath, moved his head around in a small circle, and touched the side of his head with his left hand, 'No he punched me in the side of the head, I didn't think he would try...'

Jack stopped him, 'Ye can tell me what happened later, ye need to sit down first and recover,' and then raised his voice, 'Mam come and give me a hand with Ian.'

Maggie hurried through to take hold of Ian's arm saying, 'Eee, not again, you poor thing, come on and sit doon by the fire and tell me what he's done to you.' Davy followed close behind worrying that his newfound hero was badly hurt.

After helping his mother sit Ian down in an armchair by the fire, Jack hurried to the scullery, picking up the shotgun; he took two cartridges from his trouser pocket and loaded them, leaving the shotgun open. After checking the locks and bolts on the rear door were secure, he closed and bolted the internal wooden shutters in the back-parlour and dining room before returning to the front parlour.

Jake, Rosalind and Sarah were sitting on the sofa while Davy stood next to Ian, breathlessly telling Maggie what had happened,' 'We took him te the toilet and when he came out, he ducked under the gun and knocked it up when Ian tried to shoot him and he punched Ian and knocked him doon, then he grabbed me and got his revolver from the table and shoved it in my face – here,' pointing to a red mark on his cheek,

Believing that Ian would have done his best to keep Robertson under control, Jack said nothing about his escape, instead, he concentrated on making sure they all remained safe through the night.

Standing behind the sofa he said, 'I have no idea what that bugga is going te de or where he's going, he knows he cannit use any of the trucks. He could get inte one of the barns to shelter for the night or he could even try te gan back up te Tom's place but Tom and Ruby have both got shotguns and I think they can look after themselves, it's just a pity Young Tom is not home.' He paused for a second or two before continuing, 'I am not going out to look for him while it is dark, I'll wait until it gets light in the morning, then I'll search the barns and outhouses around the back for him. If he's not here, I will walk down the road to Byrness and see if the telephones are working.'

Worry, furrowed Maggie's brow as she asked, 'What are we ganning te de tonight, son?'

'Whey I think you and Sarah, Rosalind and young Davy should go to bed, I'll stay down here with Ian and Jake to keep guard if they are up to it.'

Ian answered first, 'I'll be okay Mr Gray; I must have a thick head because I don't think he's broken anything.'

Jack smiled acknowledgement as Jake said, 'I've had a good kip teday and I can use a shotgun, so, I'll help.'

Looking at Davy sitting on the arm of Ian's chair, Sarah said, 'I don't think I can sleep, I would like to stay down here if that's okay?'

Rosalind hugged her mother's arm, 'I'm staying down here with you Mam.'

Standing up Maggie, adjusted her cardigan, and said, 'Reet, that's it then, we'll all hole up in here for the night and bugga that waster oot there, 'Aah'll put the kettle on.'

CHAPTER 22

Friday 8th February – 8 pm
To
Saturday 9th February – 5 am
Morpeth Redesdale Ashington

In his small, eight-foot by ten office at Morpeth, DI Jamie Norman, leant back in his chair, hands behind his head; he looked up at the ceiling through the heavy layer of cigarette smoke that DS Dodson had created during the past hour.

Puffing out another lungful of smoke to add to the fog above their heads, Dodson, who was sitting on a chair on the opposite side of the desk to his DI, failed to stifle a yawn and said, 'It's been a long day, sir.'

Jamie sat forward, leaning on the desk, 'That it has; a long and interesting day, now please, open the door before you suffocate the pair of us.'

Dodson stood up, stretched, and scratched his groin before reaching over to pull the door open, allowing a breath of fresher air to waft in, stirring the smoke to little effect.

Returning to the chair, Dodson asked, what else can we do tonight?'

Looking at the snow-plastered window that, acted as a mirror due to the blackness of the night, Jamie replied, 'I have to go and brief the DCI at half-eight, so let's just take stock. Dealing with the murders first; we've completed a timeline of events that clearly links Robertson to the murder of Harold Weedon. He is the only suspect and I'm sure his fingerprints when we catch him, will match with the ones on the murder weapon. We have an eye witness to his murder of his father and hopefully, he will have the revolver on him when he is caught, it is just a matter of finding him but we still need a motive for the first murder.'

Dodson lit another cigarette and took a deep drag saying, 'Well HQ at Newcastle are pretty sure that he has not gone sooth, wor best bet is that he is up on the A68, stuck in his car.'

Nodding, Jamie continued, 'Aye, that's where I think he'll be but we have to wait until the ploughs clear the road before that can be confirmed Although, I am considering asking for armed officers to walk the route, and we have the search and rescue helicopter from RAF Acklington flying to the area as soon weather and daylight permits.'

'It'll be tough for any of wor lads to walk through that, could we not get the army to help?'

'Aye, the Chief is asking the Home Office to arrange military support but we can't action that until it is confirmed he is in the area. As soon as we get word that the roads are open we will drive up,' so make sure you and Cotton are ready to go at a moment's notice.'

Flicking ash from his cigarette onto the overflowing ashtray, Dodson, moaned, 'Aye, reet ye are sir, I'll phone the missus and tell her not to expect me hyem tonight.'

Jamie stood up and stretched his long frame, loosened his tartan tie that was already askew and said, 'Right that's the outline for the hunt for George Robertson, now back to what this has uncovered in Ashington; the Weedon's activities.'

'DS Cotton and uniform from Ashington are searching his house now but I think the files that Yvonne Carter handed you have all the info we need to get warrants and carry out searches on the two Blyth and the one Ashington flat.' 'DC Routledge at Ashington is going to be dealing with the loan scam they were running and uniform are looking into the disappearance of Mrs Weedon, we'll pick up on that, once we have Robertson behind bars.'

Dodson stood up, 'That's about the size of it for noo, eh, sir; do you want a coffee.'

'Och aye, strong and black, four sugars.'

Just after four-am, standing by the window of the office he shared with four other detectives, including DS Dodson in Morpeth Police Station, DC Cotton peered out for a few seconds before using his hand to wipe the condensation and looked out again.

After a minute, he said to no one in particular, 'I think the wind is dropping and I'm sure I can see the park gates over the road, the snow must be easing as well.'

Half-asleep in his chair, DS Dodson sat up and reached for his cigarettes, asking, 'Waat did ye say?'

'The blizzard, I think it's easing,' replied Cotton, rubbing the stubble on his normally baby smooth, and aftershave scented face.

On the A68 outside Redesdale Camp, PC John Carlisle was nodding as he sat in the front of his police car that was blocking the road, while PC Wilson took his break on a bed in one of the huts in the camp.

Carlisle sat up, the reduction in the buffeting of the car by the storm had stopped, and he could hear another noise other than the howling wind. Wiping the inside of the windscreen with the back of his gloved hand, he looked down the snowbound road and saw that it had stopped snowing but more importantly, he could see lights moving steadily toward him from Otterburn.

'Snowplough,' he said aloud, and looked at his watch, it two-minutes to five.

Climbing out of the car, He pulled on his helmet and was surprised to see clear patches of sky with thousands of stars sprinkled across the gaps - the blizzard had ended as quickly as it had begun.

Five minutes later, he reversed his car off the road to allow a large, AEC snowplough and, a tractor with an enclosed cab and front scoop, to advance north along the road. A police car from Hexham with four officers on board, two of them armed with .303, Lee Enfield rifles followed them as another police car pulled to a halt by PC Carlisle.

A lean, tired looking, uniformed inspector, climbed out the back, Carlisle recognized him, 'Good morning, sir, you look as if you've had a long day.'

38-year-old Inspector Peter Thornton stretched and stamped his feet before replying, 'Good morning to you John, I've been stuck in that sodding car since two-o'clock yesterday afternoon, following one snow plough or other, any coffee on the go.'

Carlisle smiled and answered, 'Follow the cleared part of the road up into the camp, sir. It will take you to the cookhouse; the army has a duty cook on. There's always a brew on the go and he'll cook you breakfast, what's happening.'

Starting to feel the cold, the inspector fastened his coat, 'We're convinced the murder suspect from Ashington is somewhere along this road. So I'm to liaise with the army and set up a control post with a telephone to start to coordinate the search as the ploughs advance up the valley, I'm expecting twenty or more officers here between eight and nine; if the roads remain clear.'

'Major Graham and the Camp Commandant have already allocated a room for us, sir, it's in the empty visiting units' office block, I can show you the way.'

'No, you stay here John, we cannot allow anyone up the road until the situation is under control, I'll find the office block after I've had a coffee,' and climbing back into the police car he directed the driver up the hill.

PC Carlisle waited, watching an open back truck with two men furiously shovelling grit over the tailboard drive slowly past. He waved at the driver before climbing into the police car, driving forward to block off the road, switching on the revolving light on the roof, the blue light illuminating the snow-covered landscape in a cake slice chunk as it spun around.

At a quarter-past five, DI Jamie Norman placed the telephone receiver back in its cradle and walked out of his office to find DS Dodson and DC Cotton waiting, 'We heard your telephone,' said Dodson.

Scratching his head, Jamie yawned, he had been asleep in his chair when the telephone had woken him.

'The road's clear to Redesdale, Inspector Thornton from Hexham is up there now setting up a control post in the camp and they have armed officers following snowploughs up the valley, we're off in five minutes, have you got flasks?

As efficient as ever, DC Cotton replied, 'Yes sir, and sandwiches.'

Jamie walked back into his office, and closing the door behind him, he rang Jane; she answered it after the second ring,' Hello, Jane Thompson.'

'Morning Jane,' Jamie said, 'The A696 and A68 to Redesdale are both open and the storm has passed, I'm on my way up there now, we are setting up a control post and will be flooding the area with police shortly but we still have no confirmed sighting of our suspect or his car.'

Standing in her darkened hall, Jane listened intently, before replying, 'Thanks Jamie, we will be leaving shortly, I will see you up there, bye.'

Putting the phone down she turned to see Edward standing in the doorway of the sitting room where they had both been dozing on the settee. Ronnie Grundy who had been asleep in an armchair by the fire walked up behind Edward, to listen to Jane.

'The roads clear, I think we should go now, I will tell you what Inspector Norman told me as we get ready, I'll just nip upstairs first and let Mike now we are off.'

Ronnie fastened his heavy reefer-jacket as Edward held up Jane's thick camel coat for her while she pulled on her knee-high, suede boots.

Ten minutes later, sitting at the wheel with the engine of her Morris Minor Traveller on fast tick over, she waited while Edward, wearing a heavy tweed overcoat and leather gloves, scraped the last of the snow from the windscreen and bonnet. When he finished and climbed into the car, Jane engaged gear, lifted her foot off the clutch slowly, and drove carefully out of the drive into the slush of the salt gritted road leading out of Ashington. Sitting in his red Wolseley, Ronnie followed on behind as they set off for Redesdale.

CHAPTER 23

Saturday 9th February – 5:15 am
Redesdale

The snowplough made steady progress for the first mile and a half as it opened a single lane, through the two-foot deep snow in the open area of the valley where the wind had blown it unhindered across open fields. A deep drift created by a clump of five or six trees forced the plough to reverse up and allow the driver in the cab of the tractor, to use the front bucket to scoop away the deepest part of the drift.

Progress through the forest was slower; more drifts had formed in the larger gaps, requiring either, two or three pushes by the snowplough or the use of the tractor to clear them.

Just before six o'clock, the small convoy passed the tiny church of St Francis, sitting in the darkness behind a large snowdrift, a quarter of a mile from Byrness.

In the front passenger seat of the following police car, burly, Sergeant Fraser Macintyre eased the army-webbing belt and revolver holster fastened round his waist and said, 'Are you two awake in the back?'

Staring out of the side window in the rear, tall and athletic, thirty-two-year-old, PC Tom Baxter, yawned before replying, 'Yes Sarge, and ready to go, is this the area he could be in?'

'It is, Tom, but we need to find his car to get an idea where he is, Inspector Thornton wants us to do a quick walk around Byrness when we reach it, to see if his car is there.'

Hunched up next to Baxter, the shorter, PC Ray Newton, asked, 'How bliddy big is Byrness, I divvin't fancy plodging roond all night in me wellies looking for a car?'

Sergeant Macintyre, growled, 'We'll do what we have to for as long as it takes, Newton, there are more officers on their way up. Anyway, Byrness is just a couple of streets of Forestry Commission houses, it shouldn't take long to see if his car is there and the blizzard has ended, it's clear out there.'

Ray leant forward and asked, 'Will we take our rifles with us then?'

Shaking his head in disbelief, Sergeant Macintyre, replied, 'Bliddy Newton – trust you to ask that; of course, ye will, yer not much good against an armed and dangerous murderer without it, are ye.'

The driver, PC Gary Armstrong, pointed through the windscreen, 'Look, Sarge, lights up ahead on the left; that must be Byrness.'

Curled up and shivering from the cold as he lay on the stone floor between two of the dark-oak pews of St Francis Church; Geordie Robertson stared up at the beautiful, stained glass window, depicting the construction of the nearby Catcleugh Reservoir and thought he must be dreaming again. Lights danced across the coloured glass, casting, red, blue and green shadows across the inside of the unlit church as moonlight streamed through the larger, plain-glass arched window behind the altar. He was able to see the inside of the church for the first time since entering through the unlocked wooden-door in the side-porch, several hours earlier.

Grabbing the pews on either side of him, he heaved himself up onto his cold and stiff legs, his eyes not leaving the light display on the stain-glassed window as he shuffled forward, beating his arms with his hands as he tried to warm himself up, it had been a long, cold and exhausting night.

Nine hours earlier, when he burst out of Treshinish House, plunging into the blizzard, his only thought was of escape and distancing himself from the scar-faced tough man, and his shotgun. Ploughing around the parked vehicles and across the courtyard, he was unable to see more than a few feet in front of him as the driving snow sought to blind him.

Stumbling into the snowdrift that separated the yard from the main road; he fell face first into it, almost dropping his revolver; panic driving him up onto his hands and knees as he crawled through and onto his feet on the other side.

Glancing over his shoulder and not seeing any pursuers; rather than fight his way through the blizzard back to Fenwick's Farm, he turned right and staggered through the snow, heading southeast down the A68 toward Redesdale, Otterburn and the South.

Relentlessly, the blizzard tried to force him off the road and, knock him off his feet. Aching thighs and bursting lungs slowed his pace as he hugged the north side of the road, trying to find some respite from the wind by keeping in the lee of the snow banks created by previous snow ploughing. Every fifty yards or so he stopped, bending over, hands on knees, resting, and checking to see how close any pursuers might be.

It took him almost an hour of strenuous effort to cover the mile and a half to where his abandoned car lay barely visible at the side of the road. Sweating from his struggle, he considered climbing in and resting but resisted the temptation. Still worried that Jack Gray was hunting him down again, he staggered on.

Continuing to stay close to the east side of the road and with the blizzard limiting his vision, he did not see the snow-covered turn off to Byrness or the snow-covered sign for it and pushed on, falling several more times as he became more and more exhausted. He failed to register that the forest had crept closer to the road for the next half mile, affording a little respite from the ferocious wind but he did not care, he was shattered from his adrenalin-fuelled struggle and panic and needed to find somewhere to rest, safe from the blizzard and pursuers.

Stumbling past the snow-blocked entrance to an unseen farm, hidden fifty-yard from the road on his left, the wind pushed him once again over to the right- hand side of the road where he fell into a bank of soft snow that hid a small road junction. Crawling through the bank of snow, he picked himself up and saw the dark shape of a building some twenty yards off the road.

Turning to look to see if anyone had followed him, he shielded his eyes and looked back up the road but could only see a few feet into the blizzard blowing directly into his face. He turned back and with the wind, pushing him on, he shuffled toward the building stopping to climb over a small wicket gate blocked by snow, and up to a wooden door with snow banked three feet high against it.

Expecting to find the door locked, he grabbed the large, round, cast-iron handle, and twisted it. To his amazement and relief, it opened leaving the snow still standing. He pushed through and into the small porch of what he now believed to be a church and closed the heavy door behind him, shutting out the blizzard.

Groping his way inside, he bumped into a stone font and turned to his left, through an archway into what seemed to be a larger room with pews down either side of the aisle. Walking slowly down the aisle, he stopped halfway; sitting on the pew to his left, he slid along to the end and dropped onto the floor, rolling under the narrow, oak bench to hide. Stretching out, he unbuttoned his greatcoat and layback, falling into a troubled sleep, stirring five hours later cold and hungry. That was when he saw the dancing lights on the stained glass window.

As he stared the angle of the lights, slowly moved to his right, away from the end of the church nearest the road and down to the end wall with the archway he had walked through the night before.

The realisation of what it was, hit him, 'Vehicles, there are vehicles on the road, that's their headlights, the road must be cleared.'

Hurrying back down the tiny church, he opened the door to look out on a clear, storm less morning, the sky awash with stars and a half moon reflecting off the snow-covered landscape, the odd wisp of cloud still scurrying westwards. A shooting star left a silvery trail across the sky as it hurtled earthwards, the whole scene reminiscent of a Christmas Card.

His attention was drawn to the taillights of three or four vehicles, fifty yards up the road. He could see that they were clearing the road and noted that the cleared road south was in darkness with no sign of any other vehicles. Thinking only of escape, he hurried out, over the wicket gate and onto the cleared road where he hesitated to look at his watch that showed a quarter past six. Checking that his revolver was in his pocket he strode off, south along the freezing, moonlit road, flanked by banks of snow.

'Stop here,' Sergeant Macintyre ordered when they pulled level with the turnoff to Byrness protected by a bank of snow left by the snowplough pushing on, twenty yards ahead.

'Gary, stay here with the car, come on you two,' as he climbed out of the car, pulling on his helmet and turning up the collar of his greatcoat as he surveyed the hamlet a hundred yards off the main road.

PC Baxter asked, is that it, Sarge?'

'Aye, that's it, not much is it, right, I'll head off to the left and swing back to the centre, you two take a street each and work your way towards me, remember we are looking for a blue, Vauxhall Cresta, okay?'

The two PC's acknowledged and the three of them walked toward the village just as the snowplough reached Geordie's car in the bank by the reservoir.

The drive south down the AI from Morpeth to the junction with the A696 had been trouble free for DC Cotton but the route north-west toward Otterburn was more difficult forcing him to drive below thirty miles an hour.

Slush, created by snowploughing and salt gritting made the road slippery, DI Norman saying, 'Dinna rush it Cotton laddie, we need te get there in one piece,' as a southbound snowplough passed them, spraying the car and windscreen with slush.

Driving down the steep Whorrall Bank terrified Jane but she hid her fear from Edward who commented, 'Well done,' when she reached the bottom without incident. They were about thirty minutes behind DI Norman and crew.

Driving into Morpeth, Jane asked, 'So we need to go south to the 696 rather than going straight across to Belford?'

'Yes Pet, the road to Belford won't be cleared and we know the 696, is open; is Ronnie still behind?'

Looking into her rear-view mirror, she replied, 'Yes he's still there.'

It took Sergeant Macintyre and the two constables just fifteen minutes to walk around Byrness, walk back to the car, and climb in.

PC Armstrong switched the headlights back on and asked, 'Any sign of the car, Sarge?'

'Not down there, there is no sign of life apart from lights in a couple of houses, he must have got further on, if he is in this valley and we are not on a wild goose-chase, come on catch up with the snowplough.'

As Armstrong drove off the sergeant radioed Inspector Thornton's driver sitting in his car outside the office they had taken over in Redesdale Camp, 'Tell Thornton there is no sign of the suspect's car in Byrness; over.'

The driver responding with, 'Roger, will do, Sarge; out.'

Slowing the car, PC Armstrong said, 'Look, Sarge, they've stopped for something and pulled up behind the gritting truck.

Sergeant Macintyre opened his door, 'Right you two, look sharpish, out you come, let's go and see what the problem is, and yes, Newton, bring your rifle.'

The three of them squeezed past the gritting truck and found the driver of the snowplough talking to the tractor driver, Macintyre asking, 'What's happened,'

Wrapped in a huge, scruffy sheepskin-lined flying jacket, the excited driver rushed up to the Sergeant shouting, 'I've found the car yer looking for, I'm not driving any further on my own when there's a murderer oot there somewhere.'

Placing a huge hand on the driver's shoulder, Macintyre said, 'Calm down, one of my officers will travel in the front with you, now pull forward so that we can take a look at the car and confirm it is the suspects.'

A few minutes later, having confirmed the make and registration of Geordie's car, and, thoroughly checked the inside, Macintyre radioed the news through to Redesdale, the information relayed by radio and telephone to Morpeth, Hexham, Newcastle, and Ashington – 'Murder suspect in Upper Redesdale.'

The smell of cooking bacon and freshly baked bread from the kitchen drifted through Treshinish House when Maggie lifted the large tray of cooked slices from the Aga's oven, placing it on top of the hotplate lid.

Several rounds of toast and, tea, throughout the night had used up her last two loaves of bread and rather than sitting worrying about Robertson breaking in or, trying to sleep, she had baked four more in the early hours of the morning.

Sarah and Rosalind were cutting and buttering the bread when Jack walked in saying, 'By, that bacon smells good, I'm going out to check the barns; Ian will stay by the front door while I'm out. What a difference it is out there; the sky is almost clear of clouds and the wind has dropped considerably but the temperature has dropped another few degrees since the snow stopped - I won't be long.'

Only Jake and young Davy had slept more than a couple of hours during the long night, Jack and Ian checking doors and windows regularly, while Maggie and Sarah kept everyone supplied with tea and toast. Most of the time was spent either nodding off for the odd half-hour in the parlour or sitting around the kitchen table discussing events of the day before and where Robertson might be.

It was just after twenty past six when Jack finished his search, walking back into the kitchen with Ian, whose eyes were red slits between blue and purple swollen bruises, and joined the others sitting around the table, quietly eating.

Maggie handed him a bacon sandwich as he sat wearily down, saying, 'It looks as if this bad dream is nearly over. I am sure I could hear engines in the distance, I'll eat this, then go out, and meet them, we need to let the police know that Robertson is in the area and what happened here and at the Fenwick's.'

'Blue lights ahead, sir,' said DC Cotton as they neared Redesdale Camp.

Jamie Norman, sat up, fighting his lack of sleep and the heat in the car.

Shaking his head and rubbing his eyes, he replied, 'Aye, so it is, that must be the entrance to the camp and I see the sun's coming up, it looks as if it is going to be a grand day.'

The sky to the east was flushed a rosy pink from the deeper red of the horizon as the sun climbed to show its face after the misery of the past twenty-four hours. The fields of snow to the left of the car that shone a reflected, pale-pink, was disturbed by the sweeping shafts of blue light from the warning light of the stationary police car up ahead.

In the back of the car, DS Dodson opened his pack of Capstan and took out the last cigarette muttering, 'Shite, me last fag, Aah hope they hev some for sale in this God-forsaken hole.'

Jamie shook his head, 'Trust you to say that, Sergeant, this is beautiful countryside, you should get up here more often.'

'Aah, cannit see the point in that, tha's bugga aall here is there.'

Jamie did not reply; winding his window down as Cotton slowed to a halt next to the tall figure of PC John Carlisle, standing in the middle of the road, waving them down.

Carlisle placed a gloved hand on the roof of the Austin, bending down to look at the occupants as Jamie said, 'Morning, DI Norman, and Team from Morpeth.'

Looking tired and wearing a thirty-hour stubble, the PC still managed a smile, 'Good morning sir, Inspector Thornton is expecting you, if you follow the cleared lane up into the camp you will see his police car parked beyond the civilian vehicles and trucks that have been stranded here. Have you heard that they have found your suspect's car?'

Jamie's eyes widened, 'No, when and where was it found?'

'About forty minutes ago, just past Byrness but there is still no sign of him.'

Thanking the PC, Jamie said, 'Right, things are looking up, drive on and let's find out what news Inspector Thornton has.'

Cotton drove the car up into the bleak camp, which reminded Jamie of the German prisoner of war camps he had seen in films. Driving past a row of cars and trucks parked in a line on a large square in front of the brightly lit cookhouse. Cotton pulled up next to Inspector Thornton's vehicle facing the end of a wooden hut with metal-framed windows on either side of a green painted door.

Pointing to figures behind the right-hand window, Jamie, said, 'There's Thornton, talking to that soldier.'

The three of them hurried along the cleared path, and into the long hut. Inside, cream painted walls shone under long fluorescent tubes, the room furnished with desks, chairs, and a brace of filing cabinets. A door in the partition wall near the far end led to a washroom, toilet, and rear door and a number of bulky electric heaters, strategically placed below windows, struggled to keep the temperature above freezing. A police officer wearing his greatcoat with the collar turned up sat at a desk blowing into his hands as he tried to write in an 'Incident Log Book'.

Inspector Thornton turned from the conversation he was having with the QM - Major Graham and smiled when he saw them, 'Aah Jamie, come on in, this is Major Trevor Graham, he is the Quartermaster of the regiment that was supposed to be moving in here today, it is two of his lads that are missing along the road.'

Jamie shook the outstretched hand of the QM, 'Morning, sir, Jamie Norman, I'm the lead detective on the Robertson investigation.'

Pleased that the DI had a firm handshake and steady eye, the QM replied, 'Pleased to meet you, Jamie, the names Trevor, anything I or my small team can do to assist, you just have to ask.'

Dodson interrupted, 'We could de with a brew and something te eat, am famished and hev ye any fags for sale.'

Jamie, gave his sergeant a withering look but the QM smiled and replied, 'You can get something to eat in the cookhouse at any time, my RQMS is having brew kit, an electric kettle and mugs brought over here for you. As for fags, there is a cigarette machine on the wall outside the cookhouse.'

Jamie nodded, glared at Dodson and said, 'Right, let's get down te business, can you brief us on what you have so far?'

Inspector Thornton led them to a board with an ordnance survey map of the area pinned to it, spending ten minutes briefing them on the situation based upon the information they had.

He ended by saying, 'As far as we know, Robertson is somewhere beyond Byrness, but how far and where, we currently do not know.'

Outside, a one-ton army truck with a small snowplough fitted to the front had arrived from Otterburn Camp and was just beginning to drive slowly back and forth across the square, pushing the two-foot deep snow to the sides.

Shuffling along the slushy road, Robertson was just leaving the shelter of the forest, two miles from the camp, intent on finding a vehicle he could take to aid his escape. He passed a farm but did not stop to look for a car when he saw the deep snow covering the road up to it, and shuffled on.

An insipid-blue was slowly replacing the red glow in the sky to the east as the sun cleared the horizon and began its journey westward, revealing the winter landscape of snow-covered fields rising to open moorland to the north, and the pine forest half a mile to the south at the other side of the meandering river Rede.

Hearing an engine somewhere behind him, he turned to see the headlights of a truck coming slowly down the road. Unsure who was in it he scrambled up the bank of snow on his left, tumbling down the other side, rolling into the cover of the bank.

He was unable to see the gritting truck as it drove past on its way back to Otterburn for a resupply of rock salt.

Concentrating on the road ahead the driver did not notice the gap in the snow made by Robertson nor did the two men in the back, sitting hunched up out of the wind behind the cab.

He waited until the sound of the truck faded into the distance before climbing back to the top of the bank, stopping to look down the road.

'Shit,' he said when he saw the flashing blue light in the distance but then he noticed the lights of the camp to the left of the road and wondered if he could take a car from there.

Resolved to steal a car, he climbed down the field side of the bank and trudged through, pristine snow, heading off at an angle that would bring him to the range road entrance on the northeast side of the camp.

Back at Treshinish, the snowplough had cleared the road past the farm and stopped while Jack briefed Sergeant Macintyre on the traumatic events of the past twenty-four hours.

Standing next to his car, Macintyre listened, struggling not to stare, as the sun shone on Jack's scarred face.

Squinting from the brightness of the sun shining on snow, Jack said, 'I'm worried that he may have gone back to the Fenwick's Farm. Even if he did not try to get into the house, there are plenty of barns and sheds for him to hide in and surprise Tom and Ruby if they come out.'

The sergeant nodded, 'What if he forced his way into their house?'

'If he did, I wouldn't rate his chances as Tom and Ruby both have shotguns and Tom for one was itching to use it on the lad after he killed their dog.'

Macintyre climbed back in his car and radioed the PC sitting in Inspector Thornton's car, giving him the gist of the information Jack had provided, telling him to pass it on to the Inspector.

Looking at PC Baxter, Macintyre, ordered, Get back into the snowplough and tell the driver to bash on to the next farm and be careful; there's a car stuck on the road a couple of hundred yards further on.'

Turning back to Jack he said, 'We need everyone here to be available for statements, that will be after we've hopefully caught the bugga.'

Jack nodded, 'I'm going to drive into Redesdale camp shortly and see if I can provide any help with recovery, the two young soldiers will follow behind me in their vehicle as they have to report in.'

Macintyre thanked Jack, adding, 'Okay, I will leave PC Newton here just in case Robertson is still hiding around here but watch out for him, he may not be up ahead. We could have missed him on our way here or he could be lying freezing in the snow somewhere.'

Crossing her arms to stand with a defiant look, Maggie, said, 'I hope the nasty bugga does come back, I'll give him both barrels up his bum.'

Macintyre smiled and climbing back into the police car, headed off to catch up with the snowplough and tractor.

In Redesdale, DI Norman, said, 'There it is, just past Catcleugh Reservoir,' placing his finger on Treshinish house on the map in the office.

Inspector Thornton traced the road along the map, 'About seven or eight miles. I would go with you but the bus from Hexham with reinforcements is due about now, I will have to wait here and brief them, Major Graham is providing a three-ton truck and driver to ferry them along the road. Are you going up the valley?

Jamie, replied, 'The three of us will head up the road and speak to the folk at Treshinish Farm and then go on to the other farm,' and headed for the door followed by his DS and DC.

CHAPTER 24

Saturday 9th February – 7 am
Redesdale

As Jane drove up to PC Carlisle standing in the road outside Redesdale Camp, the blades of the RAF Search and Rescue helicopter beat the clear morning air above as the bright yellow aircraft flew low overhead making its way up the valley for an initial sweep to ascertain conditions and, to look for stranded vehicles. The noise as it thundered down the valley lifting a flock of panicking Rooks, kawing and screeching, from the edge of Kielder forest.

After speaking to PC Carlisle, Jane drove carefully up the slight incline into the camp, with Ronnie following behind in his Riley. Pulling to a halt in front of the collection of vehicles parked in front of the cookhouse, she was climbing out when she saw the three Morpeth detectives, led by Jamie Norman coming out of a hut twenty yards in front.

What neither her nor Edward noticed was the running figure of Geordie Robertson, who had sneaked from behind a hut, and walked unseen behind the snow plough until he was halfway across the square where he broke cover, running up behind them with his revolver in hand.

The snow muffled his footsteps but DS Dodson saw him, yelling, 'Look out, behind yer,' and started running toward them, flat-footed but surprisingly fast for a fat man.

Having left the engine of his car running to keep the interior warm, Ronnie was halfway out when he saw DS Dodson running towards him, unaware of Geordie running up behind. He did not stand a chance, one foot in the car and the other out, Geordie smashed the heavy revolver into the side of his unprotected head before grabbing him with his left hand and throwing him like a used rag into the snow.

Seeing DS Dodson charging toward him and determined to escape, fear and panic once again blinding his judgement, Robertson lifted the revolver, pointing it at the fast approaching detective, yelling, 'Fuck off ora'll shoot ye.'

DI Norman watched in horror, fearing the inevitable, as his sergeant appeared unable to stop his, impetuous rush. Robertson fired a single shot, hitting the big man high in the chest. At such close range, the point-thirty-eight calibre bullet hit him like a sledgehammer, bringing him down as his momentum carried him forward, crashing him to the ground next to Jane who had wisely, crouched next to her car when she saw Geordie with his revolver.

When Dodson slid to a halt next to her, Jane instinctively threw herself over him, protecting him from the killer.

However, she need not have worried; he had other things on his mind and climbing into Ronnie's car, he put it into gear, released the handbrake, and turning the wheel hard to the left, accelerated away.

Edward rushed forward to stop him but had to jump clear when Robertson unintentionally swung the rear of the car out, missing him by a few inches.

Wheels spinning, causing the rear end to fishtail, Robertson headed down to the main road hoping to turn left and head south. However, he found the road blocked by a large coach carrying thirty police officers to Redesdale to search for the maniac who was now escaping in front of them.

Cursing his misfortune, he swung the red Riley to the right, narrowly missing PC Carlisle and headed north up the A68.

The bang from the gunshot brought a couple of dozen curious civilians and soldiers out of the cookhouse, gathering around DS Dodson who, lifted himself onto his side, clutching his chest in pain as Jane and DC Cotton bent over, trying to help. Jamie Norman stepped in between the small crowd and his wounded sergeant, holding the crowd back.

A solidly built, middle-aged woman in a tweed suit and stout leather shoes; stepped out from the small crowd, pushing past Jamie to kneel down between Jane and DC Cotton.

Leaning forward to look at DS Dodson, she demanded, 'Out of the way please, I'm a doctor,' and looking up at the crowd ordered, 'Well don't just stand there - someone phone for an ambulance and can one of you soldiers please find a stretcher we can use to get him in out of the cold.'

Grimacing in pain, Dodson rasped to a worried DC Cotton, 'Go on then, bugga off, and catch the bastard.'

Standing up, Jane asked Jamie, 'Was that your suspect?'

Grim-faced, he replied, 'Yes George Robertson, sorry but I've got to get after him,' and turning to DC Cotton, he said, 'Come on,' and ran across to his car as PC Carlisle slid his police car to a halt, a few feet from them.

Scrambling out of his car, Carlisle yelled at Jamie Norman and Inspector Thornton, 'He's gone north and the bus is here,' the last part unnecessary as the coach was pulling to a halt on the now, cleared square.

As Jamie and Cotton climbed into their car, Thornton yelled, 'I'll stay here to coordinate, make sure your radio is on.'

Helping Ronnie to his feet, Edward asked, 'Are you okay?'

He rubbed the swelling to the right side of his head, and replied, 'I think so, but I think I'm going to have a helluva a headache.

Jane was distraught, she had just seen what Robertson was capable of, and now she was terrified at the thought of what he may have done to Ian and Jake who were still missing. She was determined to find her son and ran back to Edward and Ronnie.

Trying to control her mounting anxiety she said, 'Did you recognise him, it was definitely George Robertson, the bully who Ian had a fight with, God knows what he might have done to the boys, he looked insane. I am going to follow the police up the road, Ian and Jake have to be up there somewhere,' and climbed back into her car. Edward and Ronnie just managed to climb in before she swung the Morris around and drove out of the camp, heading north after the police car.

Outside of Treshinish House basking in bright, winter-sunshine, Ian and Jake self-consciously thanked Maggie for looking after them, promising to visit her if they had any spare time during the three weeks their Regiment was going to be at Redesdale.

Maggie smiled and said, 'It's a pity it wasn't under better circumstances but it was lovely meeting ye's; yer both canny lads. Noo Tek care and mek sure they get ye te hospital, Jake and Aah hope the swelling goes down quickly, Ian.'

Jake replied, 'I will Maggie and thanks again and you as well Mrs Dawson.'

Standing just behind Maggie, Sarah gave a little wave as Ian threw their parkas into the cab before helping Jake up into the driver's seat. He then walked across to Davy who was standing shyly by his mother.

Ian leant forward and held out his hand, which Davy grabbed, giving it an exaggerated shake as Ian said, 'Cheerio Davy lad, keep up the football and tek care of your mam, ye never know we might bump inte each other again.

'Bye Ian, I hope your face doesn't stay like that,' Davy replied, reluctantly letting go of his hand and watching him walk around the cab and climb into the truck.

Jake pulled the choke out, depressed the clutch and switched on the engine, and keeping it ticking over, wound down his window as Rosalind came up and touched his arm affectionately, saying, 'Bye Jake, don't forget to write.'

Grinning, Jake replied, I won't forget, see you soon, ta, da,' and pressed the horn signalling to Jack, who, having shovelled some of the snowbank away from the exit of the yard, was sitting in the cab of the Scammell with the engine ticking over in a steady thumping, rhythm. Tooting the horn three times, he heaved at the steering wheel as he inched the big truck forward and accelerated a little as he pushed through the remaining snow and onto the A68 heading south.

As the three women and Davy walked back inside, PC Ray Newton, pushed his right arm through his rifle sling, swung it over his shoulder and began patrolling the outside of the house.

Maggie shouted from the front door, I'll bring you a cup of tea out in a minute.'

After the ferocious storm, Jack was enjoying the dramatic change in the weather as he drove slowly down the road next to the reservoir. It was a beautiful morning, the bright sun casting dappled shadows through white, sugarcoated pine trees onto the cleared road ahead. Looking to his right through a gap in the trees, he could see the bright, white expanse of Catcleugh Reservoir, as he enjoyed the beauty and tranquillity of the valley, unaware that Geordie Robertson was speeding toward him.

Panic-stricken and driving erratically, Robertson fought continuously to stop the rear end of the sleek Riley from swinging out but failed several times, clouds of snow blasting into the air when the car's rear mudguards swung into the high banks on either side of the road. His mind was in turmoil, he knew that the snowplough could not have cleared the road over Carter Bar yet and did not know how far he could drive before he reached it.

Breathing short shallow gasps, he began sweating as his heartbeat increased with every second, his periphery vision blurring and unable to identify sounds; his mind and body were in full, 'fight or flight' response. Rational thinking left him as he drove madly on, ready to fight his way to freedom as despair and desperation fought each other to overcome him.

He was still speeding and fishtailing as he sped past Byrness where a Forestry Commission, Unimog with a snowplough fitted to the front was clearing the road up from the Hamlet to the main road.

Sitting in the front of his police car in Redesdale Camp, Inspector Thornton radioed Sergeant Macintyre, 'Robertson is driving north towards you, he is driving an early fifties, red Riley and has just shot a detective; consider him armed and dangerous and act accordingly. Block the road and stop him, but take no chances; over.'

Macintyre replied, 'Roger Sir,' and remembering what Jack had told him earlier, added, 'be warned that there may be a civilian recovery vehicle travelling south toward him, we will attempt to turn our car around and drive south; out.'

Pulling his black Webley revolver from his holster, he said, 'You heard that Gary, turn around as soon as you reach the farm just ahead, I'll get Baxter out of the snowplough and we'll pick up Newton from the farm and block the road.'

Pursuing the fleeing Robertson, DC Cotton was driving expertly, closing steadily on the Riley until he approached Byrness. The Unimog had just pushed through the bank of snow separating the A68 from the road down into the hamlet, piling snow across the road that was going to take him two or three moves back and forth to clear.

Jamie Norman jumped out of the car and ran forward yelling at the driver to hurry up as he watched the Riley disappear over a rise, half-a-mile away.

High up in the Scammell, Jack was driving slowly south, enjoying the sun as he thought of auburn-haired Sarah. He could not remember the last time he had allowed himself to think that a woman, especially a beauty, could be attracted to him but he believed he saw something in her eyes last night during a quiet chat in the kitchen that he hoped meant more than sympathy.

His thoughts disappeared as he stared in disbelief at the seemingly out of control, red car speeding toward him. There was barely enough cleared snow for the Scammell to drive through let alone pass another vehicle. He brought the truck to a halt, wondering why the driver of the Riley was not slowing.

Geordie recognised the Scammell and was raging, he knew who would be driving it, and realising that he had trapped himself, he thumped the steering wheel out of frustration but did not slow, he was beyond rational thought. Screaming like a maniac, he slammed his feet on the brake and clutch pedals, bracing himself on the steering wheel as the car slid twenty-yards, ramming into the driver-side wheel of the Scammell and the snow bank, sending a shower of snow cascading over the side of Jack's truck.

The Riley settled back, steam hissing out of its burst radiator as Geordie leapt out, running around the back of the car and up onto the snowbank, pushing along the top toward the cab of the Scammell, pointing the revolver up at Jack who had recognised him just before the collision.

Geordie's only thought at that moment was to kill Jack who he believed was to blame for his failure to escape, screaming, 'Die you bastard,' he pointed the heavy revolver at him and fired his last two bullets and then kept on clicking the trigger, seemingly unaware that the weapon was empty.

The first bullet smashed the windscreen before punching a hole in the roof and dropping in the forest beyond and Jack was already ducking behind the dashboard when the second flew harmlessly over the cab.

Hearing Geordie screaming like a banshee, he looked up and watched as he hurled the revolver at the cab before turning and wading through the thigh deep snow toward the reservoir, fifty yards away through the pine trees. Jack leapt out of the cab and chased after him, moving faster through the trail in the snow that Geordie had created.

Pulling up behind the Scammell when it slowed to a halt, Jake said, 'I wonder why he's stopped?'

'I'll go and see,' replied Ian as he opened his door and climbed out just as Geordie slid the Riley into the front of Jack's truck, rocking the Scammell and spraying snow up and over the left-hand side.

Standing between the two vehicles, Ian looked up at Jake, shouting, 'Bloody hell, what was that?'

Jake shook his head, replying, 'I don't kn...' stopping in mid-sentence when he saw Geordie appear at the side of the Scammell and instead shouted, 'It's Robertson!'

Scrambling up the bank of snow, Ian ducked back down when he saw Geordie fire his revolver up at Jack.

He waited until he heard Jake, shout from the cab, 'He's running away, Jack's going after him.' Climbing back up the bank, he saw the two men struggling through the deep snow lying between the pine trees, and leaping down, ran after them.

When PC Ray Newton heard the shots a couple of hundred yards away, he did not hesitate, he took his rifle off his shoulder and ran towards the sound.

Adrenaline fuelled Geordie's effort to escape Jack, as the realisation of his plight began to seep through his panic-driven thoughts. The effort of pushing through the thigh deep snow, slowed him down and hearing Jack closing in on him, he stopped just before the short drop down onto the ice, and snow covered reservoir and turned to face his tormentor.

Jack dived forward, hitting Geordie with a rugby tackle in his stomach, knocking him onto his back, and then pushing himself up onto his knees, he hit Geordie with a swinging right, rocking his head, shocking him. However, the big lad was far from finished; grabbing Jack by his shoulders, he swung him off and hauling himself to his knees, tried to wrestle Jack to the ground. Jack hit him with a right uppercut, rocking his head backwards, following it with a head butt to Geordie's nose.

Blood splattering from his nose, Geordie managed to punch Jack on the side of the head with a powerful right hook, bowling him onto his side. The momentum of the punch he had thrown, throwing him forward, onto his hands.

On his hands and knees, he looked up just in time to see Ian launch his army-booted, right foot toward his face. Abandoning his nagging conscience, Ian knew now was the time to stop Geordie and was prepared to use whatever physical violence was needed to put the killer down. Geordie did not have time to react, the boot smacking him square in the mouth, smashing teeth and busting his lip, knocking him onto his side. Spitting blood, he rolled over and tried to climb back onto on his knees again as Ian launched another kick. This one caught Geordie on his right cheek, splitting it open but it did not knock him over.

Pulling himself to his feet, he held his hands up too late to ward off a shoulder charge from Jack that knocked him down the five-foot drop to the reservoir. Jack lunged for him but only managed to grab his left-hand greatcoat pocket ripping part of it away. Falling head over heels, Geordie landed heavily on splintering ice below, before hauling himself to his feet to glare up at Jack and Ian.

Blood streamed down Geordies cheek and bubbled from his mouth, his eyes misted by tears, he stared without focus as his mind began to surrender to the hopelessness of his situation. Tears and snot began to run rivulets through the blood as his head slowly lowered. Self-pity and resentment washed over him as the three of them stood panting from running through the snow and the fight.

Looking down at the wretched figure, Jack shouted, 'Give up lad, there's nowhere for you to run,' and held his hand out for him.

Defeated, both physically and mentally, Geordie just wanted his nightmare to end and slowly lifted his hand to take Jacks until the sound of police-car bells and shouting echoed through the wood from the road.

Geordie hesitated and looking to his left; he saw the sweating figure of PC Ray Newton wading through the snow toward him with his rifle pointing forward.

Jack shouted at Newton, 'Stop, wait,' and turning back to Geordie said, 'Come on, don't get yourself killed.'

At the same time as Jamie Norman leapt out of the Hillman when DC Cotton brought it to a sliding halt behind the Riley, Sergeant Macintyre's squad car halted behind the army

Austin that Jake had just climbed down from, being careful not to stretch his wound.

Over the sound of the still ringing bell on Macintyre's car, Jake pointed through the trees, shouting 'Over there, he's over there.'

Bringing her Morris to a halt behind Jamie Norman's car, Jane arrived as Macintyre and the two constables waded through the snow in parallel with Norman and Cotton.

Jack's cry of, 'Don't get yourself killed,' echoed in Geordies head and thinking of last night's nightmare of hanging in the pit cage, he staggered back a few feet.

Glaring at Newton, he spat out a mouthful of blood, and yelled, 'Ye can shoot me or hang me, Aah divin't frigging care so fuck the lot of ye,' and turned to look across the flat expanse of wind, flattened snow covering the reservoir. Seeing the tree covered far bank, just a quarter-of-a-mile away, he looked back over his shoulder at the police making their way through the trees and turning back, leant forward, and began shuffling across the reservoir as the ice below, groaned a warning.

Jack grabbed Ian's arm when he made to chase after Geordie, shouting, 'No, stop, the ice is not safe, the thaw weakened it,' and then yelled after Geordie, 'Comeback, the ice is not thick enough,' but his voice was drowned out by the helicopter.

Returning from having flown up the valley, the pilot brought it into a hover above the flashing blue light of

Macintyre's squad car at the same time as the winchman spotted the lone figure shuffling across the reservoir.

PC Newton stopped next to Ian and pulled back the bolt on his rifle, sliding it forward, ramming a round into the chamber, and lifted the rifle into the aim, as he shouted, 'Stop or I fire!'

Either he did not hear or he did not care but Geordie kept on moving steadily across the creaking ice. Seeing Newton adjust his aim, Ian stepped in front of him yelling, 'You can't shoot him in the back,' and pushed the barrel of the rifle up into the air. Newton pulled the rifle back and took aim again as the approaching Sergeant Macintyre, shouted, 'NEWTON, do not fire.'

Panting from struggling through the snow, Jamie Norman arrived and tried to rush past them onto the ice but Jack stepped in front of him and shook his head, shouting, 'It's unsafe.'

Helped by Edward, Jane climbed over the snow bank followed by Ronnie who stopped when he saw his much prized Riley smashed into the front of the Scammell, he growled, 'The bastard.'

As they moved into the wood, it was Jane who saw Jake first, yelling, 'Jacob, where's Ian?'

Pointing through the trees, he replied, 'There, over there.'

She stopped for a moment and sighed deeply, tears of relief welling up in her eyes as she saw the group by the side of the reservoir and recognised the figure in the green, army combat suit.

Shuffling across the ice, Geordie felt no remorse only self-pity as he thought 'If only:'

'If only that pig Weedon had agreed to give me more money.'

'If only he had not hit me with the fishplate.'

'If only he had not kicked me, it was his frigging fault.'

'If only my fatha hadn't tried to stop me from getting away, the stupid bastard deserved to be shot.'

'If only...'

The sound of creaking and groaning increased as he moved further onto the ice but he did not slow down until he felt movement underfoot, the surface of the ice seemed to be flexing in every direction. Stopping, he turned to look back the one hundred and fifty-yards he had covered, to the line of people standing on the bank. He could see them waving at him to come back but could not hear what they were shouting, the noise of the helicopter, now hovering at two-hundred-feet above the reservoir, two hundred yards to the north, drowned out all other noise.

Aware that no one could hear him, tears again began to well up and run down his blood-streaked face as he yelled, 'Ye can all fuck off, Yer not ganning te stretch my frigging neck, Aah've had enough, ye bastards. Why couldn't ye just let me gan, Aah didn't mean te kill any bugga, they attacked me...'

Realising the futility of his shouts, he stopped and stood silent and motionless looking at the line of watchers on the bank for a long minute, before looking up at the helicopter and then back at the watchers.

He knew it was over, he was finished, but in a last show of defiance, he yelled to the unhearing watchers, 'I'll end this my way.'

Then, to the shock of those on the bank and the crew of the helicopter, he began to jump up and down on the ice, arms in the air, arrogantly waving two fingers on both hands at them.

Edward helped Jane through the snow until she was a few yards from her son.

'Ian,' she yelled and held up her hand to her mouth when he turned and she saw his battered and bruised face, saying, 'Oh my God, what has happened to you?'

They hugged each other, Ian replying, 'I'm alright Mam, just a couple of black eyes and a swollen nose, but look, we've got to see what's happening to Geordie,' the three of them joining the others to stare in disbelief at the figure on the ice.

After Jake told Ronnie that Robertson had shot him but it was only a flesh wound, Ronnie helped him through the snow to join the watchers on the bank as the helicopter dropped to a hundred feet, the pilot wondering what Robertson was doing. The winchman secured his harness ready for a quick descent as the downdraft from the blades created a mini blizzard on the reservoir below.

The bundle of pound notes he had killed his father for, tumbled out of Geordies torn pocket as he jumped higher, sending cracks across the ice all around him. The cleared area of snow at his feet, revealing ice as water began to gush through the cracks.

The fourth jump did it, the ice broke into a myriad of pieces as his boots crashed through and he plunged into the freezing water, disappearing completely for a few seconds before his head and shoulders reappeared. Gulping for air, unable to breathe from the shock of his immersion, he raked the snow and ice with his bare hands and fingernails as he fought to find a grip to pull himself out but the breaking ice gave way and his heavy, water-soaked greatcoat conspired against him, dragging him back into the black hole.

The pilot acted immediately, dropping another twenty-feet, he flew the helicopter steadily sideways towards Geordie blowing a thirty-foot-high, mini-blizzard, toward him floundering below in the ice. The winchman was already out of the door, lowering slowly as the pilot brought the helicopter to a hover over Geordie who was just hanging on by his fingertips, his shocked and terrified face showing his realisation of what he had done and what was about to happen.

More ice broke off and as he slipped back, he cried for his mother, 'Maaam,' before his head dipped below the ice-strewn water leaving just his hands reaching up, claw-like.

Watching from the bank, DI Norman muttered, 'They are making a lot of effort for the murdering swine, better to let him slip away.'

No one heard him above the sound of the helicopter as the blizzard of snow engulfed Geordie, sucking up the one-pound notes he had dropped, scattering the money to the wind.

On the bank, everyone stood silently, waiting, eyes, and attention fixed on the billowing snow, as the helicopter appeared motionless in the hover, creating a cleared circle in the blizzard, hidden to the watchers by the snow billowing up around the edge.

No one spoke on the bank, as well as being lost in their own thoughts, the noise of the helicopter far too loud for any of them to hear each other. It was a long three minutes before they saw the head and shoulders of the winchman appearing above the wafting snow as he was winched back up; the watchers all holding their breath; waiting to see if he was alone. As more of him came into view he waved his right hand, palm-down across his front, then clenching his fist, he gave the watchers a thumbs down as the helicopter lifted clear and rose high into the clear, blue sky.

The snowstorm it had created drifted off, leaving only a powdery trail in the otherwise smooth surface that led to a small black hole in the ice, then – silence.

The End

EPILOGUE

Penetrating a few feet into the dark, peat-laden water, the beam of the Royal Navy diver's torch swept from side to side as he swam slowly along the bottom of the reservoir on the first day of their search. He had only been underwater for five minutes when the torch beam reflected off, glistening circles; they were the buttons on the short belt on the back of Geordie Robertson's ex-RAF greatcoat.

His corpse was lying face down in the silt almost directly, below where he had broken through the ice and drowned, two weeks earlier.

Amongst the throng of reporters, cameramen and television film crews standing on the still snow-covered bank, DI Jamie Norman watched as the Diver surfaced next to the inflatable sitting half on the thin ice covering the reservoir and half in the opening created by the crew. Pulling out his breathing mouthpiece, the diver spoke to the men in the large inflatable; one of them nodded then stood to give thumbs up to the gathering on the bank.

Jamie waved back as DC Cotton said, 'That's it then, just the paperwork to do.'

Jamie gave a wry smile, 'Aye, Will, as far as Robertson is concerned but he has left us with an almighty Pandora's Box to sort out.'

Investigations into the Weedon's activities continue; charged with causing Grievous Bodily Harm to Edna North, Stuart Weedon is still under investigation on charges, of fraud, illegal money lending, exploitation of prostitution and controlling prostitution for gain and, the disappearance of his mother.

Edna North suffered a broken jaw, fractured cheekbone, the loss of several teeth and two cracked ribs. Charged with theft and child abduction she is under investigation for prostitution as she awaits discharge from Ashington Hospital.

It was another two days before the A68 reopened and Sarah and her children completed their journey to Scotland. Maggie Gray insisted that they remained at Treshinish until the road opened and bolted her door, refusing to speak to a plethora of reporters seeking to sensationalise any titbit they could dig up on an already over reported story. On her return to Northumberland, two days later, Sarah called in on Maggie and stayed overnight, much to Maggie and Jack's delight.

Sarah subsequently found a house to rent in Ponteland, and aided by Jack, moved in three weeks later. Their relationship continues to flourish.

Ian and Jake enjoyed the comforts of Ashington hospital for two nights before returning to Redesdale Camp in time for their Regiment arriving. Not fully fit, Jake spent three days in camp on light duties before deploying on exercise but Ian suffered some robust banter from the lads in his battery when they saw his black eyes and swollen nose.

As promised, Jake exchanged letters with Rosalind, arranging to meet up when he was next on leave.

The bullet that knocked over DS Dodson did no major damage to him or his temperament; however, the nurses at the Royal Victoria Infirmary were more than a match for him and enjoyed his sardonic sense of humour.

Ronnie Grundy said goodbye to his much-loved Riley, written-off in the crash with the Scammell. Returning to Mary and Rose at Catterick by bus two days later, Mary was so relieved he returned unscathed that she bought him a new Mini from the money her brother had given her when he sold the family business in Singapore.

Billy and Roger returned to being their normal rambunctious selves and once again enjoyed dinners provided by big-hearted, big-chested Jen.

Happily tinkering with a sickly moped in his shed, Albert Grundy stubbed out his cigarette and blowing smoke up to the roof, said, 'Whey Flo, I've been a reet silly bugga but that's aall ower with, it's nice te have a chat we ye in here again.'

Acknowledgement

My warmest thanks go to my dear Beth, whose support made this book possible.

Geordie/Pitmatic words

Aah	I
Aaful	awful
Aalreet	alright
Aah've	I have
Alen	alone
An	own
Aroond	around
Bairn	Baby or small child
Bait	food carried to work
Boond	bound
Cannit	cannot
Cowld	cold
Cyek	cake
Daad	strike
Dee	do
Div	do
Divvint	do not
Donard	stupid
Doot	doubt
Droon	drown
Fyece	face
Forst	first
Fund	found
Gan	go
Gannin	going
Gis	give me
Glakey	Silly – not with it
Grund	ground
Gully	large knife
Hoy	throw

Hurd	heard
He'sell	himself
Hev	have
Hevn't	have not
Hoo	how
Haway	come on
Hord	heard
Iviry	every
Ivvor	ever
Kna	know
Lavvies	lavatory
Lowp	leap
Mair	more
Marra	friend or workmate
Mek	make
Mesell	myself
Nee	no
Nen	none
Nettie	lavatory
Nivvor	never
Nur	no
Nowt	nothing
Ower	over
Owld	old
Owt	anything
Pinny	full apron, usually foral
Plodgin	paddling
Reet	right
Roond	round
Sackless	dozy
Shows	the fair
Shull	shovel
Sowldgers	soldiers
Sumat	something
Taak	talk
Tecking	taking
Tha	they're
Tetties	potatoes
Thowt	thought
Towld	told

Tyeble	table
Whey	well
Willicks	winkles
Winnit	will not
Wiv	with
Wor	our
Worsells	ourselves
Yarking	beating
Ye	you
Yor	your
Yorsell	yourself

Printed in Great Britain
by Amazon